THE DECISION

THE DECISION

by Nicholas G. Kolovos

Ashley Books, Inc.
Ft. Lauderdale, FL 33319

THE DECISION.
Copyright© 1991 by Nicholas G. Kolovos.

Library of Congress CIP Number:89-36775
ISBN:087949-313-5

ASHLEY BOOKS, INC / Publishers
Fort Lauderdale, Florida 33319

Printed In The United States of America
First Edition

All rights reserved. No part of this book may be used or reproduced in any manner whatsoever without written permission except in the case of brief quotations in articles and reviews. Address all inquiries to ASHLEY BOOKS, INC., 4600 W. Commercial Blvd, Fort Lauderdale, Florida 33319.

Library of Congress Cataloging in Publication Data:

  Kolovos, Nicholas G.   1912-
    The decision / by Nicholas G. Kolovos.
      p.   cm.
  ISBN 0-87949-313-5
  I. Title.
  PS3561.0436D4   1990   89-36775
  813'.54- - dc20   CIP

This novel is dedicated in the memory of my loving wife Catherine Ann, who passed away September 4, 1988.

ACKNOWLEDGEMENT

This is to thank certain people, who have helped me in one way or another with their output and encouragement over the years in the development of this story. Most especially, thanks are expressed to the late Eivar Swanson, who was the catalyst who catapulted me on the road to writing it. My thanks to Terri Sherf, wherever she may be, who saw merit in the plot and fervently urged me to continue in my writing. A special thanks to Nori Ruhnau, who cheered me on during some of the dark days, took time off her busy schedule to correct some of my misspelled words and gave authenticity to parts of my phrasing, and finally my thanks to my agent and my friend, Ray Ashcroft and his lovely wife, Mary, for being there to put in the final touches of the dream about to come true.

Illustrations by Kathryn Lewis

THE DECISION

Chapter 1

The vast, windblown prairies in North Central America are treacherous, awe-inspiring, and mysterious in scope, with millions of untold stories. On them once roamed giant dinosaurs, reptiles, and thousands of other predatory creatures, now all extinct, wiped out from some unknown phenomenon of nature millions of years ago. Then along came huge herds of buffalo that roamed the prairies, only to be slaughtered to the verge of extinction by the white man. Now, there roams another animal, far more dangerous and deadly than the others.....man. Given enough time, he, too, may exterminate himself. Here on the prairies, our story has its beginning.

The year is 1875. It is the last of June and the start of another sizzling, parched day...the seventeenth such day in a row. The fiery red sun was aglow, slowly rising in the east, harbinger of things to come. The Santee Indians who called this land their own until the white man robbed them of their rights alluded to it, "the demon sky that treads heavily on Mother Earth."

It was the most unbearable and unpleasant of seasons for both man or beast. A wizened, white-haired, tobacco-chewing octogenarian referred to it acidly, saying, "Hottest one since '37. That one was a real doozy! I remember it well, as if it were yesterday. We were on a cattle drive from somewhere in Texas. Dried-up river beds for nigh onto 500 miles as a crow flies." He stopped for a moment to expectorate his tobacco juice at a crawling insect, "Real scorcher, too!"

The hills overlooking the prairies were barely visible in the dust. Dried-up, spiny tumbleweeds hurtled, cartwheeled down the main street of Broken Bend.

Broken Bend, a western creation, was built during the pioneer days of the mountain men of the '20s and '30s. Western influence still remained

THE DECISION

in its older buildings. Aged and rundown from the devastation of unfriendly seasons and passing years, they were memorials, standing ruggedly in defiance of man and time. Broken Bend was a town of almost seven hundred inhabitants, mostly cowpokes, gamblers, transients, business people and ladies of the night. It was proud of its nickname, "The drinkiest town in all the west and America". Among its establishments were two hotels, two restaurants, nineteen saloons and eighteen other small enterprises.

From a distance, a solitary horse could be seen carrying its rider determinedly against the swirling dust. The spirited chestnut horse pranced skittishly away from the sagebrush, where coiled rattlers lay hidden in the shade. The rider was hunched down and a serape was draped over his back, protecting him from the cutting edges of the shifting sands.

He was oblivious to his steed's uneasiness and the anger of nature, being weighed down in deep thought, with problems of his own. He muttered to himself in disgust. "Damn it! Damn it! How could anything like this happen? Where did we go wrong? Betty and I were so happy. We had the perfect marriage until we were blessed with twin sons. Then it happened! How was I to know that she's to take the raising of our sons so seriously? But she did! Before we knew it, one thing led to another, then to divorce! I hope she comes to her senses and stops this nonsense. I blame myself, too. Patrick O'Shea, you're a dunderhead! You should have known better. You're older than Betty, but you weren't wise enough. I can see all our friends and the towns people having a field day at our expense, laughing and making jokes of our marital difficulties in court today. I don't give a hoot what they say or think, as long as Betty and I stay together. As it stands now, the way it's shaping up, I can't win either way in this court case. If I win the custody of the boys, I lose Betty. If Betty wins the custody of the boys, I lose both Betty and my sons. What a dilemma! Well, I guess what will be, will be, come hell or high water. Who said life is easy? Good Lord, help me!"

Patrick rode into Broken Bend to the nearest stable where he gave instructions to the owner, Zeke Cracko, "Zeke," he said as he got off his tired horse, "how's about you cleaning, graining, and rubbing down my horse? She's dead tired, and I'll be a spell in court today. How long? God only knows and HE'S not telling me. I don't know."

"Will do, Patrick," Zeke grunted, "You are both good people and I'm not taking sides. It's too bad that one of you might get hurt by it all. Wish you luck. Anyway, hope it turns out all right."

Patrick ambled over to the Buckaroo Saloon, which was packed to the rafters. Outside could be seen a long line of assorted makes of carriages and buckboards on both sides of the local courthouse. The ladies had gathered together to gossip about the coming divorce trial of the O'Sheas as their men dashed off to the nearest saloon to shake the dust from their lungs.

The saloon was doing a land-office business, furnishing drinks to the thirsty, gambling for the boys with a wad of money in their pockets, and ladies of pleasure for the daring.

A solitary horse came into Broken Bend carrying its dusty rider

Patrick sat down at an empty table for a drink of sarsaparilla. It turned out to be too warm to gulp so he sipped it a little at a time. One of the local ranchers stopped at his table, "Hi, Patrick. It's sure a hot day! Two of my steers keeled over today! A real barn-burner! And twice as hot as hell! Not quite as hot as what you'll have to put up with today though! I don't envy your position, and I hope it turns out for the best." With that he was on his way out.

The searing temperature was taking its toll on the tempers of the saloon patrons. Every once in a while, a few of the short-tempered rowdies would get a little too much liquor under their belts and they would be in a fight that was quickly broken up by the sheriff and his deputies. It didn't take too much effort to subdue the contestants, as neither one had too much inclination to continue the dispute in the sweltering heat. Nature and events stretched the fragile nerves of a few townspeople to the breaking point.

Patrick gave no heed to any of this unpleasantness. He was too involved in his own particular type of hell. His thoughts were shattered by a loud

THE DECISION

call from outside; "Hear ye, hear ye! The court will be in session in ten minutes. Hurry and get your seats before the door is closed!"

There was a mad scramble for seats. Patrick sat, stunned! First looking at the blank ceiling, then getting up slowly and walking out like a condemned criminal on his last mile.

The rickety courthouse was built in the late twenties, when the town was still in its infancy. It somehow had retained many of the original pioneer trademarks, including a large hitching post at the front of the courthouse. The building was a large, whitewashed cabin with a four-step stairway leading to the entrance. It was a simple structure built out of necessity by the pioneers of that era. The entrance had a heavy, pale brown door of pioneer construction, with a sturdy dark latch that opened and closed with a great deal of effort. Built for stability and durability, the courthouse was not for comfort, as many were to learn in the ensuing years. The floors were hard wood and well worn from the years of usage. On entering, one noticed the pews and chairs, modest in design, to accommodate about 115 people, quite a large crowd for that time.

Once inside, the first object that caught your interest was a large picture of George Washington crossing the Delaware. This prompted one observer to mutter to his wife, "I'd druther be thur than here in this dang heat," and a crony was quick to reply, "Yes, Pete, and I think old George would gladly traded places with you," that brought a loud guffaw from his comely wife.

The rickety courthouse was built in the late 20's when the town was still in its infancy.

Draped on the right wall was a picture of Jim Bridger, standing beside three bales of buffalo hides. A well circulated rumor around Broken Bend was that this cantankerous, ignorant mountain man had founded the town at the beginning of the century. Others disagreed but, regardless, there was his picture staring down at you.

Overhead, open cracks appeared over most of the ceiling. Musty grey paints was peeling off in strips. At the front of the ancient courtroom was the judge's bench, evidently showing signs of wear and in dire need of repairs. It was an uncomfortable seat, tending to make the travelling circuit court judges somewhat peevish when trying a case. During the last few years they were advised to wear leather britches because, down through the years the well-seasoned benches had become splintered. One old judge learned his lesson the hard way.

As the story goes, there was once a travelling judge, an unsympathetic character known as "Swinging Harry". He tried a man on Saturday and had him hung on Sunday, in the style of the western kangaroo court. One day in '62 "Swinging Harry" came to Broken Bend for his bi-annual whirlwind court session. As luck would have it, that day turned out to be a barn blazer too. The courthouse took on the appearance of a Turkish steambath. The judge was ringing wet with perspiration. He was short-tempered by the lack of accommodations and other trivial matters. The hardwood bench and his uncomfortable underdrawers were giving him fits!

He had a long agenda on the docket. Some were alleged crimes against the state by murderers, cattle rustlers, horse thieves. It was going to be a long, hot day for the judge. He wasted no time with the unfortunates as he knocked them off in record time, with his usual verdict, "Guilty, to be hung on Sunday!"

Finally, it came down to the last case on the docket, involving Crotchety "Pete," a horse thief of some renown.

"How do you plead?" asked the surly judge.

"Not guilty," replied Pete without hesitation.

"Guilty," countered the judge, "to be hung on Sunday until dead."

At that moment, the crotch in his underdrawers nipped him in a sensitive spot. The judge tried to shift quickly to a more advantageous position. He let out an unearthly scream of pain, "That damn seat jabbed a sliver up my ass, yeow!"

Crotchety "Pete" had a devilish smirk on his face as he got in the final needle, "Serves you right, you miserable old bastard. I'll go to my grave happy to know you got your comeuppance!"

To go on with the legend, "Pete awaited his date with destiny in jail. In the meantime, "Swinging Harry" went to the barbershop of Clipper McBee, who also doubled as the town's doctor and dentist. They placed

THE DECISION

the protesting irate judge face down on the slab, his bare ass upended. You never heard such yelling and screaming while McBee pulled out sliver after sliver from "Swinging Harry's" buttocks. The boys didn't know what pained him more, the slivers being yanked out or the 100-proof whiskey they poured on as an antiseptic. ("Swinging Harry" never came back to try cases in Broken Bend.) Someone sneaked into the jailhouse that same night to tell Pete what happened to the judge. Pete's face beamed when he learned what had happened to the judge at the barber's. Pete smiled a crooked smile. "At least where I'm going, I'll feel no pain, but that no good shyster will, every time he sits down."

In front of the judge's bench sat the bailiff and court reporter. On each side of them stood two burly, heavy-bearded deputies with arms crossed.

The creaking old courthouse was full to the brim with many interested onlookers, a "Who's Who" page out of the Wild West. Many were there for one thing: to witness and gloat over somebody else's misfortunes. Especially this day, at the divorce trail of the O'Sheas. Many were thanking God, "it wasn't them instead of the O'Sheas."

There were a few well-wishing ranchers, longtime friends of both the O'Sheas, who didn't want to see either party hurt in this trial, but were torn in their loyalties. On another side of the courtroom sat loud, cursing, belligerent cowboys, who spat at anything that moved on the dingy floors. Dirty, grub-staking farmers trod the hardwood floors in manure-covered boots. In another corner sat the painted ladies in their bright-colored dresses, giggling and gossiping about their customers; some of whom were at the trail with their plain, solemn-faced wives.

Alone and unsmiling in the back, sat a blanketed Indian. One of the locals pointed him out, laughing, "There's old blanket-ass himself. I wonder what the old coot is thinking about."

The venerable old Indian ignored the jibe. He was there to observe for himself how white man's justice worked. Last but not least, the Broken Bend Bugle had sent a reporter to report the facts of the case to its readers.

Suddenly, all commotion was stilled. The bailiff called for all to rise, proclaiming in a shrill voice, "This session of the Circuit Court of the Broken Bend Territory is now in order...the Honorable Justin G. Norbert, presiding judge."

Everyone complied. The tall, unsmiling judge entered, toting a Bible and moved toward the bench. He motioned the spectators to be seated. "This is a very serious trial," he began, "I will not tolerate any interruptions in my courtroom. If there are,...." his keen brown eyes moved from face to face. "All offenders will be charged with contempt and fined $100.00 or sentenced to thirty days in jail or both."

The spectators straightened. Not a sound was heard. Judge Norbert turned to the bailiff and nodded. The balding bailiff stepped forward, cleared his throat and said, "The Court shall hear O'Shea versus O'Shea, an action to determine the permanent custody of Masters Kelly O'Shea and Dennis O'Shea, twin dependents of the parties at contest."

The bailiff stared evenly at the spectators and then at the contestants for the moment, turned around, and sat down.

The judge peered over his spectacles, looked at some papers, and cleared his throat. "Umph!" He then continued, "This is a trial hearing. Since both of you have been unable to retain adequate legal counsel...he paused, wiping his foggy glasses, "due to the scarcity of competent lawyers in this territory," he paused again to adjust his glasses, "I will be your legal counsel to ensure that both of you get the proper advice."

He stopped, waiting for an affirmation or refusal from either contestant. None was forthcoming. "It will be my solemn duty to question you, judge your from your rhetoric and the reasoning behind your replies. I caution both of you to deliberate wisely before answering my questions. In the final summation, I alone will make the decision concerning the divorce settlement and the eventual custody of your sons."

There was a slight twitter and a scraping of feet among the spectators. They were enjoying a private scene that was raising a commotion. In the middle of the aisle was a brass, tobacco-splattered cuspidor, taking a beating from a thin, lantern-jawed farmer. His tobacco aim was perfect, knocking the cuspidor off its base momentarily, but the weighted bottom righting itself for its next battering. The "ping" of the tobacco juice hitting the metal echoed in the tiny hall. Finally, the annoyed judge angrily thundered, "What is your name?" pointing his question at the guilty part.

The red-faced farmer replied, "Jeb Clarke, sir."

"Jeb," the judge said with deliberate emphasis, "This is a court of law, not a firing range." The courtroom reverberated with roars of laughter. "Furthermore, " he went on, "if you want to remain here, Clean it up! Go outside, take that filthy habit with you, and get rid of that chaw in your mouth. Don't come back until you do. One more thing..." he said, pointing at the cuspidor, "On your way out, don't forget to take that dang filthy thing with you."

"Due to this unfortunate interruption, we have lost valuable time," the judge said evenly. "Let's go on with the trial. Call to the stand, Mr. Patrick O'Shea."

Patrick rose, batting ineffectually at the dust he had accumulated on his ride to town. In his early thirties, Patrick was a handsome, impressive-looking, well-built man of a little over six feet in height. He had penetrat-

THE DECISION

ing blue eyes that darted when he spoke. His jutting chin and firm features denoting a strong personality. He wore a tan deerskin jacket with a colored scarf around his neck. Heavy, dark pants hung over his high-heeled tan cowboy boots. Patrick took a deep breath, straightened his scarf, and dusted his pants once more before walking to the witness stand.

The courtroom was hushed with anticipation except for some shuffling of feet from the rear that brought an angry look from the judge. Patrick reached the witness chair, studied it for a moment, eyed the spectators, then sat down. The bailiff swore him in. The spectators in the courtroom were curious as to what line of questioning the judge would pursue in this trial. It wasn't long in coming. The judge began, "What is your full given name?"

"Patrick O'Shea."

"How old are you?"

"Thirty-four years, your Honor."

"Where were you born?"

"Lonely Bluff, Ohio, on March 20, 1841."

"How long have you lived in Broken Bend?"

"Since 1866, two years after my discharge from the Union Army, your Honor."

"Please tell the court how you came to own your ranch."

"I had a little pay saved from my army pay," Patrick began. He stopped for a moment to wipe his perspiring forehead with a large red bandanna. "I was an only child, thus I inherited my parents' holdings when they passed away in '65."

He had a sad look in his eye, remembering for a moment how it was, then went on. "The spirit of youth and adventure was in me, so I sold my parents' farm and headed west until I came to this territory. I liked what I saw..." Patrick smiled. "I decided then and there that this would be my home." He caught his breath, brought out the large red bandanna again to wipe the running perspiration from his sweating brow. "Then I bought a small ranch at a decent price which was to be the start of my Betty Ann Ranch. Little by little, as I prospered, I bought more land from money I earned breeding cattle and selling them for a profit."

"Mr. O'Shea, how did you meet your wife?"

"Your Honor, it was about three years ago. She was en route to San Francisco when her stage was forced to stay in Broken Bend due to an Indian uprising just north of here." Patrick smiled a wry sort of smile. "I was in town that morning on business. I stopped at the Wells Fargo office to pick up some ranch supplies that were on the stage. That's when I first met my wife..." A faraway look came into his keen, blue eyes. "She was talking to the station agent. She looked sort of...well, exasperated."

Patrick took a deep breath before he continued, "At that time, I heard her say to the ticket agent, "My good man, what do you mean I can't travel? I bought a ticket in good faith to San Francisco, where friends of mine are expecting me." Coldly, she looked him squarely in the eye and firmly said, "My good man, I'll tell you this one time and no more. Please tell your driver to be ready to drive that stage to San Francisco. I've paid my fare and I expect you to honor your end of the bargain." With a toss of her pretty head, she shocked the agent, saying, "I will stay here until hell freezes over!"

Patrick chuckled, remembering the confusion at the stage office. "The agent replied, "I'm sorry, Miss, but that's the way it is. There will be no stage leaving here until I get the all-clear signal from our patrols. It just ain't safe out there." he said, waiving his hand toward the trail."

Patrick continued, "Young man," she said, I'm completely capable of taking care of myself, I'm not afraid of any pesky Indians!"

"I'm sorry, Miss, that's final. I suggest you find lodgings until the next stage leaves here, if it ever does! When that is, God only knows and he ain't talking!"

"Oh...h, pshaw on your western humor! Rats to it all."

Patrick laughed as he thought about her last comment to the station master, then went on looking at the picture of Jim Bridger on the wall. "I was a little like that man, a pioneer of this vast, uncivilized territory. My roots are here and they'll always be here. It's been a productive era for me, far greater than I ever imagined in my wildest fantasies. I just didn't have time for women!"

He paused, searching for the right words to say, "At least, I thought that way...until that day." He reached into his pocket for a pipe, asking the judge, "Do you mind, your Honor? It will help keep my mind on the subject."

The judge nodded his head. Patrick lit his pipe, took a few puffs, exhaling billows of smoke that wafted to the courtroom ceilings like gentle clouds in the sky, and continued. "The madder she became, the more beautiful she looked with that saucy nose of hers daring the world. I guess, your Honor, it was at that moment I fell in love with her. Being a resident of Broken Bend, I knew the difficulty she'd have finding lodging here, so I interceded, "My name is Patrick O'Shea, I own a ranch nearby. If you cannot find lodgings here, you can be a guest at my ranch until your stage is ready to go."

"She replied to my invitation cooly. "Thank you, Mr. O'Shea. My name is Betty Ann Willoughby of Philadelphia. I'm en route to San Francisco where I'm a guest speaker on the topic of women and their place in modern society. I thank you for your kindness and consideration, but

THE DECISION

no thanks to your invitation, as some folks might misconstrue your good intentions with notions of their own."

"I was a little perplexed and hurt but realized she had a valid point. I thought for a moment before I replied to her statement. "I assure you, Miss Willoughby," I said, "my intentions are honorable. I'll be too busy running my ranch to infringe on your personal life or..." Grasping for words, Patrick sputtered for a moment, then went on, "or bring dishonor to you or your good name. Furthermore, folks around here are too busy minding their own business without interfering in the affairs of others." I looked at her carefully, "The decision is up to you."

Patrick continued, "On second thought, Mr. O'Shea, "She told me grudgingly, "I accept your kind invitation with the provision you allow me to pay for my lodgings."

"So be it," I said, "If you insist."

Patrick was silent for only a moment.

"Your Honor, she stayed at the ranch for a month. Then, it was two months and then three. Finally, one beautiful day, we were married." Patrick puffed on his pipe, reflecting on the joys of those days. "You should have seen her, your Honor. She was the most beautiful bride that's ever graced this earth. We were so much in love. It was heaven for the both of us. A little more than a year later, we were blessed with two fine sons, Kelly and Dennis. Then our troubles began." The irritation began to show in his eyes and his voice raised in intensity as he went on, "We immediately had problems with how to raise our sons. All of a sudden we found ourselves in different camps. Our home became a house divided. We weren't the same people! Our views were different! I believed our sons should be raised here. Betty, on the other hand, was of the opinion that she should take our sons out east to be reared, in her way of life. We disagreed vehemently and violently on the subject until our differences became insurmountable. One thing led to another, until it came to this. One thing, your Honor, I'd like to make perfectly clear to this court, Betty has been a wonderful wife, mother, and companion," his voice raised to a new pitch as he pounded the table with his clenched fist, "But I won't let her take our two sons out of my life."

"Therefore, your Honor," Patrick shuffled his feet nervously, took out his red bandanna again to wipe his perspiring brown, "I ask this court, your Honor, to award the custody of our two sons to me to bring them up in the west. If they are to survive in this rugged life of western civilization, they must first become used to it. Some day this savage territory will become civilized and be the bread basket of our nation, maybe of the world, too." Patrick proudly pounded his clenched fist on the bench, then paused for a moment to let his wrath subside, his voice softening as he went on. "This land of ours is our most valuable asset and our nation's future. Some day us old-timers will be gone and a new breed will take our place, our children. We must educate and prepare them for that eventuality. These are changing and meaningful times. We would be derelict in our paternal duties if we didn't raise our children to be worthwhile citizens, with the courage, ability, and foresight to look ahead and fight whatever adversity threatens them. We must have men who have high ideals and the gumption to fight for what is theirs. These are the kind of men who will make this nation great. As parents, we are simply their teachers. Our children are the students, for they will learn from our mistakes. Within our sons, I see the promised land I saw when I left Ohio many years ago. This is my heritage to my sons. That is why I petition the court for the custody of our two sons. In the meantime, " he paused, realizing the importance and gravity of the moment, then sadly added, "I will agree to any monetary settlement that this court sets up for my wife. It is my sincere wish that she'll never be in want."

Patrick rose slowly, looked beseechingly at his wife, as if this were some sort of nightmare, hoping against hope for some indecision on her part. Seeing none, he gradually lifted his eyes from her direction, and strode back in his seat.

The judge took a quick look at his watch, decided it was too early for a recess, and motioned to Betty, "I now call Mrs. O'Shea to take the stand."

She rose gracefully from her seat and walked briskly to the witness stand. Betty flowed with a sensuous movement that stirred the romantic beast in man. Her radiant green eyes flashed with anger as she sat down. In a few moments her anger had partially subsided and she was composed once more. As she sat in the witness stand, she was an ideal artist's picture. Her figure was slim, but immaculate and well shaped. A tiny pink bonnet that nestled on her head offsetting her yellow flowered dress. Betty possessed a special charm that still set Patrick's heart aflutter.

The judge coughed to get the attention of the court. He proceeded to ask Betty the usual questions about herself and the mounting difficulties between Patrick and herself.

Betty was the epitome of tact as she answered the judge's questions. She then gave her reasons why she should receive the custody of the two boys. "Your Honor, I too, have nothing against my spouse except his outdated, mulish beliefs on how to rear our sons. I too, am a parent with certain theories and rights on how our sons should be reared. I too, want custody of our sons, to rear them in another way of life. A life that appreciates the arts and the finer things in life. Where does it say in any court of law that a father knows more about rearing his sons, or in the

THE DECISION

Good Book, than does their mother...?'' This brought a slight clapping of hands from the ladies of the evening and a few of the plainfaced wives of the ranchers.

It was quickly put to a stop by the judge, who pounded the gavel for order and angrily admonished the guilty, "There will be no more outbreaks from the spectators such as this in my courtroom or it will be cleared." Looking severely at the guilty parties who started the uproar, he said, "Continue as you were, Mrs. O'Shea."

"I believe that society should not dictate who is to be acceptable and by what standards...or...whose standards! Does the literate gentleman or the illiterate laborer drink from the same cup of freedom, or are special cups available for each one? If that is the case, then that is wrong! Does society accept the rights of the rich and deny the rights of the poor? That is wrong also. This all stems from the ignorance of the literate and as long as you persist in this divine right theory, then you are snobs of the first class. I do not choose to raise our sons accordingly to this standard of being snobs but rather to be refined, cultured, and broadminded. Men that even Patrick can be proud of..." She looked aimlessly in the direction of Patrick, caught herself in her moment of indiscretion and then continued. "I, too, believe I should have the right of a mother to rear our sons in a way to benefit our nation, but in a different mode. Is it so wrong to educate them to be lawyers, doctors, teachers, or whatever road their talents may lead them to? Your Honor, it will take a combination of the rich, the middle class, and the poor to make this nation great. We must not be prejudiced against anyone; whether from the pigment of their skin, their beliefs, their sex, or by any other foreign creed that is contrary to ours. Prejudice stems from ignorance, which to some degree we all are." There was an uneasiness among the spectators, for her statement had hit a sore spot. She continued, "With my education, I am twice guilty: one, because it's inbred in me and, second, because I should know better. I look at you and I see your prejudices running rampant against your better judgement. The rancher doesn't like the sheep herder and vice versa. The townspeople ridicule the cowboys and the cowboys detest the Indians. The Indians don't trust the white men, nor do they trust the neighboring tribes. We all have our cross to bear, you and me. I'm not here to preach, but rather to show the court I'm capable of teaching our sons the difference between right and wrong." Betty stopped for a moment to catch her breath; some of the spectators shuffled nervously in their seats. "To reiterate: this all stems from our own particular kind of ignorance. This can only be tempered by the proper kind of advanced education I will be able to provide for our two sons in the east, an education not available here. Nevertheless, I also agree with Patrick that this country needs strong people to give it the right kind of leadership and ability to run and settle it. That is why I'd like to rear our sons to be the same strong individuals my husband alludes to." Betty paused for a moment to allow her words to be digested by the judge and Patrick, then she went on. "I, too, desire no monetary gain from my spouse. He has been a thoughtful, considerate, and loving husband in the past but is a little insensitive to our differences. I have sufficient funds of my own. I can afford to educate our sons in the finest of schools. I hope the court will see it my way and give me custody of our two sons."

She rose slowly, a gracious, proud, and determined lady in her own right. Surveying the scene in the courtroom, she walked calmly back to her seat, across the aisle from Patrick. He looked at her for a moment, as if wanting to say something, but the sound of the judge's gavel turned his attention to the judge as he gravely continued. "This is a very complex case of two people. Two, decent people with solemn rights as loving parents; however, that is not the issue here. The main issue is, what is best for the two boys? This is not an easy decision. It will take a lot of serious thinking to be fair. In all my years on the bench and as a lawyer, I've never had a more difficult case to decide. I will have to delve into the legality of it before I can make a decision. We will convene next Monday at nine-thirty." With a loud bang of the gavel, he announced gravely, "Court is adjourned."

Chapter 2

Judge Norbert stood at the window of his hotel room, gazing out at the dusty street below, his brow furrowed with concern. He was deep in thought, with no apparent solution at hand. At last he turned around and headed for his desk, in reality, just a wobbly table teetering on three legs. In the top drawer, he found a writing tablet and pencil. Staring at the blank sheet for a long time, he then began to write. Suddenly he stopped and looked down at his written words. A sigh escaped his lips as he ripped the sheet, disgusted by the words he wrote, and crumbled it between angry fingers before tossing it away.

"What should I do?" He began to pace from wall to wall, "What can I do?" There seemed no answer to either of the questions, but there had to be. He slumped down on the edge of the bed and stared at his hands, "Please, Dear Lord!" he prayed silently, "Help me to make the right decision. They are both good people, I must not hurt either one...."

After what seemed an eternity of deliberation with himself, he rose slowly and walked towards the window. The high humidity coupled with the staleness of the room was nauseating. He opened the window for relief, the air outside was fresh but searingly hot. He peered long and hard at two saddle horses ready to fall from heat and exhaustion with heavy loads still strapped on them by some inconsiderate cowboy who had forgotten them while wetting his whistle at the saloon.

The judge's shirt was saturated with perspiration, forcing him to take it off and place it on the back of his chair. He shivered, feeling an uncomfortable chill from the sudden change in body temperature. His body shook uncontrollably, like a leaf adjusting to a cool, strong breeze.

He sat down at the table and rifled through the court papers and notes he had jotted down from the first day of the trial. Each time he skimmed through the notes, he felt a sense of hopelessness; he just couldn't come

THE DECISION

up with the right answers. It was there before him, but the answer kept evading him.

Judge Norbert thought long and hard on this particular case and, the way he reasoned it, both of the parents were right in their views, and...oh...so very wrong in their approach. My, but they were set in their own minds. No amount of compromising or persuasion on anyone's part was going to change their feelings. Theirs was a sort of self-destruct warfare. Compromise was out of the question. If only some kind of solution could be found to partially satisfy and appease both parties. Who was it who said, "Love is the most powerful of all emotions and the most destructive passion known to man?"

The judge fanned his sweating brow with his open hand, his efforts affording little relief. Suddenly, he remembered something. He made a mad scramble for his saddle bag and found what he was looking for...a Bible. He took it out and laid it on the table. He hesitated, then opened it and leafed through it at random until he came upon a passage, "He, who searches for the truth, must first know the facts. He, who knows the facts, must still face the truth in time of decision. Time is relevant, though you may possess all the facts, you must still face the truth, for truth is eternal."

He felt a sudden chill in his bones and rose quickly to close the window. He placed his hands on the Bible as he sat down.

The pages had turned. What he saw now was a familiar biblical passage, "And Solomon said while weighing his decision to the true identity of the real mother, "We'll cut the boy in half and give each one their share." At that moment, the true mother said, "No, no, don't do that! Give the baby to her! Solomon had his answer as he replied, "For you are truly the baby's real mother, for only a real mother would give up her child before she would see it dead. I give you your child, for he is truly yours."

The judge couldn't seem to grasp the punch line. Somewhere between the lines lay the final answer, the one he was searching for. Who was to have the rightful custody of the boys? Who gave him the right to make one of God's decisions?

Once more he looked in the Bible and read, "Every parent should have a child and every child should have a parent."

The puzzled judge read this paragraph over and over again, trying to fathom its meaning. Finally he went to bed and spent a restless night, tossing about in a bed soaked with his perspiration. It seemed centuries before he finally dozed off.

Friday passed, with Justin wrestling with his conscience, reading over the transcripts of the trial. The more he delved into them, the more confused he became. He was a noted judge, but in all his days as a lawyer, he had never come up with such a complicated case as this. He had prided himself on his ability to comprehend the littlest details of any trial, but this one had him stumped.

Saturday came and his deliberations brought him no peace of mind. The more he reviewed the case, the farther away from the solution he found himself.

Soon it was Sunday. Still no possible clue for an answer to his dilemma. He was at his wit's end. He walked wearily to his bed, sighed and fell to his knees praying, a plaintive prayer, "Dear God, please help me. Show me the way. I know not what to do!"

At that moment, something in his inner self urged him, "Go back to the Bible, for there is your answer."

The wary judge rose slowly, concern deeply etched on his thin face. Once more he walked over to the table, looked at the Bible, opened it, and leafed through the pages at random. Finally, as if some divine power had guided him, he came to the passage, "How shall I divide my possessions with my two sons? I love them equally, but will they be able to survive the outside world? How can I test them? There is only one possible solution. I will give them equal shares to go out in the world and see how they prosper. There will be one main provision with this grant. At the end of two years, they are to come back and show me how they've prospered with their shares."

The Judge pondered on this passage for some time, then he silently closed the Bible, walked over to the window and looked down at the street below. Justin took out his handkerchief and wiped his perspiring brow as he gave it more thought about what he had just read.

Suddenly, as if God was prodding him, he thundered joyously, "That's it! That's my decision! So shall it be! Thank you, God! You have shown me the way. Amen!"

Chapter 3

The turbulent prairie winds had lessened in intensity. The searing heat of the long month had abated, bringing welcomed relief to the town. Once again the main street was crowded with buggies and buckboards with throngs of people anticipating another gala show at the divorce trial. They all awaited the climax to the drama that unfolded all week long to this much talked-about case. Everyone had a different opinion on the final outcome.

The courtroom was a beehive of activity. Some were discussing the different aspects of the trial; others were bringing up the weather, always a number-one subject. A few took time out to gossip about the lives of others. The noisy crowd of curiosity seekers was having a field day, laughing and gossiping about the coming attractions. It came to a sudden halt when the balding bailiff pounded the gavel, calling out in a loud voice, "Hear ye! Hear ye! The second session of the Broken Bend Territory Court is now in order. Everyone please stand while the Honorable Judge Justin G. Norbert takes his seat."

The sober-faced judge entered, walked slowly to his bench, and peered almost crossly at the spectators, then nodded to the be- spectacled bailiff. Nobert pushed himself forward, looking angrily one way and then the other until he was assured all was in order, then blared out, "The court will now hear the case of O'Shea vs O'Shea, an action to determine the permanent custody of Masters Kelly and Dennis O'Shea, twin dependents of the parties in contest."

The bailiff surveyed the spectators for any infractions of protocol of court procedure, paused for a moment, seeing all was in order, turned to the judge and nodded, then sat down.

The judge faced the two contestants solemnly, then spoke heavily in a low tone. "Before the court makes its decision in this case, I'd like to

THE DECISION

stress to both parties the gravity of its importance. There are many technicalities that have to be ironed out, that may be difficult to understand, but I feel it's my duty as judge to protect the rights of each party and the ones who'll be most affected by my decision...your sons. There are some ambiguous details of his case I'll discuss in length with each of you as the trial goes on."

The judge straightened some papers on his table. Enough time went by to allow the litigants to gather their thoughts before his honor continued. "First of all, I will explain carefully to your satisfaction, in detail, the different types of dissolution of marriage that are available. I'll describe each type to you. Please listen carefully as I proceed. Once you have agreed to one of them, there is no turning back for you. I trust you understand what you are about to do. If there is something you are not sure of, feel free to question me about it. Since I'm legal counsel to both of you, I'm not in the position to show partiality to either of you. As we go on, I'll advise you, step by step."

The judge peered at both parties, allowing each of them time to ask questions. Since none was forthcoming, the judge began his interpretation. "The first type of dissolution is annulment..." he dragged on while rearranging the papers in his hand. "This is a judicial declaration that a marriage is invalid due to incapacity, lack of consent of the parties, or some defect in the marriage formalities. I don't believe this applies in your case," he said with conviction.

He eyed both parties carefully, coughed, and went on. "The second type is legal separation. This permits the dissenting parties to live apart, but does not legally dissolve the marriage. I strongly advise this course of action for you."

He waited for some time to see if his advise was understood, then continued in his summation. "The third is legal divorce. This is the complete dissolution of a marriage relationship by the decree of the court. It is the immediate legal breakup of the marriage establishment and I abhor it," he proclaimed loudly.

Taking a deep breath and exhaling in short gasps, he looked at the contestants for some sign. When there was none, he went on methodically. "I will now explain the fourth and final type of divorce. It permits either party to marry again. The decree does not become final for a period of time and until then, the parties are not free to marry. The less said of this one, the better, and it's self explanatory."

The judge rose and walked over to where the two parties sat. "I will ask each of you for your decision, but first, as your counsel and friend, let me caution you. What you decide now, you'll have the rest of your life to deliberate, whether or not you did right or wrong. Think not only about yourself and your differences, but what future effect it will have on your two sons. Think well on what you are about to do. I strongly advise you to think it over carefully, as this will be one of the most important decisions of your lives. The court will recess thirty minutes to allow you enough time to meditate on it."

One of the deputies in the rear opened the door to allow the spectators to saunter outside for a breather from the stale air in the courtroom. In the meantime, Betty was thinking of the options presented by the judge. While on the other side of the room, Patrick was pacing back and forth, searching for the right answer.

Soon the recess was over, the bailiff called out to one and all that the court was again in session, and ordered the spectators to take their seats before the door was bolted.

The judge entered the noisy courtroom and motioned wearily for the spectators to sit down, then began in a serious tone, "I would like a little quiet in the courtroom! We re through the preliminaries of this case. Both parties have had ample time to make up their minds." Then Judge Norbert turned to the ashen-faced Patrick, "Mr. O'Shea, what type of divorce do you prefer?"

Patrick replied with a worried look on his drawn face, "Your Honor, the decision is simple for me, after great deliberation, I prefer legal separation."

This brought a faint smile of relief to Betty O'Shea's face as the judge posed the same question to her, "And now, Mrs. O'Shea, what is your decision?"

"Your Honor," she answered emphatically, "I, too, have decided on legal separation."

The judge thanked both parties for their quick decisions, then went on, "This is not the end of the trial. We have only arrived at a satisfactory vehicle of divorce for both parties. Now we come to the most important part of the case. What to do about the custody of the two boys? I caution the spectators to keep their emotions down regardless of views about either of the two parties at contest here. This has been a trying time for them. Do not think in your wildest dreams that this trial is for your entertainment. No, no, it is not! A divorce trial is not a sideshow for scandal mongers or gossip vultures to have a field day preying on the bones of the unfortunate. I will not condone any of this type of action in my court."

His menacing look straightened the backs of some of the more outspoken and critical of them who viewed the courtroom drama with amusement. He glared again at them, then went on slowly and deliberately. "I did a lot of soul-searching during the weekend. Asked the Lord for divine guidance. And in his mysterious way, he showed me the road for an ap-

THE DECISION

propriate and fair solution concerning the two boys. I read and researched the Bible, and as I said before, with the help of the Lord, I believe I have come up with the right decision. I earnestly think it will benefit the children most in the long run, along with the parents. If it were possible, I wish I could be here to witness the final conclusion of today's momentous decision."

Someone sneezed in the courtroom. It caused a ripple of laughter that soon died down when the judge showed his displeasure at this interruption by glaring at the miscreant. "At this trial, during the interrogations of both parties, even the slightest infraction from any of you in the audience hinders justice. If you must sneeze or anything of that order that upsets the court procedure with your actions, please have the courtesy to go outside. Now, to get back to my thoughts before I was rudely interrupted, I listened intently to both parties during the cross-examinations; what delighted me the most with both of them," he pounded the gavel for quiet among the spectators, "was that I found no rancor or hate in their present relationship. This is encouraging, yet...they do have philosophical differences. This barrier, that is breaking up their marriage, stems from their stubborn belief about how to raise their children. At the present time, reconciliation is not the answer. Only time will solve that. These are two people of separate worlds."

The judge rubbed his chin thoughtfully, scrutinized both parties, then made his opening remarks to Patrick, "Mr. O'Shea, you are a true westerner. A man to its ways and you have learned to adjust to its changing ways. You have become a success, extracting a living from the good earth, which, I grant you, at times does not come easy. You began your spread from a small ranch you had bought to the large holding you now own. There were many pitfalls and adversities. You are one of the new breed of cattlemen to make this your new home. I admire you! You're always looking to the future, as your success in breeding your cattle to be the finest in the west will attest. With your foresight and selectivity you helped make a better strain than there were at the beginning. You, and others like you, are the molders of the west, as we now know it today."

Patrick fidgeted in his seat in embarrassment to the words of praise from the judge. He was not used to compliments. Patrick bowed his head, determined not to show the slight blush of red on his swarthy face. The judge sipped a drink of water slowly, then proceeded. "Someday, this will all change to a new world that we can hardly envision, Mr. O'Shea..." Looking at Patrick straight in the eye and speaking quietly, he continued, "It will take people like you to make this dream come true. Your desire to raise your sons in this mold, to carry on your life's work, to think as you do, to be like you...well...that is commendable and understandable. All parents have the same aspirations for their children."

Justin stopped for a moment to catch his breath. The thin air made it hard for him to breathe properly. Then he turned his attention to Betty. "Mrs. O'Shea, you are an honest, intelligent, and beautiful young woman. In my discussions with you, I couldn't help but notice your excellent choice and use of words. That comes from a good education and social background that will help you in whatever vocation you may undertake. I like that! Those are sterling qualities that are absolutely necessary in raising children in today's world. Studying you, I've learned that you are a person of rare convictions; the ability to know right from wrong. That is also vital in raising your sons. The principles and ideals that you possess, will teach them another way of life. I can't fault you on that. I can readily understand your primary concern," the judge smiled encouragingly at Betty, "Your views are admirable; someday there will be more women like you raising their voices in this man's world."

The judge looked straight ahead to include both of them as he went on, "We have shown two different ideologies on how to raise children. One by hard work and perserverence in the ways of the west, while the other emphasizes a good sound education as a basis for furthering their careers. They both have merits! I'm not in the position to find fault or condone either one...only time will furnish the answer to that."

Justin took a sip of water, looked disapprovingly at some gossipers in the back row of the courtroom, then went on. "The most encouraging part of this trial was the lack of hostility by either contestant and the good taste that each used in answering the questions presented to them. It's quite evidence that there is still compassion and love between them, but...for the present, it appears to all of us, it will have to be shelved for the time being for the more pressing concern for their children. This is nothing new in today's world. We see it every day. Children rule the destiny of their parents. The fault lies not with the children but with the parents who made it so. As we can see, this is the main cause of the rift in their relationship. Their personal philosophies that decree a continued conjugal discord. We can accept that...but can the children?"

Once more the tired judge paused to take a drink of water. "No parent," he said gravely, "should be deprived of his or her children, and no child should be deprived of its parents. If the court were to give custody of both children to the mother, then we'd be depriving the father the blessings of the children. On the other hand, if the court were to give the children to the father, then it would be negligent in its solemn duties by depriving the mother of her motherly rights."

"Before I go on..." he said with conviction and with restraint, "there is another important aspect of married life that both parties are not fully aware of. Our red brothers refer to it as the totem pole theory of marriage between brave and squaw. Its precepts are quite simple. They believe that

THE DECISION

marriage is more than a union of brave and squaw. It's a union that stabilizes the tribe. It would be well if we could follow its simple formula. The Indians believe that a marriage is like a totem pole with all its ledges. On the top ledge, stand only the brave and his squaw. On the ledge below them, are the children to be guided and loved. Below them on another ledge are the parents. They have their rights too, the rights of love and respect of the inhabitants of the upper two ledges. There are other ledges on the way down comprised of close relatives, friends, warriors, and associates, with one main difference. They can not be interspersed from ledge to ledge to attain the status of the top three ledges, but can move from ledge to ledge below those top three ledges. That is known as the totem pole theory. Our contestants are not of that opinion; and no matter how much rhetoric will be expounded here, it will not change that. Therefore, the court has recorded the signed decree of legal separation of Patrick O'Shea and Betty O'Shea. Just hold off all celebrations for the present, there is more to this decree! There are special stipulations to this decree that are congruent to the divorce. I expect both parties to follow them to the letter of the law. What I'm about to divulge is of the greatest importance to all concerned. They are...."

The judge glanced quickly at Patrick, then at Betty, before continuing with his judgment, "The court decrees that Kelly, one of the sons both of this union, will be given to Patrick O'Shea, to raise in his way of life. Dennis, the other son, will be awarded to Betty O'Shea, to raise in her way of life."

The courtroom was in an uproar over the unexpected decision. The judge pounded the gavel furiously as Patrick and Betty started at each other in utter disbelief. The bedlam in the court subsided when the judge thundered in a stentorian voice, "One more outburst like that, and the whole lot of you will be spending the weekend in jail. I know this decree doesn't set too well with some of you, but I'm not here to please you or what you may think. Perhaps it will not meet with the hearty approval of either contesting party. I do not claim to be Solomon. I'm only a backwoods judge called upon to make an important decision. I believe it to be the wisest for, and fairest to all concerned. Furthermore, the court has one more provision that is of the utmost importance to this decree..."

Justin wiped a tiny bead of perspiration off the end of his nose, cleared his foggy glasses, raised his head to glare at some scuffling of feet, then went on, "The court also decrees that the parent of each child will have custody until each son attains the age of nineteen, at which time, according to this provision, they are to be exchanged for a period of two years. This will allow each child ample time to rediscover his other parent, and to learn about them, and love and understand them. God in his infinite wisdom has shown me to the way to this decision."

"To both of you," the judge stared fixedly at them while making his point, "this will be the greatest challenge of your lives. You will live two lives. One for the next several years, then another for two years. Who knows? There may be a richer one for you after that. Let the record show that on June 10, 1875, this decree was signed and put into force by me, the presiding judge, with the stipulation that on June 10, 1894, by court decree, the parents are to exchange their sons for a period of two years. I've instructed the court reporter to print enough additional copies of this decree to suffice all parties and one to the District Court in St. Louis. A copy will be kept on file until the time this decree goes into effect. I expect both parties to honor it at that time."

With a quick rap of the gavel, the judge curtly announced, "Court is adjourned!"

Chapter 4

With the echoes of the divorce still ringing in his ears, Patrick set about the herculean task of getting his troubled house in order. These were going to be difficult days ahead in his life. Inheriting the taxing responsibility of raising an infant son, of which he had no knowledge or how to begin, or from which end, was going to be a trying experience for the rancher.

Out of necessity, Patrick was forced to hire a woman from Broken Bend to care for his son while he was on the trail, taking care of the ranching business. Within a week she quit. Then, in the space of four months, eight others were hired and left for one reason or other, but mainly for one reason, logistics. All the women were hired came from Broken Bend, a small western cattle town in the northwestern part of Kansas, about twelve miles from O'Shea's Betty Ann Ranch. It took the women between four to five hours daily to make the trip by horse and buggy, besides having the additional burden of listening to the complaints of their hungry husbands and the caterwauling of their own young charges. Patrick paid them a handsome wage, but any wage under these trying conditions wouldn't have been enough to make up for the domestic difficulties they had to put up with.

Patrick had just finished hiring his tenth caretaker for his young son, Kelly. Her name was Matilda Rotaille, a large, heavyset, domineering woman with a loud, biting, abrasive voice. Patrick kept a respectful distance from her. He had been at his wit's end when he hired her, having been refused by every available woman in Broken Bend. Patrick was so desperate for help at that time that he would have hired the devil's mate if she were available.

One of the ranchers, Nate Williams, suggested to Patrick "Joe Pedigree had the same problem with his three motherless children. Guess what he did? He sent them off to a kinda school for children in the neighboring town of Sagebrush, about thirty miles from here. Reckon it wasn't too good an idear, 'cause in a week, his children showed up at his front door, dirty and hungry. They had walked all the way back.''

Patrick exploded, "Hope! That's not for me! Nate, I promised the judge when he awarded me Kelly, I'd raise him to the best of my ability, which, at the moment, is not too good. That's what I said when I promised him. Consarn it! So be it! I won't let no stranger from out of town to do my job. Darn it! Never!''

Patrick wouldn't admit it, but he still carried the torch for his beautiful wife. The hurt from the divorce haunted him. It was noticeable to his close friends, in little telltale signs here and there. It was quite evident to them he wasn't the same jocular, considerate person they had always remembered. He had grown into a somewhat morose, short-fused man who became easily frustrated with small problems that he used to shrug off with a snap of a finger.

One day he confided to an old friend, Zak Targol, "You know, Zak, if it wasn't for the love I have for my son, Kelly, I don't know how I would ever had survived the divorce. He's such a game little critter! He gurgles, laughs, and tries to talk when I'm holding him. He has given my life a new meaning. When Betty left and took our other son with her, it took the guts out of me. I was a beaten man! At the time, I cursed the judge for splitting up my family with his decision, but as it turned out, I should have thanked him for giving me a son to build a future on. Who knows what path I would have taken if he hadn't? There's another thought that's entered my mind, Hm-mm! Perhaps Betty has the same misgivings as I have about it. In fact, I'm sure does! You know, Zack, divorce is hell!''

It was slow going at first for Patrick but in the process he was carefully putting his wrecked life back together again. He was getting a new lease on it, and every day it was wound around by the pride of his life, little Kelly and his ranch. Each had a special niche in his heart. Since his talk with Zack, he never again mentioned his wife by name. It was like a festering sore that refused to heal by itself.

The ensuing days had been kind to Patrick, aging him gracefully. A twilight shadow lightened his sideburns while a slight, unnoticeable, middle aged bulge began to appear at the waist. He was beginning to shed his hardnosed image, becoming more tolerant of the little foibles of his close friends and associates. Some of his cronies recognized the Patrick they once knew. Patrick was laughing again with his former vigor and gusto, so much so that it would infect others to join in his loud outbursts. Patrick had made a complete circle. He was again with the living and loving it.

One bright sunny day in the spring, Patrick called out to Tex Andrews, "Say, Tex, we're going out on the range to check on the steers. Saddle up!"

Little did Patrick now that this was going to turn out to be an important day for him. An important one before it was over. The worrisome problem of a caretaker for his son would be solved forever in a manner he hadn't dreamed possible by someone he had never imagined.

The pair had ridden for quite a distance when Patrick spotted something on the prairie not to his liking. He stopped and pointed it out to his foreman, "Tex, do you see what I see?"

About a quarter of a mile away, five drunken cowboys were trying to force their attentions on a lone young Indian squaw. She was in her early twenties and ragged but fighting with a demonic fury to protect her honor.

One of the burly cowboys grabbed at her worn, deerskin blouse, half ripped it, exposed a firm, well-formed breast. The sight aroused the liquor-soaked cowboys to a new frenzy. One of them tried to take advantage of the situation but was rewarded with a healthy swat on the nose that drew blood by the Indian woman.

The cowboy uttered a vile phrase as the blood flowed from his injured nostril. "I'll get you, you heathen savage." He cussed again, "I'll be the first to give you what you want. You will be mine! Nothing or nobody will stop me! After me, the rest of you galoots can get your share of funning."

She snarled, fighting back furiously, "Paleface dogs! Dogs! You no men, you squaws! Ph....ooey!" She spat at them.

"Let's burn leather, Tex," roared Patrick, "She can't hold out much longer against those varmints."

"Giddap!" yelled Tex, whipping his horse to the limit, "Patrick let's even the odds."

They arrived on the scene in the nick of time as one of the cowboys held the squaw firmly on the ground while trying to unbutton his baggy pants. Patrick yelled out to him, "Hey, you dirty polecats! Get your filthy hands off that woman!"

The man swore at Patrick while the rest yelled obscenities at the two, "Who's gonna make us, big man? You and what army?" as the first man continued to molest the squaw, "Besides, we're only funning! She's only an Indian squaw! We'll even let you have your turn with her after we're done!"

Patrick made one leap off his horse, landing on the back of the cowboy who was attacking the squaw, knocking him away from her.

THE DECISION

The drunken cowboy fumed in anger at the intrusion, then took a swing at Patrick, but Patrick moved faster than he and drove a hard right to the other's unprotected jaw, flooring him for good. Then in a quick move, he grabbed two of the others by the neck and conked their heads together with a loud bang.

Tex, in the meantime, was handily disposing of the other two. It was over in a matter of minutes.

The fiery Indian squaw was ready to do battle with the two newcomers, snarling and baring her teeth like a cornered wildcat. She awaited their first move. As far as she was concerned, they were all the same, hated palefaces. She still had plenty of fight in her as she hissed at them, "I kill you, palefaces!"

"Whoa!" pleaded Patrick in surrender, holding up his hands, surprised by her hostility towards them. "We're friends, not enemies." Laughing loudly at her display of anger, he said, "Not all palefaces are bad, nor are all Indians good. There are bad and good in both our people, Please..."

Patrick talked to her in a slow, low monotone that calmed the frenzied woman. Soon her anger subsided and her voice softened, "You no try to have fun with me? I die fist! I am Omaha! Me good squaw!" She was very outspoken and emphatic about this assertion by crossing her arms across her bared breasts.

Patrick studied her. She had to be in her early twenties and had long, smooth black hair that glistened in the hot sun. She was thin as a rail and anyone could see she hadn't eaten for a long time. Her face was dirty and cracked from the cruel winds of the prairies. Patrick spotted a certain quiet beauty under all the dirt. It was classic beauty, in the amber Indian mold, and just as wild as nature.

She wore fringed, soft deerskin clothes of the prairie Indian tribes, that were now in shambles from the battle with the drunken cowboys. On her feet were beaded moccasins. She had the look of a proud, resolute woman who had put her self respect first and her life second. She possessed a regal bearing that separated her from the common people.

Patrick reached into his saddlebag and handed her some dried beef which she grabbed and hungrily devoured. Tex took a blanket off his saddle and placed it around her shoulders, covering her exposed breasts while she munched away on the dried beef.

After waiting for her to finish the meal, Patrick gestured to her, "Peace!" by gently offering a friendly hand to assist her on the horse with him. She eyed him in distrust, still not sure what kind of devil this genial, smiling paleface was, but in the end, his earnest, pleasant face won her over. "I'll take you to my ranch where no one will ever bother you again. You'll have a chance to clean up, eat, and sleep in a clean bed until you feel better. Tomorrow, we'll see what is in store for you. If at that time, you want to leave, you will be free to go. No one will stop you."

"Ugh!" she grunted grudgingly, "Mebbe you good paleface," nodding her head, then shook it, "Mebbe not! But I believe you just the same. You have good face. Me! Shatoma! You and you! What name?"

They both laughed at her innocent but naive inquiry. Patrick replied, "Me, Patrick O'Shea. This is Tex Andrews," putting his arms around his foreman, "Now tell us how you happened to get tangled with those drunken buzzards?"

On the way to the ranch, she unfolded a frightening story about how she and her husband-to-be, Bawata, and a small band of Omaha braves were attacked by a war party of hated Crow warriors. Shatoma went on to relate, "Bawata say to me, "Hide behind the trees. Don't let the Crows take you alive! Don't be a Crow squaw! Better to be dead, I fight to save you. If they kill me, don't move! Don't yell! Don't cry! Hide! Live for tomorrow! No good to die today! Bawata care for you! Soon I will be gone! You must not die! You must live to tell what happened here. I go gladly die for you. Someday, you will join me in death. I wait for you, Shatoma. Goodbye!"

She sobbed a little and continued with her story. "The hated Crows killed Bawata and all the Omaha braves, then scalped them. They sang, drank, and danced all night, celebrating their scalping party. In the morning they ride away. I come out of hiding. I cry when I see Bawata. I bury him so the birds and animals don't pick on his bones. I find some food! Go before hated Crows come back. I eat off the land until now. That was twenty moons ago. I tired and hungry. I sad, I lose Bawata. I lose good man! I walk, walk, walk. I don't know how far! Long time, long ways! Then today I meet bad palefaces. They try to have fun with me. I die first before I let them. Then you two come and fight for Shatoma. Good fight! You win! I glad! Now I rest easy on horse. Me tired."

Matilda met them at the doorway. "Where did you find that stinking, filthy savage?" she roared in her authorative voice, "Why did you bring her here with you? She isn't stepping inside this ranch as long as I work here. I will not be associated with that heathen. Her Indian friends killed my brother and his family. I won't forget that to my dying day. I've hated Indians ever since. Get her out of here!" She made a move to evict her.

Patrick put up a hand, "Oh no, you don't. This is my ranch and I'll say who can stay here or not. She has suffered enough indignities without you getting on your high horse. She's had her brave killed and scalped by the Crows. Shatoma hates them as much, or more than you do, with damned good reason."

THE DECISION

"Maybe she means more to you than just work! You've been without a woman for so long that you'd even take a stinking squaw to satisfy yourself. You've got a hankering for that Indian bitch, eh?"

Patrick exploded, "That does it! You've said enough," Patrick reached into his back pocket and counted out some silver, "This will more than suffice for your employment here. I will not have my son raised by the likes of you."

"Hr....mph!" she explained in disgust, then marched out of the room with her nose in the air.

The yelling between Patrick and Matilda woke little Kelly. Matilda got in the last word as she walked out, "I hope your son keeps you awake all night. It would serve you right for bringing that damned squaw here."

Kelly's cries continued unabated until Shatoma said, "Little papoose hungry. It yells for food! Bring papoose to me!"

Patrick climbed the stairs and returned with the sobbing child. Shatoma took him into her arms and looked under his clothing, exclaiming in surprise, "Him brave! Heap strong brave! Good strong voice!" She sang softly to him but Kelly still cried. Then Shatoma did a strange thing. She pinched his nose a few times and soon he stopped crying, "Bring some milk for young papoose. Him hungry!"

Patrick was curious, "Why did you pinch him on the nose while he was crying? How come he stopped?"

"The Indians do this to stop the papooses from waking the chiefs. The squaws squeeze the papoose's nose so they can't breathe, and soon, little papooses get smart, and get the idea. It's better not to cry than not to breathe."

?Well, I'll be hornswoggled!" explained Patrick.

Patrick was impressed with Shatoma. What he saw, he liked. Chance had found Patrick a new caretaker for his son and ranchhouse. Quickly, he put the question to her, "Shatoma, how would you like to live here and take care of the house and papoose for me?"

She asked a fair question, "Where is your paleface squaw? Why she not care for him?"

"It's a long story, "Patrick tried to evade the question but she would have none of it.

"Me wait! Got lotsa time! Make story good for my ears. Me hear! Me judge!"

Patrick began slowly, not knowing how or where to start, to tell it as it was: the whole truth. After all, the Indian woman was no fool. "Paleface squaw and I live apart. Big White Chief separate us many moons ago. He gave me one brave papoose and one brave papoose to my paleface squaw. The Big White Chief said it was to be so for many snows."

Shatoma sneered at the answer, "Palefaces have funny laws. Make Indian laugh! Indians no do that! Indian laws are straight as arrow. Paleface man too soft! Paleface squaw too hard!"

Patrick persisted, "Will you take the job?"

Shatoma appeared in no great hurry. Finally, after what appeared like ages to the impatient Patrick, she had made up her mind, "Me take job on one condition. You chief of everything outside of these walls. In these walls, all will do as I say! Run by my laws!"

Patrick roared with laughter, "You are just as hard as paleface squaw. It's a deal! Inside is your domain and I'll notify everyone of this arrangement. Peace?" as he held out his hand to seal the agreement.

A mutual bond of respect had crept into their business arrangement. They would never break that bond! Shatoma had found a home in the paleface's world with a young brave to love as her own son, the papoose that was denied to her with Bawanta's death. Patrick had found someone he could trust in caring for his son. It was as if this arrangement was made in heaven by a fairy godmother.

As the days went by, Shatoma proved to be a hard disciplinarian, running the ranchhouse and raising Kelly under the harsh training of the Omaha warrior. She spared no one, neither Kelly nor Patrick. The house was her domain. Her law was final. Little Kelly fell in love with her from the first day. Her stern but fair ways ruled him in the daytime. She loved him with tenderness, singing Indian songs to allay his nightly fears, and hugging him whether he needed it or not. She instilled in him the Indian theory of right and wrong, the simple philosophies of a regal people.

As Kelly grew older, Shatoma patiently answered most of his steady stream of questions to the best of her ability. Once in a while she would take him out in the woods to teach him about nature and its wonders. Shatoma taught him tracking, how to read a trail, and judge how old it was. She showed him how to make camp without arousing curiosity of others, and how to break it down without leaving any telltale traces. She was patient as she taught him Indian discipline, the ability to accept orders and obey them, and to issue orders fairly and confidently to your subordinates.

Kelly learned many valuable lessons in the forest from Shatoma. She taught him that animals have rights. They should be respected by all mankind, and any indiscriminate killing of them was just plain murder. She warned him about the perils of the woods, to walk softly and carefully in the forest, lest he step on a coiled rattler. Their ominous warning was their way of saying, "Don't step on me and I won't bite you."

Shatoma cautioned him often, "Kelly, remember one thing at all times: have fourteen eyes in your head. See in all directions. Trust nothing but yourself, whether in the woods or in the paleface's villages. You must

THE DECISION

be wary of the many dangers that you may encounter in these places, from both man and animal, but man is the most dangerous of all."

The things that Shatoma taught Kelly about life in his growing years couldn't be measured in words, found in school books, or learned in the paths of the woods. No amount of money could ever repay its worth.

In the following days, Patrick was to learn many things about Shatoma that were to change his life. He thought he knew her in his short association with her as a person of strong character, one who kept her feelings hidden from the outside world, yet she seemed to be completely happy in the paleface environment. She ran the house like her own home and care for the young brave as her own son.

Shatoma had regained most of the weight she had lost in her ordeal on the prairies, adding color to her swarthy Indian complexion that magically transformed her into an Indian woman of rare and unquestionable beauty. It seemed that everyone on the ranch noticed the transformation of Shatoma except Patrick, who was blind to the obvious.

This incredible situation would have probably gone on indefinitely if it hadn't been for one fateful day in the bunkhouse. Patrick happened to be taking inventory of the supplies that day when, by chance, he heard some of the men talking behind a thin, partitioned wall that separated the two rooms. He wouldn't have listened except that the mention of his name linked with Shatoma's caught his attention.

One of the cowhands blurted out, "Christ sakes! Did you ever get a gander at Shatoma's breasts as she walks by? I almost fell off my horse the first time I saw them. They're firm as spring apples and probably twice as sweet. Twin mountains of heavenly pleasure. Boy, would I like to enjoy a little of that! I tell you, Buck, and that straight black shiny hair, falling to the small of her back, is something to behold. Every time she walks by, I turn in my saddle to get a better look. I'll never work for any other ranch as long as she's here to raise my emotions. I wonder if Patrick has taken note of her? He'd have to be blind not to have noticed her beauty."

Another cut in, "Shur 'nuff, Enos! I wonder if Patrick is getting any? He'd be a fool if he isn't. He doesn't look the type who lets any moss grow under his feet. The way I look at it, as long as she's in the house night and day, she's there for the pickings! Let's face it, Patrick has been divorced for a long time now and he's got be a little hard up for a little lovin'. I know I would be! Can you imagine what you would do with Shatoma shasaying that pretty little butt of hers around the house at all hours of the day and night? It would make a Baptist preacher throw away his Bible! I know I would never go out on the range if she were in the bunkhouse waiting for me. I know what I'd do! I'd make my big play for her. She's a real prairie beauty! Darn it! I wish I could put my brand on her."

"Craps and tarnation!" exclaimed a third, "She's not only beautiful, but she also walks like an Indian princess should, with her head held high in the air like an untamed deer in the forest. She's a sight for sore eyes. All the hands are in love with her, but she doesn't give them the time of the day. She's friendly and polite to all but well reserved. She's the most beautiful woman I've ever seen, Indian or white. I agree with Buck about Patrick. He's got to be blind as a bat if he hasn't noticed Shatoma by now. He's been without a woman for so long that he's probably forgotten what it's like to be with one. After all, he can't be a saint! Here in the west, there are no saints to be found. Just think of the stiff temptations, ha-ha, he must have to face each day watching her prance by with that wonderful body of hers staring him in the face. It's no wonder I can't sleep at night thinking about it. It would drive a saint to drink....I wonder if it has any affect on that thing between his legs? He's not that old, you know. I wonder if it can still rise to the occasion? I don't care if she is an Indian squaw, I'd marry her in a minute if she'd have me."

Patrick heard enough. All that the men had candidly said of a possible relationship between Shatoma and himself had merit. It opened up a bright new world that he hadn't dreamed existed before.

Patrick reasoned logically. He couldn't fire the men for what they had said. They had done nothing wrong except air their personal opinions. He remembered when he was in the Union Army during the Civil War. There were many remarks that he and his buddies used to make about women, some far worse than the men in the bunkhouse had said. Besides, wasn't he in the wrong? He was the one who had invaded their privacy by eavesdropping on their conversation. What were his men to believe? After all, wasn't he living in the same house with Shatoma? In a way, he was glad they had opened Pandora's box. If they hadn't, he probably would have missed out on Shatoma's wonders. Only one thing bothered him. What if somebody else was thinking about moving in and he didn't know about it. Maybe he has already caught Shatoma's attention? What a fool he would be to let something like this to happen right before his eyes!

Patrick tried to excuse his lack of foresight by backtracking his thought to the day he first saw her on the prairie; a ragged, scrawny, frightened, unkempt Indian squaw fighting for her honor. She wasn't much to look at then! How could anyone in his right mind have noticed anything special about her beneath all that dirt? Then he remembered how she took over the responsibility of raising his son and running his ranchhouse. He recalled the gentleness and love she bestowed on Kelly, and the million and one things she did to make his home a happy one. He should have

THE DECISION

noticed all this sooner, yes, and her, too, but his eyes were closed to everything except his son and the ranch. He should have told Shatoma sooner how much he appreciated all that she had done for him. Appreciation! Hell! What he should have told her was more than that. It was another word that seemed to get stuck in his craw.

Patrick did turn over a new leaf. He began to pay more attention to Shatoma. And he learned one startling thing! The men were right! Shatoma was beautiful! She was desirable, so desirable! Something he couldn't control, or didn't want to control, possessed him whenever Shatoma passed by, a feeling he had forgotten existed. She had blossomed into a rare beauty right before his eyes. He had been too blind to see what everyone else had.

Suddenly, a change came over Patrick. His eyes had been closed to her beauty. Miraculously, they were opened by some unknown power. A sensation he had forgotten existed was within him once more. It was wonderful! He was so alive again! The lure of Shatoma was unbearable to him, he felt possessed by her beauty. The sweet scent of her body was like the wondrous fresh aroma of the forest in the springtime. Her sparkling dark eyes captivated him with every glance, and when she spoke, her voice enslaved him like a hypnotist's spell.

He began to feel again that pleasant sensation in his groin. He still had that old feeling for his divorced wife, but they were apart now. Shatoma was here, and...he was a man. Patrick knew he was treading on dangerous ground. What if Shatoma didn't feel the same way about him?

Desire and propriety battled on even terms in his head, with no apparent winner. Patrick was in a dilemma. What to do or not to do? That was the question in his mind. Then he remembered an old saying of his father's, "Propriety is fine in church, but it doesn't warm the bed at night."

Patrick thought over carefully his options. They were limited! Perhaps the talk he had heard in the bunkhouse had stimulated his interest in Shatoma. Perhaps it was no idle talk! Wasn't it possible that others in Broken Bend had arrived at the same mistaken conclusions as the men about Shatoma and himself? For Patrick to explain his position to anybody would be admitting his guilt, but he was an innocent party. Who would believe him?

His only other immediate concern was Kelly who was too young to know anything. Then what of tomorrow when he grew older and had to listen to the snide remarks of his playmates who had been informed by the local gossip? To ugly rumors that are formulated by narrow minded, ill informed gossips. Fortunately, Kelly was his staunchest ally! He loved Shatoma and would ignore such malicious tripe.

Patrick knew it was a perilous course he was following. Where it was leading him he didn't know. He did know that the rewards in the end appealed to him. He had to tell Shatoma how he felt about her. If she felt the same about him, then it was worth the gamble. If her answer was negative, and she threatened to leave the ranch, then all would be lost. The thought of this frightened him, yet, for all concerned, it had to be resolved one way or the other.

The beauty of Shatoma had aroused his desire to a new high. He had fantasized in his mind what it would be like to have Shatoma in bed in a warm love embrace. What was he to do? She had never offered any encouragement in the past, nor had she ever teased him with provocative looks to sizzle his blood. She had kept a low profile in their relation, remaining expressionless through the most delicate situation.

What the men had brought out in the open that day in the bunkhouse preyed on Patrick's mind. It was like the serpent in the Garden of Eden, enticing Eve to eat the forbidden apple. Patrick wondered if Shatoma was to become his forbidden fruit. He had to learn the truth.

Patrick a began low-key courtship of Shatoma in the next few days. At first, he was a little shy. He could only bring himself to talk about the weather. Shatoma only grunted at his childish attempts, "Me no worry about the weather. If you no like, it will change with the new moon."

Then Patrick tried another tactic. He asked her how little Kelly was getting along and she replied, "Little brave eat, sleep, and dirty bed."

Then Patrick tried to talk about the ranch operations. She stopped him cold, "Me no good for that! You care for the cows, I care for little brave and Big Chief. I no tell you what to do and you no tell me what to do."

Every time Patrick tried to start a conversation with small talk, Shatoma was equal to the occasion by keeping it in that vein...small talk. She didn't try to enlarge or continue with it. One day she told Patrick, "Heap many words, but no meaning!"

She was either too busy, didn't care, or too smart to let Patrick know how she felt. She let him cook in his own stew. Whatever it was she was thinking, Patrick didn't know.

Then Patrick decided to try a more direct approach. He started looking over her shoulder as she was preparing the nightly meal. He'd give her a smile of approval with each delicious repast. Her closeness hungered him more, the fire in him was being stoked by a great desire of passion. If he had any doubts before, they were all put to bed now. He hadn't lost that old feeling. It had just remained dormant, like a slumbering volcano waiting for the right moment to erupt. His newfound emotion caused an ache in the groin. He wondered if the ache was love or lust. He wasn't sure, but it felt so wonderful, whatever it was. It wouldn't be long before he'd find out.

Patrick continued his courtship of Shatoma by being gentle in his approach and suave in his demeanor so as not to frighten her. He had to be near her, always hoping to touch her if the possibility occurred. At

THE DECISION

first, it was a little pat here and a little pat there. All this filled him with more desire than ever. However these little innocent acts didn't go unnoticed by Shatoma either. She was keeping her daily score. She knew Patrick was up to something, but what it was she wasn't sure. Shatoma had the naive belief that Patrick had found someone else to replace her, perhaps a paleface squaw from Broken Bend. Little did she realize that this was the farthest thing from Patrick's mind.

This sticky situation was getting out of hand for poor Patrick. His emotions were beginning to betray him. He had to find the answer before something embarrassing happened. One day it almost occurred when Shatoma accidently brushed against him. His whole world seemed ready to explode. He couldn't take this much more! He was human after all! After that, it always came down to two choices for Patrick when Shatoma passed by: either take a quick cold bath or saddle up his horse and go count the steers on the prairie until he cooled down.

Shatoma didn't know the constant torture she was putting him through. If she had been more observant, she would have seen the bulge in the front of his riding pants that manifested itself like a magic wand, waiting for the opportunity to create its own magic.

Patrick had fears of getting too close to Shatoma. He knew that if he touched her for any length of time, all hell would break loose. Then one day, the one thing he feared the most, happened. Shatoma was in the parlor when she half-tripped over a curled up rug and fell helplessly into Patrick's waiting, eager arms. He caught her before she could fall and hurt herself. He felt her soft body brush against the warm hardness of his lower self. Shatoma didn't flinch from the first contact. She just went on with her work, unsmiling, as if nothing happened. Poor Patrick was beside himself! He was devastated with unbridled inner emotions! He knew that this couldn't go on. It was time to talk to Shatoma!

That night, Patrick asked Shatoma to sit at the table with him. He explained that he had something important to discuss with her. Shatoma fidgeted and fretted; Patrick had never asked her to sit with him. Why now? As she sat down, her worries started anew! Her fears were beginning to surface. She believed Patrick was going to ask her to leave.

"Shatoma," he began gently, "You know I have white squaw I am still married to, but she is far away. I'm a man, and as a man, I have certain needs. For these needs, I need a woman. I have found that woman."

The one thing that Shatoma had feared the most had come to pass. She said fearfully, "White Chief, you want me to go so you can bring in paleface squaw to care for young brave and horse? What I do wrong? Me sad! You want me to go?"

"No, no, Shatoma." Patrick protested, "It's not another woman I want to bring here. The one I want is already here! Shatoma, do you understand what I'm trying to say? It's you, Shatoma, I love! I cannot marry you became I'm still married to white squaw in the east. I do want you to be the squaw in my house. Here, you will have two men that love you, Kelly and I. Shatoma, I've loved you for a long time but my eyes were closed too long."

"You want me to be your squaw?" she asked in disbelief, "Why, White Chief?"

"Shatoma, I'm lonely for the love of a woman. A man has certain needs that only the right woman can supply. Sure, since the day my wife left me, I could have had a lot of paleface women, but none have excited me as much as you did. They could never be like you. You are kind, gentle, and loving. Kelly loves you and I love you! Shatoma, I want to ask you a question. Is it wrong for a man to love two women like I do? One paleface and the other Indian?"

Shatoma was stunned at the sudden turn of events, then by his personal question. She thought it over somberly and then answered. "There's an old saying among our people, "Love has no boundaries; age, color, tribes, or beliefs. Love is good medicine for sickness of the heart, and sometimes, bad medicine too." White Chief, we all have more than one love in our hearts. When we born, we love mother, then father, then sisters and brothers. Time goes by, we love others we grow up and play with. Then one day, we no children no more! We find someone to spend all our days with. When I found my brave, I became his squaw! I was happy! When he was killed, I was sad. Now, I too, am lonely! I too, need a man! Your paleface squaw not here, no good for you. My Bawata is dead, no good for me! Just we two left. You want me to share your tepee? Maybe we no love each other now, but we keep plenty warm in winter together! Palefaces call it love, Indians say it's a need for each other to be together all the time"

"Does that mean," Patrick asked hopefully, "You will accept me?"

"I no say that," teased Shatoma smiling, "I need time to give right answer."

"How much time do you need?" asked Patrick impatiently.

"White Chief, say one-two-three," she said impishly.

"What kind of game is this?" asked Shamus, not quite sure what to make of it, "Well, all right. I'll go along with it. One..two..three."

"Me make up my mind, White Chief," she said with a snap of her fingers, "I accept you to be my brave. Remember, White Chief, me still boss of tepee!"

THE DECISION

Patrick roared with laughter as he hugged her. "You still are harder than the paleface woman. You are my love. Not just for today, but all the days to follow. You'll be the mother to my son. I will cherish you forever as my wife. One other thing, Shatoma, please call me Patrick from now on. Welcome to your tepee!"

Shatoma smiled as she confessed, "You know, White Chief, I mean, Patrick. There's never been a doubt in my mind about you. I've loved you a long time, since the day you fought for me on the prairies. I never forget! You big man for me then, now bigger man for me! I no let you escape! I no want to escape! Our bed will always be warm."

"Why didn't you let me know of your feelings then?"

Shatoma looked at his strangely, trying to say the words that kept eluding her. "Easy to answer! Mebee, Patrick, you no remember. Me, just squaw to you at that time. Mebbe me too, still no trust the paleface either! Mebbe me want to learn if paleface talk with forked tongue or straight as a stick!" She lengthened her arms to pantomime to describe what she meant. "Mebbe I want you to tell me first. Better for squaw that way! I asked you, Patrick, the same question, why you no tell me before you like me?"

"I guess, Shatoma, for a lot of reasons, but mainly, I was afraid of my true feelings until now. Now I do! Yes, I do! We can't get married because I'm already married! Really, we will be married as man and wife for all the tomorrows of our days. I love you, Shatoma! You have made me very happy. Paleface...Indian...mean nothing to me, except our love. That is all that matters, what we fell about ourselves."

"Good words, Patrick," she said as she kissed him. "Me like the ring to them. One last word, Patrick: To have happy tepee, squaw must be squaw and brave must be brave in tepee. No good if squaw try to be brave, or if brave try to be squaw in tepee. No good for both of them."

That night, Patrick and Shatoma consummated their love. As they lay there holding each other, Shatoma said in soft tones, "You make me very happy, Patrick," then impishly went on, "Paleface warrior still have plenty of fire."

Patrick laughed, "What good is a fire if you have no stove? Your stove sparked my log into a barnburner tonight!"

"Love's heap good medicine for brave and squaw." sang Shatoma, "When squaw is satisfied, much better for brave. From now on, we will have more loving and less talking in this tepee!"

Chapter 5

The dark clouds of scandal hovered over the peaceful skies of Broken Bend, caused by choice bits of gossip circulated by naive, loose-tongued, inebriated cowhands. Town talk centered around the love life of Patrick and Shatoma. The story was picked up eagerly and magnified out of proportion by the flap-tongued gossipers of Broken Bend. It was a smoldering brush fire at first that soon blazed into a conflagration of unlimited proportions. It reached its boiling point on Sunday morning at church. The usual services lasted for an hour. Patrick and Kelly were the last ones to leave. Outside the church, various groups congregated, discussing favorite topics. One of these groups, and the most vocal, aired their views concerning the carrying on between Patrick and his Indian squaw.

The whole town was divided in its sentiments about the affair. There was no middle of the road. Most of the ill feelings were directed at Shatoma. Many believed that she was some sort of evil witch with a strange power over Patrick.

There were about nine in one unrestrained group who were jabbering and laughing, pointing fingers at Patrick as he came out of church.

One of the most outspoken of them called out to Patrick tartly, "Where's your Indian squaw, Patrick? Why didn't she come to church with you? Aren't we good enough for her or would she feel more at home in our church if we had a totem pole?"

Most of the group laughed. Patrick had had his difference with her before. The woman's acid tongue cut him to the quick, but he was equal to the embarrassing situation.

Patrick looked her evenly in the eye. "Mrs. Dumboldt, I'll answer your questions. My relationship with the Indian lady is none of your business, but since you've chosen to make it so, I will satisfy your curiosity. She didn't want to come today because she didn't want to be associated

THE DECISION

with the likes of you. By the way, Mrs. Dumboldt, she's more of a Christian than you are or ever will be. She is my woman because I love her! I expect you and others like you to keep a civil tongue in your mouth concerning her and that applies especially to you, Mrs. Dumboldt. Off the record, she's a faithful woman to all my needs. Keeps my bed warm at night so I don't stray down to the Buckaroo Saloon, where some of your husbands are to be found at night. Not that I blame them with what I have seen here today. I think, Mrs. Dumboldt, I've covered everything for now. Good day!''

Patrick started to walk away but was stopped by a frail, pleasant lady. ''Patrick,'' she said, ''I hope you don't believe I cotton to all that Aggie said about you? Heavens no! You have a perfect right to live your life with anyone you wish. Patrick, if it's alright with you, I'd like to visit your Indian lady. Yes, I would like that! There are many of us here who don't think like Aggie. Most of them fear that vicious tongue of hers. That's why they listen to her! I'm glad you horse tied her. She's had it coming for a long time. She's a vixen!''

Patrick broke into a wide smile. ''Of course, Olivia, anytime you'd like. I'm sure Shatoma would like that! Just name the day.''

Olivia thought for a moment, then replied, ''I can't make it Monday, that's my washday. How about Tuesday? Yes! I'll be there in the morning, about ten.''

''Thank you, Olivia, we'll be expecting you at that time. I'll tell Shatoma. A pleasant morning to you. Come on, Kelly, let's hit the road. It's getting late, time to be getting on our way.''

On Tuesday, Olivia rode up to Patrick's ranch in her horse and buggy. She knocked at the front door. In a little bit, the door opened and the unsmiling Shatoma stood there. ''Good morning, my dear. I know I'm going to like you. My name is Olivia Wilson and you are Shatoma. May I come in?''

Shatoma eyed the petite paleface suspiciously. The dainty white lady was a little over five feet tall. She wore a blue bonnet, a modest print dress, and brown flat shoes. Shatoma finally answered, ''Yes, come in, please, paleface squaw. Me glad to see you! Patrick said you would come. You paleface lady with good heart. Your voice sings good words. I like you, too.''

It didn't take long for the both to become friends. The need was there on both of their parts. Before the morning was over, they were chatting and laughing like old friends, exchanging private little stores about their menfolk. It was the start of a long and worthwhile friendship that was to stay with them for many years. A little after three o'clock, Olivia left for home with a promise of returning the following Tuesday. Their socializing went on for sometime. Always on Tuesday. Then one day, Olivia brought Ann Sombers, another wife from Broken Bend. They got to be a regular threesome for a few months. Within six months the group had grown to six ladies who formed a special club to help the needy.

One day the group talked Shatoma into going to church with them. Shatoma had a certain amount of suspicions, distrust and calculated worry about meeting the church folks. Shatoma gave in and went to church. At first, it was a trying experience for her. In the end, she made a few more friends, with the exception of Aggie Dumboldt and a few of her friends.

Shatoma liked her new life with the ladies she had come to know. The group exchanged cooking recipes with Shatoma, and in return, Shatoma taught them how to keep their husbands away from the wild women of the Buckaroo Saloon. "The Great Spirit," said Shatoma, "made the earth with braves and squaws. Each is different in body and head. Man think one way, woman another way. To keep your braves happy, be a good cook. Talk very little and keep the bed warm at night. Heap good medicine! Help keep your brave away from other paleface squaws. All want good brave! Some don't care who they get! Give your brave plenty of loving and food. Him too tired to go out at night. Good medicine for squaw too."

They roared with laughter with her simple philosophy of how to hold a man's interest. In their hearts they knew that Shatoma was right. It should be noted that homelife improved for their husbands from that day on.

One day, four of the ladies showed up, missing was Shatoma's dearest friend, Olivia Wilson. "Why," she asked, "Olivia, she no come?"

Ann Sombers replied, "We just learned last night that Olivia is ailing with a contagious disease. The doctor won't even allow her husband to be with her. Poor Bill, he's distraught with her condition. Poor Olivia! We want to help but we're afraid of the disease."

"Me not afraid!" Shatoma said quietly, with conviction, "I call Patrick to take me. Olivia is our friend, and what good is friend if they no help? Mebbe just to drink coffee and talk. Goodbye, ladies, I must go to my friend now!" Shatoma went outside and called Patrick. He came running to see what was the matter.

"What do you want, Shatoma?" he asked.

"Take me to Olivia's house right away. She very sick! Mebbe die if I no help! Hurry, Patrick!"

Patrick rushed out and returned in a few minutes with the buckboard. "Patrick," she confided to him, "Ann tells me Olivia has bad disease. Medicine man allow no one inside! Not even her brave! This is squaw's work! I go help! She good paleface friend to me. Now she need my help! I help friend!"

THE DECISION

"Whoa!" roared Patrick, "How serious is the disease? Is it contagious? If it is, I won't let you go. I love you, Shatoma. You mean very much to me."

"Me love you too, Patrick, but our love must be for others too. That is the Indian way! No talk more, hurry!"

Patrick realized any further talk was useless. Shatoma's mind was already made up and nothing would change it. They arrived at the Wilson home. A quarantine sign was nailed to the front door.

"Patrick," Shatoma whispered to him, "You go home and pray to your God for Olivia. Don't worry about me. Me fine! You go see Olivia's brave, he need help! I worry about you. You going to be the squaw in the family now. I don't know when I'll be home. I stay here until Olivia better. Goodbye, Patrick. I must go now. See you...when better. Not until then."

Patrick gave her a lingering kiss, said goodbye, and then watched her disappear in the Wilson home. Dr. Shelby met her at the door. "Shatoma," he exclaimed in surprise, "what are you doing here? What do you want? It's dangerous for you to be here! This might be a contagious disease!"

"Medicine man, stay out of my way!" she said determinedly, "I here to help Olivia. What disease she have?"

He scratched his head, "Frankly, I don't know! It's one I've never seen or heard of before. It's got me stumped! Shatoma, I'm glad you came. Olivia can sure use a nurse! None of the other women would come. They were all afraid! I couldn't blame them."

"You take me to Olivia now!" she ordered. He took her to another room where Olivia was resting. Shatoma was shocked by what she saw. The room was dark, the blinds were shut, and the windows closed. The air was filled with a stench of different odors. The offensive smell of Olivia's body hung like a shroud over a corpse. It was a damp, cold room that breathed death in its wake. No one could live under those conditions, mush less a frail person like Olivia. Then Shatoma saw Olivia! She was appalled at her sight! She was deathly pale, perspiring profusely. With feverish eyes, Olivia noticed Shatoma. A weak smile appeared on her drawn face, as she weakly said, "Oh, Shatoma, my dear, you came! You shouldn't be here, but I'm glad you came. I knew you would!" she gasped, trying to get her breath.

"Quiet now, Olivia! Shatoma is here to help old friend. Tell medicine man to go now to other people. I care for you."

"Doctor," Olivia said weakly, "You can make your other calls. Thank you for all that you have done. I'm in good hands now. Don't worry about me. Shatoma is good medicine for me."

"Good," the doctor replied, "I do have numerous cases to look in on tonight. Glad you came, Shatoma."

As soon as the doctor left, Shatoma asked, "Where you hurt the most?"

Olivia coughed, gasping for breath, "Mostly in the lungs, Shatoma. I can't breathe! I can hardly talk."

"Don't talk now," Shatoma ordered, as she put her hands up to her lips. "Shatoma try good Indian remedy. I go out in the woods. Will be back soon. Go to sleep! Need lots of rest!"

Shatoma covered Olivia with a blanket, then lifted the blinds and opened all the windows to the house. "House needs Great Spirit's air! More sunlight help too! Now feel like Great Spirit's home."

Within an hour, Shatoma had returned from the woods with an armful of various herbs. She took some of the herbs, put them into a pot of water, and boiled them for a long time. Shatoma kept adding various herbs until they formed a soft salve. The strong pungent odor filled the room. Shatoma let the salve gel while it cooled. Then Shatoma took another batch of herbs, added water and sugar, boiled it until it reached its maximum temperature. Shatoma then added vinegar and another herb to the concoction. After it had boiled for a time, Shatoma let it cool to room temperature and then poured it into a gallon jug. In the meantime, the salve had gelled and Shatoma rubbed it gently on Olivia's throat and chest. Then she gave Olivia a drink out of the jug that Shatoma had prepared. It was a bitter drink and Olivia couldn't swallow it. "Drink, drink! Don't stop!" ordered Shatoma, "Keep drinking! More, more, more! That is plenty! Now you can go to sleep! Don't talk!"

Olivia downed the awful-tasting concoction and within a few minutes, she was resting comfortably.

Shatoma stayed at her side for five days and nights, wiping the perspiration off her body. She changed Olivia's bed sheets. Shatoma knew these days were important. She had to be with Olivia to meet anything that may arise. Finally, on the fifth day, Shatoma helped Olivia to a chamber pot.

Her fever had broken. Olivia gasped, "Oh, Shatoma, I feel so much better."

Shatoma laughed, "Good! Smell of death has left your body. You will now feel better!"

"Yes, Shatoma, I feel better, but oh, so weak. Help me to my bed. How can I ever thank you for all you have done for me? Shatoma, my friend."

Shatoma carried her gently back to her bed, covered her with a blanket, and said, "Stay quiet, Olivia. Don't let this all go to waste now. You no well yet! You just young papoose that cries for milk. Mebbe you eat tomorrow! Now you sleep! Tomorrow we talk. You rest now!"

The next morning Olivia awakened to see Shatoma asleep on a nearby chair. "Shatoma," she called out. Shatoma awakened from her call. "Have you been sleeping in that chair all night? You couldn't! You shouldn't

THE DECISION

have done that. You should have got your rest in bed instead of a chair. I am feeling a touch better now, thanks to you and your Indian remedies. You'll have to teach them to me someday."

"Someday, mebbe, but not now."

"You know, Shatoma," Olivia said weakly, "There are things you should know about some of the women of Broken Bend. One of the main reasons they were all against you for corralling Patrick was not because you were Indian, but because you were another woman. Any woman at that time was a threat to them., Patrick was the prize catch in Broken Bend. You'd be surprised how many chased him before you appeared on the scene, and not all of them were single." Olivia coughed hoarsely.

"Enough stories!" Shatoma was adamant, "You too tired! Go to sleep! We talk after new moon. Stories wait, I wait too!"

Before Olivia went to sleep, Shatoma rubbed her throat, chest, and legs with the salve. Around seven at night, Shatoma heard a quiet rap on the front door. She opened it and there stood Patrick! "Shatoma, my love! How're you feeling? How is Olivia? When will you be coming home to Kelly and me?"

"Not too fast, my brave! Too many questions! Don't know when I come home. Mebbe six or seven suns! Only Great Spirit knows! He no talk! Olivia feel better, but weak! How is her brave?"

"Bill is worried sick about Olivia. He's so grateful for all you've done for her. He can't thank you enough. All the hands send their regards. They all love you and say if you need any help, just let out a whoop and a holler and they'll come running. I never knew how much I loved you until you were away. Kelly misses you too. He says to hurry back."

"Me thank the men. If I need their help, I will tell them. You tell Kelly to be strong brave while I'm away. Me love him plenty! You go home now, Patrick! I hear Olivia breathe hard. She need me! Come back on new moon. Soon I keep your bed warm again."

Patrick left and Shatoma went to the house, "Was that Patrick?" inquired Olivia, "He's such a wonderful man."

"Me know," Shatoma smiled approvingly as she proceeded to rub Olivia's chest with the salve to help her respiration.

"As I was saying" Olivia began, her voice a little stronger, "I can talk a little easier, thanks to that potion you have been rubbing on me, Shatoma. Now where was I? Oh, yes, Patrick was a good catch for the single women but it took a special woman like you to win him over."

Shatoma kept rubbing Olivia's chest, then quietly asked, "Tell me about Patrick's white squaw? Why did she leave him? Me no understand about paleface women."

"Shatoma," Olivia began slowly, trying to say the right words as they should be said, "It's a strange story. Betty was a wonderful woman. A beautiful woman! Perhaps she was a little too educated for Patrick. Who are we to say? They were very much in love. She had to pursue a dream and it cost her a husband and a son. The price was a little too heavy, even for her to pay. She was very foolish, but at the time, also very stubborn.''

''Why did she leave Patrick?'' Shatoma insisted.

''It's like this. They both had needs that devoured them. ''I, I, I,...and not enough of you.'' That means both of them wanted to do what they wanted to do, without thinking about the other person's wants and feelings.''

''Like Indian says, ''Me brave, you squaw! You take care of tepee, I take care of hunting. You do as I say.'' Shatoma laughed, thinking of the situation.

''Not quite, but pretty close.'' Olivia continued. ''Both were to blame. Betty wanted to take both sons out east with her to rear them in the finest of schools. Patrick, on the other hand, wanted to rear them as he was raised, in the mold of the western rancher. A wise old judge solved the problem for both of them. He gave one son to Betty to rear as she wanted, and the other to Patrick to rear as he believed it should be done. The judge also said when the sons reached nineteen years of age, they were to be exchanged for two years by Betty and Patrick. What a solution! I wonder who will do the better job? Betty or Patrick? As I said before, Shatoma, Betty is following her dream, but I think she was a foolish and vain woman.''

''Mebbe so,'' agreed Shatoma. ''Mebbe not! Mebbe Great Spirit in the sky have the right answer. It will be hard on paleface woman! No brave to keep her tepee warm in winter. Papoose no can do that! Long time ago, ancient Indian believe, ''When squaw marry, then no include their mother in tepee.'' Too much trouble with two squaws in same tepee. Good thing for paleface women to know. That means young brave, too. Teach him place in tepee comes after brave and squaw. Long time ago, Indians say, ''Wise chief never asks squaw to war council, war starts before arrow start flying.''

''Shatoma,'' Olivia was hilarious with laughter. ''You know you Indians have a unique, delightful approach to husband-wife- children situation. Maybe you have a better solution to it than we palefaces do.'' She started coughing again.

Shatoma quieted her. ''That's enough talking, Olivia! You say too many words! No good for you! I like your words! Tomorrow I like them better. You rest now! We talk again. I be here, no place to go.''

In the days to follow, Broken Bend was to know a new era. Significant events transpired to make it so. The first of these was Dr. Shelby's announcement, ''Olivia Wilson has passed the crisis and is on the road to recovery. The major credit goes to God and Shatoma, who, with her

THE DECISION

Indian remedies and faithful nursing speeded up this miracle. Shatoma showed no concern for any danger to her own personal life and health and safety."

Bill Wilson came home to be happily reunited with his lovely wife, Olivia.

The next important event saw Shatoma return to the Betty Ann Ranch where she was greeted by Patrick, Kelly and a host of cheering cowhands.

The most important event that Broken Bend had seen in years was proclaimed "Shatoma Day", honoring Shatoma. Even Aggie Dumboldt grudgingly admitted Shatoma did rather well under the circumstances.

Mayor Breech started the festivities. "Broken Bend applauds and welcomes Shatoma, who taught us a precious lesson of love."

There was a loud clapping, whistling, and calls from the exuberant crowd. Breech continued, "I'm glad we had the chance to discover Shatoma when we did, even if Olivia half scared us to death in doing so." Everyone roared with laughter.

Mayor Breech went on, "From now on, Shatoma will be our public treasure, and by God, we'll hang on to her! Our own Indian princess! May she long reign!" the crowd broke out again into loud cheers, then Breech concluded, "And now, what you have been waiting for, the one you'd like to hear, from our guest of honor... Sha...to...ma!"

Shatoma rose slowly to the crescendo of cheers and stepped effortlessly to the front as Patrick watched proudly from the rear. A beautiful, humble Indian princess in deerskin stood before them. When the cheering subsided, she spoke in low tones to the crowd, "Me glad we are friends!" Loud cheers broke out again, but ceased when Shatoma went on, "Me glad your God and our Great Spirit smoke pipe of peace. Mebbe they same person! Like we are same people! You paleface! Me Indian! We all take different roads to God and Great Spirit, but we meet at same place." The crowd exploded with rounds of cheers as Shatoma tried to go on, ₉Wise Indian chief once said, ₉You can break one twig easier than a bundle of twigs" Now we bundle of twigs. As long as we stay that way, no one can break us." Another loud round of cheers burst our as Shatoma tried to go on. "You make me happy! They say Indian no cry, but my heart cries now. What I do is not too much for friend. If you have the chance, I know you will do the same. You are all good people! No more paleface! No more Indian! We all one people. You are good friends! Patrick say, "Come one, come all to ranch! You all welcome! Big time!"

By the time Kelly neared sixteen, he had grown into a sturdy young man of 190 pounds. His well-muscled frame stood at six foot two inches. He had light brown, curly hair and blue eyes that sparkled mischievously whenever he faced a humorous situation.

Kelly finished school at fourteen years of age, as was the norm in Broken Bend at that time.

Patrick, with the help of Shatoma, had spent a lot of time training and grooming Kelly for the day he would take over the Betty Ann Ranch. Kelly was very good, he listened to both Shatoma and his father.

Then one day he had a chance to prove his worth. Patrick took his fledgling aside. "Kelly, your time has come. Your apprenticeship is over. You are now going to earn your food and lodging! Now we will see what you have learned about running this spread. This is your chance to show me. I have urgent business in Broken Bend that will take three or four days, perhaps more. That will stop me from making my monthly rounds of the outlying areas of the spread. You will have that task to do alone. I'm sure you will be up to it, son. Take a rough count of the stock, the way I did when we went on the trip together. Inspect the condition of each area and see if the hands are well cared for. Don't forget, Kelly, we are only successful if they are good employees. You will also be responsible for bringing in new supplies for the men. Don't forget, our men are like the army. They travel better with full stomachs! You'll have to take this trip alone. I have utmost confidence in you, and by the time you're though, I expect a full and exact report of each area. Do you think you can handle it?"

"Well, Dad," Kelly answered, "I had the best teacher in the world. If I don't know now, then it's time I saddled up and learned. You've been very patient with me. Taking me everywhere with you, advising me every step of the way. I think you've taught me well. The rest is up to me! I won't let you down or disappoint you, Dad."

Kelly went home to pack his saddle gear. Shatoma was waiting for him at the door. "Young brave, your father has already told me of his decision to send you out alone to do his work on the range. Our people have a saying, "A young brave is honored twice in his life. Once when he takes the place of his father in the tepee, and when he brings in squaw to share it with him." You are now taking you father's place in the tepee. Walk softly! Talk softly! When you get back, I pray you will be a man! You are like my own son and I love you like my own son. Tonight, I will cross the logs on the fire to bring good spirits for your trip tomorrow. They will watch over you on this trip. I look forward to your return with pride."

Kelly put his arms around her, patted her dark black hair, and kissed her on the cheek as he said, "Shatoma, you're the only mother I have known. I love you so much! I will not bring dishonor to you."

With these final words, Kelly gathered up his gear, went to the barn where the supplies were in the supply wagon, saddled up his horse and rode out into the cool morning air.

THE DECISION

Abutting the Betty Ann Ranch on the northeast was the Diamond Ranch owned by Jeff Cravath, a huge mountain of a man, with a thunderous voice that commanded attention and respect. His big voice covered up a tender heart that had compassion for all his fellowmen.

Just south of the Diamond Ranch was a spread run by Sid Sayd. Sid claimed that his ancestors had sailed the seven seas as pirates, and that his father served with LaFitte at the Battle of New Orleans. He related so many horror stories about himself and his notorious relatives that his listeners were in doubt where the facts ended and the fiction began.

To the west of Sid was the Great L Ranch owned by John Logan, fondly known as Pop by all who knew him. He was one of Patrick's closest friends, from the first time that Patrick had settled in the area.

Patrick had an inkling as to why Kelly was so anxious to make the trip alone. It all revolved around John Logan's fetching daughter, Annie, a sprightly, redheaded tomboy. Their relationship had been a tumultuous one ever since Kelly had pulled her braids in grade school and she retaliated with a painful kick in the shins.

Actually, Kelly had first met her at a school function in the lower grades. The only way he could get her attention was the curl pulling affair that got him the proper notoriety. After that fiasco, they sort of drifted into a comfortable relationship that their parents noticed with approval. They hoped some day it would blossom into a permanent relationship.

John Logan's wife died when Annie was born. Like Patrick, John had the identical task of raising a child and running a ranch at the same time.

Naturally, Kelly's first stop on his inspection trip would be at the Great L Ranch. It was the nearest to the Betty Ann Ranch and at the same time give Kelly the chance to renew old acquaintances with the beautiful Annie.

John Logan was rocking on the front porch, smoking an old corn cob pipe when he spied Kelly in the distance. He called out to Annie that Kelly was coming.

Annie dashed out, then remembered the unsightly way that she looked. "Oh, fud..de..dee! Look at the way I'm dressed!"

She was wearing cowboy chaps, a dirty plain shirt and scuffed brown boots covered with manure. Not too impressive a sight for a young lady. "Pshaw!" she exclaimed in disgust, "That's the way I am and that's the way I'll be! Serves Kelly right catching me at such an awkward time.

Nevertheless, she strode out to greet him. "Holy grass 'a fire!" she yelled, "Why in tarnation are you out here alone? Anything the matter with your dad?"

Kelly smiled, then laughed aloud, when he saw what Annie looked like. It was the same old Annie, curious as a Cheshire cat and always good for a laugh. She had an upturned nose that challenged anyone who disagreed with her. Her cool green eyes flamed in changing emotions.

"Hi Buck," Kelly said with a snicker, "Oh, excuse me. Is that you, Annie? I didn't recognized you. You must've got tangled up in a fight with some wildcat."

"Darn it!" Annie let out a bellow that could be heard in the next ranch, "If you don't button your lip, you'll see what it's like to tangle with a real live one. You sod buster! Just you keep it up. Holy Tarnation!"

"You even cuss like our hands," Kelly laughed. "Yeah! About your question, Dad's all right. He's in Broken Bend tied up in some sort of business deal he wouldn't tell me about. The only thing he said to me was, "Kelly it's about time you started earning your keep around here and learn the ranching business from both ends of the steer." That's why he's sending me out on the range to inspect the outlying areas and learn more of the cattle business. Actually, it serves a dual purpose, it gives me a chance to look in on you and see what modern ladies are wearing these days!"

"You'd better check your bedroll at night for rattlers. They'll crawl right into your sleeping roll and they're not the friendliest of critters," teased Annie.

"Go on, Annie, I ain't afraid of them."

Her father puffed on his sweet-smelling pipe. He loved to hear the young 'uns rattling their spurs. He rose from the rocker and held out his hand to Kelly as he warmly greeted him, "Well, Kelly, so Patrick has finally took the wraps off you and let you sprout your wings. I guess I was your age when my dad let me test the water. I came through all right and I predict you'll pass yours well. Take care on your trip. One piece of advice I'll pass on to you that my dad passed on to me a long time ago. Always have your men look up to you. Don't expect them to do anything you won't."

With this bit of prairie wisdom, Logan wandered off to some imaginary task that had just come up. Kelly made another attempt to pull Annie's hair. She laughed as she squirmed away warning him, "Darn it, Kelly, don't you ever learn? Have you forgotten already that last kick in the shin you got?"

"You're a real loaded pistol, Annie," Kelly answered back, You're a wild, unpredictable young lady that I'm going to tame some day."

"Holy grass 'a fire!" she exclaimed laughing, "You and what other saddle burner are you going to get to do the taming?"

"You're a regular wild bronco," laughed Kelly from the hollow of his stomach. "I don't know what I'm going to do about you. I get some funny feelings when I'm near you. It's a hankering I've never had before. Something too wonderful to explain. You're such a tiny wisp of a thing, and yet, you've got me horsetied."

THE DECISION

"Maybe you're loco in the head," Annie purred. "I hear it runs in certain families," then she exploded, "You're a man, aren't you? You should know about women and things and what they can do to innocent dopes like you. Holy Tarnation! If you ever learn what that feeling is about, let me know, please? I'll be waiting patiently for the news but I won't hold my breath. Before you shove off, how's about a little kiss?"

Kelly blushed at her forwardness. Tried awkwardly to grab her. She gingerly danced out of his grasp. She laughingly teased him, "You missed your chance, Ha-ha!"

After this playful bantering of words with Annie, Kelly eagerly said, "Annie, this has to be the best part of the trip of me. You are really something, Annie. Something real special. I like you a lot. A whole lot! I hope I can stay longer the next time around. Don't forget, Annie, you owe me a kiss. I've entered it in my log book. Until then, goodbye!"

"Consarn it! It will be a wet spell on the prairies before you collect that kiss, Kelly. Pshaw! But nevertheless, I'll take pity on you and save it for you."

The short stop at the Great L Ranch pepped Kelly up for the rest of his stops. The romantic fantasies of Annie played tricks in his mind as she kept spinning round in his brain. Kelly knew there had to be plenty of young gaffers on the prowl in Broken Bend trying to get to Annie but none could beat his time. What a girl she was!

It was the northwest station, overseen by Buck Jardine, a garrulous halfbreed who chattered on and on about nothing in particular. Still he was a very capable foreman for the Betty Ann Ranch. He greeted Kelly warmly, "Hi Kelly! Where eez Patrick? Eez he sick or what? Eez ze young fry getting in ze frying pan at last? Maybe ze pere eez going to let you make ze trips by yourself. N'est pas? I'll give ze lowdown on what's what as soon as you get off ze horse."

"Buck," Kelly said after dismounting, "My dad couldn't make this trip due to some pressing business in Broken Bend. That is why I'm here alone. I presume by now you're down to your last bean. Give me a hand and we'll put the supplies where they belong. What do you say we get started early in the morning for my inspection station? We'll see what has been done and what needs to be done."

"Sacre bleu!" shouted the halfbreed, "Why so early in ze morning? Let's eat a good breakfast, rest, zen break camp. Maybe you need rest?"

"Buck, there's nothing I'd like better to do on my inspection here, but my load is a heavy one. I've got to do ten days' work in seven days' time. Dad is expecting me back then with my report. You know, Buck, how precise my dad is. Besides, Buck, I've some other danged important things to do."

"Ho..ho..ho!" laughed Jardine, "You let ze cat out of ze bag! I'll bet dat important business eez, Annie," giving Kelly a playful nudge in the ribs. "Oui, bon homme, am I not right? I'm ze old romantic dog! I know ze score. She ees ze prettiest jeunefille in ze parts. If you don't lasso her soon, some fast-talking hombre in Broken Bend will rustle her away from you. Remember what I said! I give you ze warning first, ami!"

With that parting remark, they spread their blankets under the starry skies and went to sleep. The next morning came much too soon. The cook rudely awakened them with a loud clang of the bell. After a quick breakfast, they started on a methodical tour of Buck's territory. It took most of the morning it inspect it all. In the end Kelly was satisfied that everything was in order except for a few minor problems that couldn't be corrected by Buck. As Kelly was leaving, he told the halfbreed, "You outdid yourself, Buck. Everything was in tip-top shape. My dad will be pleased with this report of your area. Keep up the good work."

"Remember what I said, Kelly," reminded Buck, "About Annie, she can't wait forever for you."

Within a week, Kelly had inspected all the range areas that Patrick had laid out for him to check on and arrived back at the ranch for his reports for his dad. Patrick showed satisfaction after going through the lengthy reports. "Kelly, these are very good reports. Everything as I wanted to see in them. From now on, you'll be making the rounds by yourself. Of course, there will be times I'll trail along with you in an advisory capacity and nothing more. I'm quite satisfied you're capable enough to do the job without me babysitting you."

"Thanks, Dad, that makes me feel good."

Shatoma had already prepared a buffalo hump roast for her two men, "A feast for my two men can only be the best."

After the trip, the relationship between father and son meshed together another notch. It cemented the respect and love they had for each other. Shatoma smiled, for she knew that the Great Spirit was favoring them. So, as time went by, nature took a firmer grip on Kelly's shoulder and began to mold him into his father's image.

Chapter 6

In the eastern part of the country, Betty was picking up the shattered pieces of her troubled marriage. She and her son, Dennis, were now living in Philadelphia. The enjoyment of Dennis being with her, as well as being able to watch him grow, gradually helped to release the bitterness she had felt in her heart. Was Patrick having the same misgivings about their separation? The added burden of raising a son seemed to offer no solace for loneliness.

Betty was rearing Dennis to be a gentleman and scholar. She started his education at an early age under the most competent tutors. To qualify as Dennis' tutor, they had to meet Betty's high standards and rigid qualifications. Under the personal tutor's training Dennis was ready to enter grade school on a higher plateau than other students of his age.

During Dennis' early grade school years, he met a young lady who was to play an important part in his life. Jessie Longstreet was a willowy blonde with large hazel eyes that sparkled. Her infectious smile could warm the coldest of hearts. Her voice was warm, with a touch of homespun southern accent that captivated the listener. She moved with a graceful, flowing stride that brought "Oh's" and "Ah's" from all the young men.

Jessica had moved to Philadelphia with her mother about the time Dennis was starting his fourth year of school. They found a home in the same block where the O'Sheas lived. Dennis was playing in the front yard when he spotted Jessica and her mother unloading their furniture and belongings. He rushed over and offered his help which they gladly accepted. It was then that Dennis first caught sight of the beauty of Jessica. She was the most beautiful girl he had ever seen.

It didn't take long for the two to get along. It was inevitable! Jessica, with her bubbly personality, and Jason, with his quiet, calculating nature. As the summer progressed, their friendship developed into a strong bond.

THE DECISION

Of course, their relationship would have its ups and downs. Sometimes Dennis would exasperate her with his cool, self-assuring manners. This wasn't what Jessica looked for in a boy. Not by a longsight it wasn't. What she wanted was someone to sweep her off her feet, perhaps a knight in shining armor would suffice. Sometimes Dennis' reserve frustrated Jessica. Like any romantic young lady, she liked her men to be self-asserting and masculine. On occasion, she'd cry out, "Oh, you make me so mad! You're so sure of yourself! Do you always have to be so precise and methodical in everything you do? Don't you have the urge to grab me and hug me? What's the matter with you? What's the matter with me? Hug me! I won't break! I'm not made of glass!" she berated him laughingly as she scampered down the street making faces at him.

Betty was fond of Jessica. She reminded her of herself at that stage in her life. Jessica was just what Dennis needed the most. Someone to shake him up. A female companion to arouse certain instincts in him, with reservations of course. Betty loved her son but there were times she had her doubts about him. He wasn't like the other little boys in the neighborhood. He was just too straightlaced in everything he said or did. Betty wanted her son to be a gentleman, but at the same time she didn't want him to grow up to be a sissy. All she desired of him was to be was just like any normal, growing boy who got into a little mischief at times. But that wasn't Dennis. He had to read the textbook of life from cover to cover and leave nothing to chance. God knew she had never meant to raise him that way but a parent never knows how a twig will bend and grow with the seasons. Dennis had always been a wonderful and obedient son; however, every good little boy needs a bit of the devil in him to keep parents on their toes. With Dennis, Betty didn't have those kinds of parental problems. Of course she was thankful for it, but pshaw! Why couldn't he be more spirited?

Jason seemed to know what he was doing all the time, as if he had his life mapped out and he was running straight on course. Betty liked Jessica because she was just the girl who might ignite the spark that would light a bonfire under Dennis.

Jessica made it a habit of coming over a couple of times a week to talk with Betty. Betty was pleased to have Dennis' friends come over and keep her company. One day Betty asked Jessica, "Jessica, I love your company, you light up my day, but why aren't you out with others your age?"

"That's easy to answer, Mrs. O'Shea. I happen to like you a lot. That's the main reason. The other reason is that the others are such children! All they want to do is play with their stupid dolls and talk about boys,

boys, boys and rot like that. I think there are other subjects more interesting. Don't you think so, Mrs. O'Shea?"

"Why, Jessica!" Betty looked at her in surprise, "What's so wrong about that? I used to do it with my girl friends when I was your age. It's a growing-up process we all go through."

"Shucks, Mrs. O'Shea! I know that! Mother keeps telling me that all the time!"

"By the way, Jessica, not to change the subject, but how is your mother? I understand she's not feeling well. Is there something I can do to help?"

"Not much, ma'am, she keeps getting worse and worse."

"How dreadful, dear! Please let me know if I can help. May I come over to see her?"

"I think she'd like that, Mrs. O'Shea. Yes, I know she would!"

"Well then, Jessica, now is as good a time as ever to see her. Wait until I get a wrap."

Within a few minutes they were beside the ailing Mrs. Longstreet. Betty whispered to her, "I've wanted to meet you, Mrs. Longstreet. I can see the resemblance between Jessica and you. It's plain to see where she gets her beauty from you. She's a lovely, talented young lady. Every so often she drops over to visit me. She's a delight to have around."

"Yes, I know, Mrs. O'Shea. She's already told me what a wonderful person you are."

Betty cut in, "Please call me Betty, now that we're friends, and I'll call you..."

"Dorothy. My maiden name was Dorothy Templeton. I'm from Georgia and I married a fine man there, Broderick John Longstreet, a southern gentleman. Six years ago he was trampled to death by a runaway horse while trying to save a child that had run in front of it. It was a terrifying experience! I have never been able to get it out of my mind. Some four months later, we left the south, Jessica and I, and never returned. I never did recover from the shock of losing my husband. But you didn't come over to listen to my miseries."

"Dorothy, that's what friends are for. To unburden yourself and confide in. I live just down the street a spell. Perhaps, I can be of assistance until you get back on your feet again."

"Jessica, dear," Dorothy said softly, "Why don't you go out and play. I'd like to talk with Betty."

Betty looked at the middle-aged woman with silvery white hair. She had a face that was beginning to show the signs of a few wrinkles. Her eyes were a light blue, like a sky without a cloud in it. Yet sad, they were surrounded with haunting memories. She talked in a whisper, seeking not

THE DECISION

to offend anyone with her words. She sat there quietly, lost to everything around her except her doubts and problems.

"Well, awright, Mom, I'll go," Jessica said, scampering out and slamming the door behind her.

"She's such a dear! I love her," Betty said as she straightened her hair.

"I know, Betty, and she thinks the world of you. She's told me that a thousand times or so! Betty, there is something I'd like to talk about with you, but it's difficult. Let's call it a woman-to-woman talk. This will be strictly confidential between you and me. Please don't tell Jessica. It would devastate her. I'm not a well person, as you can probably see. My days are few and I have fewer friends. To be honest with you, we have none outside you and Dennis. You have a precious son! He is special! Probably more of a man that he shows. Jessica cares a lot for you and Dennis…You and I both know that. What frightens me the most, should anything happen to me! How would it affect Jessica? Who would care for Jessica? I know I haven't the right to ask this of you, but I have no recourse, no one else to turn to. When my time comes, would you contact my lawyer? I've already instructed him in my will what I want done with Jessica in case of my death. Will you help him with final arrangements? Jessica will need a woman's love and care in those trying moments. She will need someone to care for her until she gets over her loss. I know I'm asking a lot from you, but as you said, "What are friends for?" Will you take over the responsibility of Jessica?"

"Dorothy, nothing is going to happen to you. You'll probably outlive all of us. You're worrying for nothing! You've got something that will soon pass. Then you'll laugh at your needless worries."

"Betty, I know different, please!" she pleaded, "I'd feel more secure in the knowledge that you're caring for her. I know I'm asking a lot, but who else can I turn to?"

"Well, Dorothy, if it will make you feel better, then I promise to care for Jessica as if she were my very own. However, I know it will not be necessary. I promise you!"

"Bless you, Betty," Dorothy said happily, "I feel so much better already."

"I have to go now, Dorothy, but I will call on you again soon. It was a pleasure talking to you. Goodday."

One morning, Jessica came running over to the O'Shea home, screaming and crying, "Mrs. O'Shea, my mother's dead. I tried to waken her this morning but she wouldn't move. She wouldn't even answer! I'm so scared! What shall I do? What must I do?"

Dennis came bounding down the stairs when he heard the news to console the sobbing Jessica, "Oh, you poor girl! I'm so sorry, so sorry!"

He took the grieving girl into his strong arms, "I'll tell you what you're not going to do. You're not going back into that house again. Ever! You're going to live with us. We'll take care of you from now on. In the meantime, I'll go over and pick up some of your clothes. Just tell me what you need for the present. Mother, you care for Jessica while I do what is necessary."

"Dennis," Betty said, "After you've done that, I'd like you to contact Mrs. Longstreet's lawyer. Here is his name and address. I'd like to have him over as soon as possible to make the final arrangements."

The next day, a slender man arrived at the O'Shea home. Betty opened the door and asked, "Are you Mrs. Longstreet's lawyer?"

"Yes. I'm Jeremiah Bender, the late Mrs. Longstreet's lawyer. May I come in?"

"Please do. How rude of me! I was thinking of something else. I'm sorry! Please come in."

Betty escorted him into the spacious parlor as he commented on it, "Mrs. O'Shea, you have a lovely home. Now to get down to the business at hand. As the late Mrs. Longstreet has probably noted to you, I've been to her home a couple of times. The last was a few weeks before her untimely passing away. She instructed me in the setting up of her will. There are certain conditions that you may or may not be aware of. One of her main desires was in making you trustee of the estate and the guardian of her daughter, Jessica. Shall we proceed?"

"Why, yes," replied Betty hastily, as she sized up this pleasant, understanding man. He was over six feet tall with a rangy, sturdy build. His dark eyes twinkled when he smiled. He was middle-aged, carefully groomed, with a touch of gray around his temples. There was something about this man that Betty liked.

"Mrs. O'Shea, we're going to be spending a lot of time together in the future, what with the funeral and carrying out the will's codicils. I think it would be more expedient for the both of us if you called me Jerry and I called you Betty. One of my duties is to counsel my clients and trustees in sad situations like this. Please let me in on your wishes on how you'd like this to be accomplished. Between the two of us, maybe we can bring a smile to a sad young lady. What do you say?"

"I can see we'll have no trouble in communicating or getting along, Jerry. What is the first thing that has to be done in things like this? You're more knowledgeable in this sort of thing than I am."

"Betty," he said cautiously, "Let's do this one step at a time. First, let's make the funeral arrangements."

"Yes. Jerry, and after that, we can take the other things that may pop up. In the meantime, Jessica is living with us. At a time like this, she needs a woman's love and the surroundings of a happy home."

THE DECISION

The funeral service were short. Jessica clutched Dennis' arm, holding to him desperately as she paid her final respects to her loving mother. She wept hysterically. Betty held her in her arms, consoling her, "You're not alone, Jessica. We'll always be with you."

Each passing day brought Betty and Jerry closer together as they ironed out the final details of the will. Betty had taken a liking to this gentle man. She had learned by asking questions that Jerry was and always had been a bachelor, one of the more eligible in Philadelphia. There was one more thing she liked about him. He reminded her of Patrick in everything he said or did. She enjoyed these new feelings.

In the next few weeks, Jeremiah took her out to the finest restaurants and the latest new stage shows. He was gallant, treating her as a lady. However, things had gotten past the stage of fencing. She noticed that they were exchanging less short "hello's" and more lingering "goodbyes".

Betty got to wondering at night, "Am I falling in love with Jerry? Do I have the need for such a man as he? I wonder if it's just a passing infatuation, or what is it?" Whatever it was, her Quaker upbringing kept her inner emotions in check.

Then one night, after a delightful evening at the opera, Jeremiah invited her to see his home. It was located in a posh district. Betty had never seen such an elegant house. It was just what she had always dreamed about.

"Betty," Jerry said seriously, "You know I'm in love with you. I want to marry you."

Betty pressed her fingers on his lips. "Jerry, you mustn't! You know I can't! I'm already married. As far as I'm concerned, my estranged husband and I are still man and wife in the face of God. We've been legally separated for some time now, but as long as that document is in force, I can't marry you."

"Remember, Betty," he reminded her, "I'm a lawyer and it can be broken."

"No, no! I won't permit it! My husband still has my other son with him out west. I can't do it."

"Betty, even though I'm a successful attorney, I'm still a lonely man. What good is my success without the woman I love to share it with me? I've never loved another woman as I have you. Do you know what I'm going through and what you're doing to me? I can't hold out much longer. I really need you!"

"You must, in God's good name," pleaded Betty, "because we both know it's wrong."

Her passions were beginning to betray her. She was reminded of an ancient French adage: "In every chaste woman, no matter how pure of heart, there comes a time when the right man comes along at the right moment, under the right conditions, that the woman will succumb to the desire of the flesh."

Before Betty knew it, she was that woman! She was in the midst of a romance with Jerry. He held her in his arms and kissed her passionately. She moaned in ecstasy, "Patrick, Patrick." But the fires of passion had gone too far. Neither could stop this consuming fire of love. Soon they had become one as their passions erupted into inferno.

They lay there motionless, all the fire out of them. Without a sound in the room, except their deep breathing. After what seemed an eternity, Betty regained her composure and dignity. She dressed and combed her straggling hair and calmly said, "Jerry, that was wonderful. You were perfect, but it was wrong! Neither of us was at fault. It just happened, we needed each other at that moment. I am ashamed of my weakness. It will never occur again! It mustn't! Jerry, I promise! It won't! Please take me home."

"Betty, it was the most wonderful moment of my life, but the spectre of your husband will always be in your thoughts. If we did have a continuing relationship, it would always be like this, the shadow of your husband lurking in the background. You are, Betty, and always will be, a one-man woman. You have ideals and principles of the highest caliber that no man will change. I thank you for my moment in heaven! I know you can not accept me or any other man as an equal to your husband. And that I cannot bear! Goodbye, Betty."

The time passed quickly. Betty had become used to not seeing her other son. It was like a fading dream that comes and goes in a flash. She had never disclosed her problems to anyone except her favorite uncle, Bobby Brooks, a delightful, liberal-minded Scotsman who owned a coal mine in Andura, Pennsylvania. Betty had always been the apple of his eye. Bobby was a confirmed bachelor, her uncle on her mother's side. He was a small, fearless man in his early fifties, semi-bald, stocky, and extremely popular with his miners. He talked with a charming burr and wore the Scottish kilts with tartan woven plaid patterns of the Scottish Highlands. Bobby had saved his money with a zeal that thrifty Scotsmen are noted for. When the opportunity came, he bought the Black Diamond Mine from the heavily indebted owner who spent most of his time in the local bars.

In time, Brooks was able to make the Black Diamond into a profitable venture with his new management methods. He made it a point to know all the men who worked for him, calling them by their first names, and caring for them as if they were family. The miners loved this Scottish highlander.

THE DECISION

The cagy Scotsman listened patiently to their many problems and helped solve many of them with cash donations or advice. In fact, outside of Betty and Dennis, the miners were the only family he had. When Betty came to him with her marriage problems, he listened sympathetically to her account of the separation, but took no sides and offered no advice. He warned Betty only that there would come a day of accounting with Dennis that she would have to face. Betty had feared this for some time, but felt she would cross that bridge when she came to it.

In her beliefs Betty was a liberal woman, far ahead of her time. Maybe in that way, she felt at ease talking with her uncle, who shared the same ideas. She tried in instill the same type of reliance in Dennis. She wanted him to be kind, courteous, and considerate of others.

One day she took Dennis to a poor neighborhood on purpose to see how the other half lived. "Dennis," she said, looking him straight in the eye, "I want you to remember this the rest of your life. Look close! Get a good, hard look! What do you see?"

Dennis looked over the area and the people carefully. The rundown condition of the buildings, the threadbare clothing of the poor, and the hunger in their eyes. "Mother," he replied, "their clothes are worn to the last thread. They look so thin, as if they hadn't a good meal for a long time. They have a certain frightened look in their eyes. What does it all mean?"

"First of all, Dennis," Betty explained, "what you see here is the face of poverty at its worse. It's bad enough to see it in other countries but it's disgusting and degrading to see it right here in America, the land of plenty. Let me go into this a little more deeply. From our early beginnings, we were all in this same state of affairs. Our ancestors were poor and uneducated and lived in this type of world. However, each succeeding generation of our family improved on its lot. That is how you and I were able to live the affluent life we now enjoy. What about the people you have observed here? Dennis as you stand before me, I want you to promise me that you will do your best to improve upon the situation you have observed here. Promise?"

"Mother, I do promise you that I will do everything to the best of my ability to help the poor and unfortunate. I really will!"

"Dennis, if you do this, the most rewarding day of your life will be when others will stand up and point you out and say, "He is a friend of man.""

Betty's parents had been a well-to-do Quaker family of old Philadelphia who made it possible for her to be educated in the finest of schools. Betty graduated from a local university as a journalist major. Upon graduation she became the first lady reporter on the Philadelphia Post. Unfortunately, the first story she covered was a train derailment that involved the death of her parents. The tragedy left her in a state of shock for a long period of time. Then one day she took a leave of absence from the paper to go to San Francisco to talk about woman's rights at an early women's suffrage gathering. This was the trip that forced the stopover of her stage at Broken Bend due to an Indian uprising in the territory. There she met Patrick O'Shea. Fell in love and married him. She had never met anyone as exciting! He was tall, handsome, and masculine, with a strong, pleasing voice of deep resonance.

Betty tried to determine the moment her marriage went all wrong. It shouldn't have been for it was a happy time for them in the first year of their marriage. Then fate smiled on them when they were blessed with twin sons. Their happiness was boundless! They were so proud of their sons and started making plans for their future...then something went wrong, soon things started to go downhill.

Betty remembered telling Patrick of her great expectations for their sons. "Patrick, I'd like you to agree on what I have in mind. I'm going to take our sons to Philadelphia to get them a proper education. They cannot get that education here in Broken Bend. They just don't have the facilities here to do them justice. We can arrange it so they spend the summer vacations on the ranch, but I do insist they are to be educated in Philadelphia."

She recalled how furious Patrick was when she mentioned her plan. He had answered in no uncertain terms, "Betty, I will not stand idly by for this. You have some high ideals and standards! Basically, I agree with you on most of them, but not if it means you hijacking our sons out of my life for nine to ten months a year to satisfy your thirst for a higher education in the east. I have my ideas on how they should be raised and that doesn't mean raising them in Philadelphia. I believe they should be reared in a climate they were born in, educated to the western life style. How in the Good Lord can an eastern education teach them to ride the range, rope the steers, and raise stock? There is no way I'll consider changing my mind under these circumstances. I see no good coming out of this conversation. I've made up my mind and that is final!"

Betty reached back in her memory, living each moment as if it were yesterday. "Patrick, you're a stubborn old goat! The issue is not closed! It's not final! Do you realize the advantage they'd have in a modern school with competent teachers compared to the schools you have here? I won't allow that, and that is final!"

Suddenly, those differences in rearing their sons were magnified to gigantic proportions. It put a solid wedge in their once happy marriage. Patrick was steadfast in his views and Betty was adamant in her beliefs.

THE DECISION

Then one day in court it all came to a head when the judge laid down his historic decision. She recalled some of the more pleasant times with Patrick, but those happy memories of the past soon faded into oblivion as the years took their toll.

Jessica went away to finishing school and Betty was left with Dennis. From the time Dennis was eight years old, Betty and he spent the summer months with Bobby Brooks in Andura, Pennsylvania. Dennis loved Brooks, watching him bug-eyed filling his briar pipe, and was hypnotized by the giant circles of smoke coming out of his mouth. Why, you could almost stick a finger in each one as it wafted by. Bobby Brooks and Dennis were like father and son. Year in year out, Betty and Dennis would count the days until they joined lovable Uncle Bobby Brooks in Andura. Those were happy times for them.

On Dennis' fourteenth birthday, they visited their jolly uncle on their annual summer stint. Bobby Brooks greeted them warmly, but this time Betty noticed a sign of worry in his eyes that she hadn't seen before.

"My bonny lass," he gleamed, "you bring me a touch of the old highlands whenever you visit me. I so wish you could stay a mite longer. It's a dark day for me when you go back. The days pass so quickly when you're here! It seems like forever before you return." Bobby paused a moment to swat a buzzing fly on his forehead, "The most difficult of all is the waiting to see you again."

Brooks's voice got serious as he continued, "You bring such joy to an old man with terrible problems. I don't want to burden you with them, but I feel my days are numbered here. I can see the handwriting on the wall. I'm blessed with good, hard-working men making a living in my coal mines. They are close friends of mine. Most of them are foreigners of many lands who came to this country for freedom and a happy life. I've been able to supply that to them, but I'm afraid for their future. What I'm about to say to you is true. There are many unprincipled men who want to steal my mines. They're not humans, they are beast who treat their men like animals. Right now, they are in a midst of a coal war that hasn't reached me yet. The powers to be are too busy fighting each other to gain control, but the day will come when one will conquer all. Then that group will methodically take over the small mines, one by one. That day will come soon! When they've taken over the small mines, they will be looking in my direction for their final victory. It will be a showdown between them and me."

Betty put her arm on his shoulder consoling him as he spoke on, "I have no one to confide in or help me in a time like that, no one to trust except you two."

Betty cut in softly, "Dear Bobby, what bothers you the most? I'd like to hear about it. How can we be of help to you?"

"I'm afraid," Bobby started seriously, "If something were to happen to me, who would care for my men? They'd be so alone and defenseless! That's what I'm afraid of the most, the safety of my men and their families."

Betty thought for a while and then answered with great conviction, "Uncle, I intend to help you. As soon as we get home this fall, I will learn about the coal business! I will scour the libraries, researching the business of coal"

Dennis added, "And I shall cover the newspapers to learn more of the groups who are trying to rob you of your mine. I believe in the end that good will triumph over evil."

A peaceful smile radiated on the Scotsman's face, "I feel so much better already. Maybe the three of us can kill Saint George's dragon. At least now, I'm not alone! It's comforting to know! We are kin, and the bond is deep. I love you both."

True to her word, Betty haunted the libraries for research material on the history of the coal business. Dennis, in the meantime, plagued the newspapers in his spare time, scanning the tabloids for information on the imminent feuding of the coal barons.

Within a month, Betty set her notes down in an orderly fashion, thanks to her experience as a reporter. She read them to Dennis as they exchanged information, "The first mention of coal, Dennis, was in 320 B.C. by Theophrstus, the pupil of Aristotle. He used the word "anthrakes" to describe it. The next mention of coal was in about the 13th century when Marco Polo discovered coal in China. He wrote home about "the black stones that heated homes.""

"The first of the moderns," Betty continued, "to run a coal mine in a commercial operation were the Welsh," Dennis' eyes gleamed with interest as Betty went on, "The first American miners were Negroes. Slaves working in what we would call strip mining near Richmond, Virginia, about 1750. To the north of them, Connecticut Yankees moved into Pennsylvania, taking over large reservations in the Wyoming Valley, beneath which lay huge, rich beds of anthracite coal. A famous wit of the day proclaimed, "the last word in coal, the super product of nature.""

"One more item of interest, Dennis," Betty said, as she leafed through her papers until she found the right article, "the next report we hear of coal is in a region of Pennsylvania. It's an area of 120 miles long and 50 miles wide, perhaps the richest find in the world. Mother Nature had done her work well in creating this precious material. It must have taken

THE DECISION

her millions of years." "Mother," Dennis hastily pointed out to her, "here are some stories that I've dug out that will astound you and they are cause of future worry. I've been doing a lot of late night working. I've come up with a lot of pertinent data and information that has to deal with Uncle Bobby's problems. This old periodical states that by the middle of the 19th century, English immigrant miners, predominantly Welsh and Scot, began arriving in America to work in the coal mines. The mines had been previously worked by native farmers and their sons. A little later this force was augmented by immigrants from other nations in Europe. In some mining towns, there were as many as a dozen different tongues spoken. In time, these people, through necessity, learned to correspond with each other by banding together in acts of compassion. They aided one another and were able to cement a strong bond of affection and friendship.

"Here's another article in the Philadelphia Post that states, "The coal mines of Pennsylvania have been a miserable existence for the miners, being treated far worse than the black slaves of the deep south. They unsuccessfully tried to unionize themselves to combat the high prices of the company stores and the low wages at the mines. Those conditions kept them constantly in debt and at the mercy of the coal companies. Another infamous act of the coal mines and a constant source of agitation was the fraud that the coal owners perpetrated on the powerless miners by the weighing of their daily production at the tipple. They were shortchanged on their everyday output by this unfair weights measure."

"That is deplorable," cried out a fully aroused Betty, "I know that Uncle Bobby is not involved in any of wrongdoings like this. Not our lovable Uncle! Never!"

"Here is another shocker," Dennis said, "It points out here that the average wage of the miners for year was below $300.00. This was working ten to fourteen hours a day, seven days a week, 365 days a year without any time off for holidays. The highest wage scale in the mines were the foremen and the brutal strikebreakers who were paid a little more than twenty cents an hour. This scale was graduated downward to five cents an hour for dynamite men and to as low as two cents an hour for eight and nine-year-olds picking out slate from the coal. It was common to see these youngsters working with fingers and sometimes whole arms missing because they were lost in the breakers while picking out slate from the crushing mills."

Betty shuddered as she listened to Dennis' article on brutality in the coal mines as she exclaimed, "This makes me want to vomit. To think that the greed of man would go to such extremes to do this to their fellowman. These type of people should be exposed to public scrutiny and scorn. They are lower than the lowest beasts, with apologies to the animals."

"According to this exposé," Dennis explained, "written by Clifford Dunette in the Post last year, the major coal companies are now battling each other for supremacy in the Pennsylvania coal fields. Warfare has erupted and spread like wildfire between the coal companies, forcing the owners to hire enforcers to keep the miners in line. These enforcers are being used to thwart incursions into their territory by hired henchmen of rival mine owners. Caught in the middle of all this were the helpless miners, who had no place to turn to in this undeclared war. Once more they tried to unionize themselves and once more they were brutalized by the unsympathetic enforcers of the owners with statements like this, ''This will teach the bastards once and for all."

Betty agonized at this revelation by Dennis, "What kind of people are these? Have we sunk so low as human beings to make the dollar our God? No, no! I can't believe it! I won't believe it! I know it isn't Uncle Bobby they're referring to. It couldn't be! I think I know now what he meant when he said, "I worry about the future of my brave and loyal men. What will become of them? I wish I knew." You know, Dennis, he may be marked for death by those awful men and we are powerless to do anything about it. How horrid!"

Dennis continued, "If you think that is shocking, wait until you hear this. The article goes on and names the seven most dastardly coal mine owners. Let's begin with Iron Mike Finnegan. He got his start as an enforcer for Big John Williams, keeping the helpless dissident coal miners in line. He did such a brutally efficient job instilling the fear of God in the illiterate miners that Big John rewarded him by giving Iron Mike an interest in his mine. It was learned later from reliable sources that this benevolent act by Big John was speeded up when he found out that Phillip Gaston was making overtures to Finnegan to work for him at considerable more money. Williams never forgave "the Frog" for this. Within a year, Finnegan and Williams became equal partners in the mine."

Dennis held off for a moment when Betty sensed a cough that didn't materialize, "Big John Williams was the first of the unsavory seven to work his reign of terror among the coal miners. He was a huge man! Foul talking, yes, a foul brute, who took a sadistic delight in beating up helpless people. The only good thing that could be said of him was that he was no worse than the rest of them. Another of those godless brutes was the one known as "the Frog", French Phillip Gaston. He was a perfumed dandy out of the French courts with the impeccable manners of an aristocratic slob."

Betty turned up her nose in disgust.

"You haven't heard anything yet, Mother. Just have patience and you shall learn more. Listen to what our eminent reporter has dug up. He

THE DECISION

writes, "Slippery Adam Havell is a small gnome of a man. If you want to call him that. He has tried to parlay a loud, caustic voice into a fearful ogre, that he is!" He is a cruel man with calculating eyes, perhaps the most treacherous of them all. And feared the most! We mustn't forget Black Jack Murphy, a black Irishman of Spanish lineage who uses a resounding voice to frighten others into doing what he wants, because of the fear of his ill temper and cruelty."

"One minute, Dennis," pleaded Betty, "while I get a drink of water. This is quite an ordeal I'm going through hearing about these louts. It's more than I can bear with a thirst. There now, I feel better. Proceed, Dennis, with your story."

Dennis straightened the papers in front of him, found the missing page, then went on with the expose, "Another disgusting compatriot of theirs was Herr Adolf Wantens, formerly a Prussian officer, who was a stickler for regimentation."

"Finally, we have come to the seventh of the Devil's henchmen, Crazy Olaf Johanson, an illiterate Swede, who got his start in the coal business by outworking any six men in a twelve-hour day. He then beat them up at night and robbed them of their money, which in time furnished the funds to buy his own mine."

"Mother, these are the Big Seven who hated each other with a passion and anyone else who crossed them. The line has been drawn between them! They are now battling each other for supremacy of the lucrative coal business."

Dennis took out a handkerchief to blow his nose and clear his mind for what he was about to say. "There is only one coal company that won't buckle under their rule of terror. The Black Diamond Coal Company, run by the fearless Bobby Brooks, the beloved Scotsman of his employees. He advocates the paying of higher wages than the rest of the others. He adheres to the principle of shorter hours for his men and practices mine safety. He is the first coal mine owner to install a first-aid center for his men and the first to bring out the prohibition of child labor. Bobby Brooks, being a religious man, was against Sunday work, urging his miners to attend the church of their choice on the Sabbath. He also instituted work programs to better the living conditions of his men. This was all contrary to the views of the greedy Big Seven."

"Bully for dear old Uncle Bobby," cheered Betty.

"Here's an ominous note," cautioned Dennis, "the article goes on to say, "I predict that once these coal mine vultures have stabilized their petty squabbles, they will turn their full fury on all the small coal mine owners. When they have devoured them, they will have one last stumbling block to complete domination of the coal industry, Bobby Brooks! That will be a black day in America!''

"How dastardly to live with such scum! I'm afraid for Uncle Bobby's life. If only I were a man.''

"In the meantime,'' Dennis continued reading from the article, "The canny Scotsman has amazed the coal industry by installing fans in the breakers and erecting steam heating pipes in the screen's rooms. The fans collect dust and carry it away, keeping the air fresh and clean. The newly added steam heating unit is giving warmth and comfort to the miners in the winters while the carbide gas lights hung from the beams to light up the early mornings and late afternoon shifts. The farsighted Brooks introduced mechanical picks to take the place of hand pickers in a more progressive mode of safety. It also increased the mine's yield. Brook also negated the idea of cracker bosses as being too tyrannical for 'his lads.''

"I don't know where Bobby gets all his ideas! He must have spent all his spare time dreaming of all the good he could do for his men rather than the evil that others are foisting upon them. Still, I worry about the old dear.''

"Here is another excerpt from the same article, "None of his liberal thinking has set too well with the Big Seven. They have been too busy fighting their own private vendetta to consider any action against him for the present. They've snickered remarks when his name was mentioned. Thought him a senile, public nuisance, a menace to their way of thinking. They believe in their heart some day there will be a trial test between them and Bobby Brooks, but now was not the time. They could wait, for time was their ally. They will eventually try to take possession of the Diamond Coal Mine, the richest prize in all Pennsylvania. Its coal was assayed as the best grade in the world, with veins so deep that no soundings of them have been recorded. The coal is smokeless and odorless, commanding the highest prices in the land over all brands.''

Betty smiles, "Bobby has a bonanza in his coal mine and his unscrupulous competitors know it. There is only one thing he has to worry about, and that is how to hold on to it. Mm-mm! How are we going to help him?''

"I don't have the answer, Mother, but the article goes on to say, "We know from private sources that some of the Big Seven have approached Bobby Brooks. Even offering him a large amount of money for his holdings. He has turned them down. They've tried to intimidate him with threats but he cares not. He is one owner that can't be bamboozled or controlled.''

"Shocking!'' lamented Betty, shaking her head. "Poor Uncle Bobby.! He worries more for his men than he does for himself.''

THE DECISION

"I'm afraid, Mother," sighed Dennis, "the day isn't too far away before the Big Seven will make their move."

"Dennis," Betty remarked sadly, "that's the reason I want you to finish your law course at Harvard as soon as possible. I hope you can graduate in time to help your uncle."

"You're right, Mother! I will do my best and graduate in time. I hope it isn't too late to help Uncle Bobby."

Unbeknownst to them, time was molding a new Dennis, dedicating himself to helping the oppressed and weak, but there were dark clouds brewing on the horizon.

Chapter 7

As the years passed, Patrick's ranch prospered beyond his wildest dreams. The Betty Ann brand had become widely known throughout the country for the finest steers in the land. His spread had grown to over 50,000 acres of the most fertile grazing land in the territory. His lands stretched farther than the human eye could see or imagine. Tens of thousands of Betty Ann steers dotted the landscape, each a testimony to the rich land on which they grazed. The ranch had outposts in six different areas, each run by an experienced foreman and manned by a crew of dependable cowboys, calloused drovers, and tobacco-chewing cooks.

The pastures of the Betty Ann were close to clear rivers and lakes. Patrick had discovered "ecology" long before modern science had prompted its importance. He used a system whereby his cattle grazed for a certain period in one area, then were taken to a new location in order to rotate the use of the lands.

Kelly observed this for some time, then finally one day asked his dad for the reason why.

"Kelly," Patrick answered, "The reason is simple. The land, like anything else, needs a rest once in a while. It's like the cattle, the ranchhands, and you and I. If not given a rest, we'd be all worked to death. You must remember one important thing about the land. We work for it for the future and not the present. If we're good to the land, the land will be good to us."

"Dad, I learn more and more from you with each passing day. When will I learn all there is to know?"

"Son, you will never learn all there is to know. Life is a school of experience; if you carefully observe all that you see, view each day as a day in school, you might make it. It all depends on you. You are the master of your fate. You can learn by your mistakes and from those of

THE DECISION

others. Only fools prosper by their wiles, but not for long. You can pray that the Good Lord has given you enough time and sense to soak up some of the wisdom of the prairie and the Indians. There will be days when nothing goes right for you. Then there will be other days. That is life in a nutshell, but don't let it discourage you. What you can't do today, somehow you'll manage to do tomorrow.''

Patrick recalled the early dark days as he was talking to his son. The problem he had raising Kelly while trying to run the Betty Ann Ranch at the same time. If Shatoma hadn't come along when she did, he shuddered to think what would have happened. Then, magically, it all seemed to fall in place. The times had been hard on Patrick and the other ranchers. It was a wild time when they were harassed with land sharks, cattle rustlers, outlaws, crooked town officials, and many other shady characters trying to make a dishonest dollar at their expense. In the end, Patrick and the ranchers overcome it all by their perseverance, courage, and the help of their loyal hired hands. In later years, their sons became old enough to meet all the challenges and won the battle. The ranchers were a team that gained the respect of the townspeople, and they were feared by their enemies.

One day, it all disappeared like a bad nightmare with the passing of the bad men. The Betty Ann was to know a new era, a happy, progressive, prosperous one. The ranchhands were a content and happy lot. The cattle became fat and plentiful. The ranchhouse was enlarged and its western decor transformed into a beautiful, spacious prairie castle. Only Shatoma grumbled, ''Much too big for three; big enough for the whole Omaha tribe.''

One day while Kelly was in Broken Bend on business, he met a favorite friend of his in an embarrassing position. Carrying packages in both of her arms, it was the irrepressible Annie. He was set to say hello but, before he had a chance, she tripped and fell to the ground. Kelly hurried over to pick her up and help her retrieve the scattered packages.

She was furious at her plight and herself, and especially with Kelly's knowing smile, and then laughter. She angrily lashed out a him, ''Laugh, you old sow's belly, laugh, consarn you! You really must think I'm a clumsy dodo to fall down like I did! You'd think I could have picked a better time to show off my ballet training? Holy grass 'a fire! I'm sorry to blow off steam, but anyhow, thanks for helping me up.''

Kelly replied with a twinkle in his eye, ''That's what friends are for! You sure looked funny sprawled all over Main Street with those packages flying in all directions and you cussing like an army trooper. What can I say? No one looks as beautiful as you when you're mad. What do you say we smoke the pipe of peace with a drink of sarsaparilla? That should cool you off.''

"Kelly, I know you're doing your best to cover it up, but you are a not! What makes you think I'm angry? I'm nut angry, I'm just disgusted with myself. What would my dad say if he found out about this? He'd probably think I was drinking four fingers straight up! Heaven knows I can't stand the smell of whiskey, much less drink it! What are you grinning at? You look like the cat that swallowed the canary. Let's go and get that drink!''

As they walked toward the cafe, Kelly was thinking to himself, "Ain't she something?"

Annie was something special! Still in her teens, she turned many an eye and stirred many a heart whenever she came to Broken Bend. Annie had that certain kind of female magnetism that turned on all the eligible menfolk, beside a few on the married ones too. She stood five feet four inches tall, which seemed like a good size for Kelly and boasted a perfect figure. Her intriguing green eyes sparkled with mischief and her bright red hair fell to her shoulders. Annie was just as fiery as her hair and outspoken in her views.

Through their teenage years, Kelly and Annie had developed a firm friendship that bordered on the edge of love. They were a lot alike in many ways: quick-tempered, garrulous, and stubborn. Friends rumored about their companionship, figuring it was a matter of time before they tied the wedding knot, but, so far, nothing had really developed in their relationship.

Kelly loved and admired "Pop" Logan, Annie's father. He was a softspoken, gentle, balding man, who always seemed to be smoking a sweet smelling corncob pipe. Pop talked to Kelly more like a friend than as a perspective father-in-law, though he wished that too with all his heart. "You know, Kelly," Logan mentioned to him one day. "your father and I are of the old school. We agree on one thing. This is a young man's world we are living in. If we don't keep up with it, it will pass us by. I like young folks! Whenever they're around, I never feel old."

"You'll never grow old, Mr. Logan, thinking the way you do. You'd be at home during any age in history. How do you do it?"

"Well, Kelly, I could have been bitter but that would have served no useful purpose! I'm thankful I have a daughter like Annie. My wife died while giving birth to Annie, and her death was almost the end of me. I was so in love with her! If it wasn't for your father, I would have been the town drunk. He realized and sympathized with my problem. It was almost the same as his, raising you. So you see, Kelly, time heals everything, even that tormenting ache of mine in my heart. I know a lot of people are saying I'm spoiling Annie, but I will not dim the fire in her spirit. It's special to me! She's just like her mother used to be. Your dad and I go back a long way. That comes from mutual respect, the kind you

THE DECISION

have to earn from each other. We've both paid our dues on that score."

That night, Kelly was home thinking about what Mr. Logan had said to him. He tried to put it into proper perspective as he sat down to supper with Patrick and Shatoma. "You're late, son. Where have you been so long" questioned Patrick. "Supper is getting cold and Shatoma was getting worried about you."

"I was over at Annie's place," Kelly answered as he took a bite of food, "I had a nice long talk with Mr. Logan. He sure has some young ideas in his head."

"Kelly, I've been meaning to talk to you about Annie for a long time. She's a delightful young lady. Shatoma and I have been wondering.... and we both have come to the same conclusion. When are you and Annie going to tie the knot?"

"Make wedding soon, before I get too old," Shatoma said, "need a lot of papooses around here."

"I love you both, but right now, we're not ready for marriage, so please don't rush me! Whenever we make up our minds to do it, you'll be the first to know."

That was the only concession Kelly would make to Patrick and Shatoma. From time to time, Patrick and Pop compared notes. Logan told his old friend that he also had the same response from Annie. So they both agreed to let the matter drop for the time being.

In the days that followed, two traumatic events were to take place in the Broken Bend Territory. The first of these was to affect Patrick and Kelly and concerned the O'Shea household. For years, Shatoma had taken care of the needs of Kelly and Patrick without thought for herself. As the years progressed, Shatoma became thinner and thinner, and her movements had slowed down rather noticeably to all but Kelly and Patrick. Neither gave a thought to it as they were both involved with their everyday life. Then one day, while they were supping, they heard an ominous thud in the kitchen followed by the crashing of dishes. They found Shatoma lying unconscious on the kitchen floor. Kelly picked her up gently and carried her to the parlor. Patrick sent one of his hands into town to get Doc Mertes. In the meantime, Kelly and Patrick made Shatoma as comfortable as possible.

As soon as the doctor arrived, he asked them to leave the room while he examined her. In a short while he told them of his findings, and then he asked one simple little question, "Why didn't you call me out here sooner? I might have done something to prolong her life but now her days are numbered. She has contracted the tuberculosis, commonly known as consumption. There is no hope for her, but good care will make her last days more comfortable."

In the sad days that followed, Shatoma grew much weaker. The women of Broken Bend came to attend her as she had once done for Olivia, but there wasn't much they could do. Shatoma knew she was dying. She asked Patrick to take her out and leave her on the prairie to die, according to her Indian tradition. Patrick exploded, "Shatoma, I love you! You've given Kelly and me everything, without a thought for yourself. You've given us your life, your love! You've taken care of us through thick and thin, without complaint. Now it's our turn to care for you."

True to his word, Patrick hired ladies of Broken Bend to sit with Shatoma and care for her needs whenever he and Kelly were unable to sit up with her. The ladies refused payment when Patrick offered it to them. Olivia reminded Patrick, "Shatoma taught us to care for each other. If it wasn't for her, I wouldn't be here now. Patrick, how could you expect me to take pay for service to a very dear friend? We all love her, and we'll stay with her as long as it is necessary."

The disease proceeded to its end, which came mercifully fast. Kelly and Patrick were at her side when Shatoma said to Patrick, "Leave room, please. Must have council with young brave."

Patrick left with a deep sigh. Shatoma whispered weakly to Kelly, "Listen close! Must go soon to happy hunting grounds to meet with Bawata, my chief. We no have son but Great Spirit gave you to me to love as a son. Time is like quicksand, we all fall in same trap, and it won't let go!"

Tears streamed down Kelly's cheeks as he held her close for the last time, not wishing to let her go. "Shatoma, I know I should have told you this more often in the past, but I thought we would go on forever. I love you like the skies above! I love you like the waters that run deep! I love you like the breezes that rustle through the trees! I love you for many things, my mother who raised me. You were there to dress me and care for my wounds. You tried my tears and quieted my fears. Now, I'm powerless to help you. Please, God, what am I to do?"

Shatoma pressed her hand to Kelly's lips as she whispered, "I am not your true mother. Only borrowed from your real mother. I've never seen her but I always felt her at my side when I throw angry words at you. Some day you will see her and love her. Tell her for me, Shatoma thanks you for allowing her son to be mine. Kelly, the day will come when your father will say good words about your mother. She will be beautiful like the sunset and her words will be like the sweet sounds of the birds. I will be in happy hunting grounds with Bawata, smiling down at you. One more word, Kelly. Ask your father to tell you of your mother when time is right and he is ready, and not until then. He will tell you all the good things you want to know. Him feel heap bad about your mother. I know he still loves her! The time is here for me. Call Patrick."

THE DECISION

Patrick came quickly at Kelly's call, "Hold tight, Shatoma, the doctor will soon be here."

Shatoma silenced him with an upraised hand, "Oh, big chief, Bawata and you would have been heap good friends. I tell him pretty soon about my white family. Don't cry for me, but feel happy that I will soon be with my ancestors in happy hunting grounds. Will be one big feast and celebration when I get there. Will smoke pipe of peace for greetings. Hold me, Patrick, I'mmmm..." With Patrick's name on her lips, a sign left her weakened body and her spirit went to meet the Great Spirit in the sky.

The funeral services were held twice, the white man's way and an Indian ceremony. Ranchers and town folks were lined up outside the small church, teary-eyed in grief. The many who knew her and who loved and respected Shatoma were there to pay their final respects. The reverend eulogized her as an Indian saint in a touching funeral that left many, even the hard-hearted, in tears. The Logans were there with Annie, holding Kelly's hands during the service, consoling him and sharing his grief.

The situation around Broken Bend remained quiet for about six months after Shatoma's death. There were the usual scuffles down at the Buckaroo Saloon among the drunken patrons but nothing spectacular. Then one day, the second event occurred that would turn Broken Bend into an armed camp, inflaming the citizens into a fever pitch, causing the ranchers untold worry and concern, banding them all together against a common enemy, the railroad.

The cause of this commotion was a story that appeared in the Broken Bend Bugle with the blaring headlines, CrossCountry Railroad Company Lays Claim To All Land In The Broken Bend Territory. The story went on to say that the courts would given the final verdict, but no date had been set for a court session. The action included all the ranches in the area. The territory was estimated to exceed a half a million acres of prime land. Among the most noted of this edict to be affected were the Betty Ann Ranch, owned by Patrick O'Shea, the Great L, owned by John Logan, the Effendi, owned by Sid Sayd, the Cross Bar, owned by Jeff Cravat, and over a hundred other, smaller ranches.

The injunction held that the railroad had valid claims to all the lands in the Broken Bend Territory due to a mandate of the Homestead Act that had it hidden in the small print of the Act. According to it, the party or parties who had homesteaded the land or bought it from a homesteader were supposed to have it registered in their names by a certain date or it would belong to anyone who registered it after that date. Thus through a hidden codicil, permission was given to any person or corporation to file a registration of said properties in their name or names.

The CrossCountry Railroad Company had registered all these lands in its name, according to the fine print of the Act. They were now the legal owners of all the properties in the Broken Bend Territory. The article went on to say that the present owners were squatters and would be forced off their lands.

Patrick called a meeting of all the ranchers to be held at the Betty Ann Ranch. They gathered in angry little groups, vowing vengeance on the railroad and discussing ways and means of beating this new ploy of the railroad. The meeting turned out to be a heated one, with plenty of spit and vinegar erupting from every sentence uttered by the angry ranchers. They were ready to fight the world, if necessary.

The spacious parlor of the Betty Ann was filled to capacity with spiteful, yelling, cursing ranchers. It almost became a free-for-all between old friends as they differed in their views and expressed their violent beliefs. It was a yelling match until Patrick let out a loud whistle and a holler, "Hey, hold on a minute, friends! Quite please! You're waking up the cattle! We'll have a stampede in here if this keeps up. Let's do this orderly. We're friends, not enemies, it's the railroad we have to fight, not us! We're all on the same side, fighting the same enemy, the railroad. The way it looks right now, we're in a heap of trouble. Hold it! Don't go off the deep end! No matter how much you may curse, scream, or yell, it will not solve the problem. Quiet down, so we can talk about our strategy in a sane and normal manner. You will all have a chance to have your say, one at a time. We called this meeting for one purpose only, to find a possible solution to our dilemma. It's sink or swim for all of us. What we need to know is, "how can we stay afloat?"

Sid Sayd yelled out, "Let's do it like my daddy did it when he fought with LaFitte at New Orleans against the British. Don't give up the ship or an inch of territory. I'll personally hang the first son-of-a-bitch that steps on my land and slit the gullet of the first railroad bastard I see!"

Big, burly Jeff Cravat blared out, "We've got to make plans on defending our ranches to the last man."

"Hold it, men!" Logan tried to reason with the man. "I know how you all feel! I share the same anger, the same anxieties, and the same concerns as you. Deep down in our hearts, you and I know that we can't win it that way. The railroad has too much money and can muster too many men against us and generate too much power of the likes of us. We've got to put our heads together to find the final answer. Somewhere, someplace, someone will lead us to the final victory."

Kelly rose slowly, not knowing what he was about to say or how the older ranchers would accept him. "I know I'm still wet behind the ears,

THE DECISION

but in school they taught us that the courts were for the poor and rich alike. It didn't matter what type of trouble you were in, or who you were! All that mattered, just as long as you were in the right, and by God, we're in the right, we should win. But, right is not always right, so let's explore that street first, the courts. Let's not do anything drastic that may hurt our case. But when the time comes, we will fire our best salvo, and, friends if it gets down to that...I reckon you'll find me in the middle with you all the way."

The meeting lasted until midnight. Nothing much was accomplished. They were no closer to an answer than when it began. It was evident that the ranchers had one weakness known to the railroad. They had no knowledge of the law or how it operated. Most of them had never been any farther than the limits of their property. They never worried about the law because they were the law in their domain. Now the railroad had changed the rules of the game and the ranchers would be held accountable by the American courts and its laws. What could they do? What must they do? Those were the questions uppermost in their minds.

It was damned if they did and damned if they didn't. If they took up arms, there would be bloodshed and violence. The railroad wouldn't get hurt; they had countless men to do their dirty work. If they couldn't bring the ranchers to their knees, there would other devious ways. They could create an incident whereby the army would be forced to come in to fight the ranchers. The ranchers realized it and tried not to make this incident blow up in their faces. Fate had dealt them a low blow, but perhaps not a fatal one.

They said that trouble begets trouble, and Patrick was to find this out the very next day. He was at the ranch, discussing the railroad problem with Kelly, Annie, and her father, when a messenger rode in with a special delivery letter from St. Louis. Kelly asked, "Who do you know in St. Louis, Dad?"

Patrick replied candidly, "As soon as I open this letter, we'll both cure our curiosity."

Patrick opened the flap and started to read the letter when he exclaimed, "Oh, my God! I forgot all about it!"

He passed the letter to Kelly who read it aloud, "This is to inform you that you are subject to the mandates of the Legal Separation decree of 1875 between Patrick O'Shea and Elizabeth O'Shea. You are now instructed to follow the provisions of that decree by sending your son Kelly to Philadelphia to be with his mother for the next two years. You are also notified to expect your son, Dennis, on June 10, 1894 as per court ruling of the degree, duly signed by both parties with witnesses."

As Shatoma has prophesied on her death bed, the time had come for the chickens to come home to roost. The time had come for Patrick to tell his son the true story of his marriage and separation. Patrick started slowly, beads of perspiration dotted his forehead. "Kelly, I know I should have told you about your mother a long time ago, but I kept putting it off until the right moment. I guess that time is now. Before I start, I'd like to have John and Annie listen in, as I consider them family."

Annie popped up, "Wrangle your spurs! I wouldn't miss this for the world. Grass 'a fire! I want to know all about this dark secret."

Patrick told the complete story, without leaving out any of the details. He didn't miss anything, from the time he met and fell in love with his wife and about the final days before their separation. He offered no excuses for himself nor did he find fault with his wife, "We never hated each other, even after the separation. We just went out separate ways until now. I guess we were just two stubborn fools. Perhaps I was the worse one. It was the matter of ideology that was the cause of our misunderstanding. Betty was of the opinion that she should raise our sons in the east, in the finest of schools. I was dead set on raising our sons in the east. It was that simple difference that caused us to drift apart. Deep in our heats, I know there is still love for each other. Kelly, I'm sure you will love your mother; she is a wonderful woman. Take good care of her, for the next two years, as she'll be lonely for the temporary loss of her other son. I know she'll love you as I have. I'm sure the day you arrive in Philadelphia, your mother will be waiting for you. She'll be easy to spot! She'll be the most beautiful woman at the station."

"Jumping sidewinders!" gushed Annie. "Just think, Kelly, you didn't lose a father by this latest turn of events; you gained a mother. Wow....eeee!"

Kelly laughed, "Annie, you make a lot of sense. Probably as much as anyone around here at this time. There's got to be a silver lining out there someplace in our battle with the railroad and I'm going to miss all the fun in finding it. I'll especially miss you, Annie. Who knows, Dad, maybe my brother will be a little help when he gets here. After all, he's still an O'Shea. Give him a break to get started, Dad. You too, Annie. It will be a strange world for him. Don't hold it against him because he's a tenderfoot. He's just a victim of circumstances of the court, as we all are."

With that off his shoulders, Kelly strolled to his room and started packing his belongings. Annie followed him, sad and dejected. "Kelly, what about us? I care a lot for you and I know you feel the same way about me. What will become of us?"

THE DECISION

"Annie, you wildcat! What can I say? I'm at a loss for words, just like you are. Too many things have happened lately that's changed our lives. You are the best thing that's ever happened to me, Annie, my dear. We've had fun, even argued, but through it all, we've enjoyed each other's company, doing the things we loved. We're both young, with a full life ahead of us. The feelings we have for each other are wonderful and will always be there. We don't know if it's love or friendship. Maybe this separation will furnish the answer for us. For the present, there'll be no commitments between us. No promises. No guarantees. Just plain honesty! Are we in love or just good friends? We can't truthfully say but time will furnish the answer."

"Kelly, that is the way I feel! Holy grass 'a fire! Now, how about a long kiss for a very good friend of yours or who knows what?"

Two days later, Kelly was on his way to Philadelphia, leaving Annie, the Betty Ann Ranch, and his loved ones behind. Kelly felt especially concerned for his dad, for he had raised him for such an eventuality but fate had changed the script and locale.

Patrick, in the meantime, mused to himself. "I wonder what kind of a son Betty raised?" His guess was a perfumed dandy who sniffs snuff. "Wa...hoo! Fate sure has dealt me a cruel blow!"

Chapter 8

The days slipped by, Dennis was busy with his law courses at Harvard, exerting every effort to finish them in time to assist Bobby Brooks with his troubled coal mine in Pennsylvania. Betty, in the meantime, true to her promise to her uncle, kept him informed as to what Dennis and she had learned about the nefarious activities of her enemies. She cautioned him to be on his guard at all times as the Big Seven were capable of any foul deed in order to take over his mine.

In the spring of 1894, Betty visited Bobby Brooks at his home in Andura. Shocked to see how he had aged since she had seen him in the previous spring, hugged and kissed him. "Oh, Uncle Bobby, how are things with you? You're not your smiling self! You look so worried!"

"Aye, my bonnie lassie," agreed the Scot, We are now living in terrible times. I don't know how much longer I can hold out against them."

He puffed harder on his briar, exhaling little clouds of smoke. "The worse is yet to come. I've been informed by good sources that the coal war between them heathen devils is o'er. There's a lot of reasons for it, but primarily it's the loss of production by one t'other and the heavy damages they continued inflicting on each other. Sabotaging each other's mines, and add to that, the costs of derailment of valuable carloads of coal that caused a terrific drain on their resources. Last year, that slippery snake of a man, Adam Havell, called for a truce. A meeting was held among the unholy group to straighten out their difficulties and differences. Out of this meeting came an agreement of the seven feuding coal companies to merge together into one large combine to be known as the Big Seven Coal Company, with equal power among all members."

"Aye, my lassie," bewailing the troubled Scot, "There's over a hundred or so independent little coal companies barely making a living from their mines. They are now left at the mercy of these brigands. They've

THE DECISION

already started taking over. They're using intimidation, threats, harassment, and yes, even murder to get their way. Why last week, my old friend, George Hendres, was found murdered. The police say it was robbery, but I know different. It was murder! Their plan is quite evident. To eliminate the competition, one by one, then control the coal industry by setting the coal prices at a higher rate for a much larger profit. Aye! That's their main motive! More profit! Their next move would be to lower the wage scale of the miners by creating their own coal monopoly. The wolves are beginning to emerge from their dens, devouring all who get in their way. After they've gobbled up all the small, defenseless companies, their only obstacle left is the grandest prize of all, the Black Diamond Coal Company! My mine!''

"Shame, shame!" cried Betty, "Isn't there something that the government can do?"

"Nay, lass! They've bought out the government agents, who now look the other way while the Big Seven continue their ways."

"Have faith and hold tight, my darling. Dennis will graduate this coming June. As soon as he does, we'll be back to see what can be done within the law."

"Lassie, aye! I hope it's real soon, but I have my doubts that I'll be around to see it. I've had tremendous pressure put on me by them devils. There have been six definite offers to buy at any price of my choosing and the same number of forcible threats."

In the meantime, the Big Seven didn't let any grass grow beneath their feet. Slowly they were taking over all the independent coal mines until there was none left except the Black Diamond Coal Company, run by an uncompromising "Bonnie Bobby" Brooks! The time had come for a showdown between them. His was the last bastion of defense of free men. The Big Seven had offered Bobby Brooks money many times for his company, but he disdainfully called them "the brothers of the devil" They tried other methods to intimidate him but he was adamant in his refusal. He was the last independent owner left they had to defeat before they could lay claim to all of it. This was the subject that the Big Seven owners were discussing as they had gathered in their spacious new conference room.

Sitting at the had of the table was Chairman "Iron Mike" Finnegan, the ruthless enforcer of the old days. On one side of him sat Adam Havell, "Black Jack" Murphy and "Crazy Olaf" Johanson. Across from them were Adolf Wantens, Phillip Gaston, and "Big John" Williams.

The notorious Big Seven carried their power right to the legislature, where they had many in their back pockets, thus laws for their benefit were easily passed.

The meeting opened with Iron Mike Finnegan pounding the gavel. "The meeting of the Big Seven Coal Company is now called to order. We'll skip all preliminary business and get right down to what we have in the back of our minds. What are we going to do about that bastard, Bobby Brooks? We're getting loud rumblings of discontent from our miners about the good wages Brooks is paying his miners. The Scottish bastard is paying them more to work a ten-hour shift than we are paying for a fourteen-hour shift, besides having Sundays off. Why should they have Sundays off? They aren't going anyplace! They have no church or preachers to call their own. Besides, how does Brooks do it? Why does he do it? It isn't right to pay foreigners like that. Most of them can't even speak English. People like that just don't have feelings!''

"Yah!" yelled Crazy Olaf, "Dat is so. Dey's lumberheads! Vot dey need is a bingo on der noggin. Remember de fun ve used to have in der goot olden days scaring de hell out of der mine owners while ve were beating de hell ou of dem up near Pittsburg until dey sold out to us at our prices. I luvved dose days.''

"Dot is right!" echoed Adolf Wantens, "Vorkers like dot are inferior people! Der vorse den jackasses! I know!"

Gaston piped up in a squeaky voice, "Monsieur, the main question is how do we get rid of Brooks? His liberal movement has made us the laughing stock of the miners,'' fluttering his handkerchief in the air, "besides, I don't like anybody laughing at me! Mon Dieu!''

Finnegan called for order as he bellowed out, "Quiet, I've got some very important news for you that just might help us out of this damned mess. A few weeks ago you authorized me to find someone to break the Black Diamond's back, and that goes for Bobby Brooks' too. I think I've found the right man. He knows our problem and he has the ready answer. He won't come cheap, but he will be worth every cent we pay him! He's as mean a man as I've ever seen and I've seen some of the worst. We're hiring him for one purpose, to get rid of Brooks! One way or the other, head first or feet first. He'll be kaput, Herr Wantens,'' he grinned knowingly.

"He promises," Finnegan continued, 'he'll be out of your hair, once and for all! Will you agree for such a man to undertake this job before I bring him in?''

The sullen member promptly agreed, but not before Iron Mike had one parting sally, "We must give our man unlimited power to do his job, and enough money to carry it through to its successful completion. I repeat: his job will be threefold. First of all, get rid of Brooks. Second, shut down his mines. Third, to buy the Black Diamond mines at our price. Are we all in favor?''

French Gaston squealed with pleasure, "Mon Dieu! Wonderful! Bien! Anything to wipe out Brooks and his liberal movement meets with my approval! In fact, I'd go for hiring the devil himself to do the job.''

THE DECISION

"I guarantee," thundered Finnegan, "That this man is the devil incarnate himself, as Brooks will soon find out."

"Let's see who dot vunderman is," asked Adolf Wantens.

Finnegan walked to the adjoining room and returned in a few minutes with a hulking monster of a man who dwarfed even the huge Big John Williams. His sinister smile promised unpleasantness for anyone who crossed his path. Fierce eyes seemed to search out his victims sizing them up at the same time. He was large, over six foot six inches in height, with not an ounce of surplus fat on his bones. His large, black cigar filled the room with massive billows of smoke. He eyed them all as if he was interviewing them "instead of the opposed" from one end of the table to the other. Finally, the eyeball-to-eyeball confrontation between them was over as Finnegan introduced his find. "Gentlemen, this is the man I was telling you about. His name is Joe Dvorak, your new troubleshooter. I've explained to you and to him his new duties with our company and he knows what is expected of him. Are there any further questions?"

Crazy Olaf asked, "How much vill it cost us? How many men vill he need? How long vill it take for him to close down the Black Diamond?"

Joe Dvorak blared out in a sharp voice that left little doubt as to who would be in charge. "The cost will be small in proportion to your gain." This caught their attention. "I've looked over the area and the operation. The Black Diamond miners are loyal to Brook and will fight like hell for him, which is more than I can say for the miners you have working for you. The first thing on the program is to get rid of Brooks! That will be my job! When that job is done, the fight will go out of the miners. The rest will be like shooting fish in a barrel."

This brought a loud laugh from the members. He was saying all the right words at the right time. "Step two will be a little more difficult, but it can be done. Give me enough men, and we will stop the miners from working and close the miners. For this, I will need at least a hundred good head knockers for a start, maybe more later on. This will be expensive! It will cost you over five dollars a day for each man, along with my salary and expenses. That should run you in the neighborhood of a thousand dollars a day. In the long run, it will be the best investment you ever made. Within a month, I'll rid you of Brooks. Within two months, I'll have the mine shut down and boarded up. From then on, you can pick up the mine at your leisure and price."

"In the meantime," Dvorak continued, with a nasty curl on his heavy lips, I've been doing a little research on my own. I hired a geological engineer out of my pocket, which will be included in my expenses. You'll be pretty interested in his findings. I know I was! In his report, it is stated that the coal dug out of the Black Diamond mine is the cleanest in the country. The veins are so deep that no soundings have ever been reached to the bottom. His report also notes that the Black Diamond mine's worth is in the millions. Now with information, I ask you, "Is the money you're investing worth the grand prize at the end of the rainbow?" If I know you guys, the answer is definitely yes, but the decision is up to you."

Murphy roared, "Begorrah, laddies! May the saints preserve you! How do you suppose we made it so far? Of course, with a little larceny in our hearts! I'm all for hiring Dvorak right now! The rewards will far exceed the expenses for the mine. I've convinced!"

Adam Havell leered at his cohorts, then in a calculated, unruffled voice answered, "What are we waiting for? I move we accept Dvorak as our troubleshooter."

Big John Williams screamed, "Jesus Christ, Adam, let's talk it over. We're not ordering a meal at a restaurant or anything as simple as that. This is serious stuff we're thinking of! I like the deal but I want to know what it involves."

"Yah! Dot is right!" agreed Adolf Wantens, "I also vant to know vat vere getting into."

Dvorak put a stop to all the disputing. "Hold on! Here is what I propose! I'll tell you for the last time, so don't waste my time or yours. Here is what I've promised to do for you. I'll outline it to you for the last time. First, get rid of Brooks, and second, close the mines and finally, you get to buy the Black Diamond mine at your price. For my end, I do the work, get well paid for it plus a hefty bonus. It's as simple as that. If anyone around here blows the whistle on our operation, we will all be implicated on this venture. I don't look for any blackguard here doing that, eh? Are you, or are yo not in favor?"

Adam Havell looked out with vengeful, glaring eyes that were filled with greed, replied, "We're all in this together. No one before has ever argued or disputed our methods on how we acquired some of our mines. Why should this be any different? Why should we change now? I'm in favor of hiring Joe Dvorak right now to carry out his duties as our troubleshooter. I move we hire Dvorak."

The vote was carried out with all in favor of hiring Joe Dvorak, with the added provision that he be given free rein and unlimited powers to carry out their orders.

One month later to the day, the first point of Joe Dvorak's program was carried out when "Bonnie Bobby" Brook was found shot in the head and robbed of his money. The police claimed he was a victim of robbery and shot when he put up a struggle.

THE DECISION

Dvorak got in touch with Finnegan, "We've carried out step one and we're proceeding to step two. I expect to accomplish it within a month or so."

Finnegan replied with great gusto, "Terrific, Joe! Good job! I read about the sad details in the paper, ha-ha! I've also learned through the grapevine that the person most likely to inherit the Black Diamond mine is some socialite in Philadelphia. They're having trouble trying to locate her. What a snap this will be. Keep up the good work! I'm laughing, ha-ha! They're still trying to locate her...She doesn't know beans about mining, or anything except parties...ha-ha...nor would she have the guts to do anything about it. As soon as you close down the mine and board it tight, don't let anyone near it! Guard it night and day! Don't let anyone try to open it again. We have to keep it closed until September 30 of this year, and then it can be sold to the highest bidder, and you know who that will be! Go ahead and put plan two in action."

"I've hired a hundred of the toughest, roughest strikebreakers in the business. We're going to start bringing them into Andura a little at a time so as not to create suspicion on our part. In two weeks to a month, we'll be in full business of shutting the mine down."

"Good, keep in touch with me on your progress."

The following Monday, the henchmen started arriving in Andura a few at a time. Within two weeks, they had their full complement on the scene. Then strange things began to happen. Little things started to go wrong at the mines. One day a cable snapped and a runaway car injured a score of people. Each day brought a new danger at the mines to the men. The frayed nerves of the miners were at the breaking point.

To compound their miseries, Dvorak's musclemen started their nasty business of harassing the miners and their families. This resulted in many open clashes between the two factions, with the defenseless miners getting the worst of it. The goons continued to plague the miners at every opportunity by insulting their women and routing their children from their favorite playing areas while painting obscene descriptions and pictures on their homes. It had become a lawless town with the miners afraid to leave their homes.

In a little more than a month, Dvorak's paid enforcers succeeded in closing and boarding up the mine, establishing a guard around it day and night. Step two had been carried out. All that was left to stop step three was a frail, defenseless, unsophisticated woman in the coal business who knew nothing of it.

The miners wept openly when they learned of the death of their beloved owner. Tony Dinardi, the miner's spokesman, went to the payroll office to learn what would be done now that Brooks was dead. He was told that there had been a reading of the will, an the only heir to the estate was a Mrs. Patrick O'Shea. There was one main stipulation to the will; if the mine was not operating on September 30, 1894, it must be sold to the highest bidder. In the meantime, Tony learned they were having trouble locating Mrs. O'Shea but would try operating the mine until they received notice to the contrary from the new owner. Mr. Brooks' lawyer finally got in touch with Betty by mail but had received no answer as yet.

Betty arrived back in Philadelphia after spending a month at a retreat in New England. She was surprised to be greeted at the station by Jessica, who she thought was still in finishing school, "Jessica," she exclaimed, "What a pleasant surprise! My, how you've grown! You've blossomed into a rare beauty."

Jessica hugged her, "Betty, you look wonderful, beautiful as ever! I just graduated from finishing school, couldn't wait to get here! Got in yesterday, learned from your gardener you were coming in today and here I am! I'm glad to be back home with you again."

"You know Dennis is away at Harvard studying to be a lawyer. I believe I wrote to you about it a few months ago."

"Yes, Betty, and I treasure that letter. Let's hurry home! I want to see it again and I have so much to tell you."

They arrived back home by carriage, Betty was tired, "I'm looking forward to a long rest with no headaches. It seems every time I go on a vacation, I'm anxious to get home and rest up. It's great to sleep in my own bed again. Jessica! Look at the stack of mail staring me in the face. Will you be a dear an go through it with me?"

"That would be fun, Betty, I'd love that. I'll take this half and you take the other half. I just like reading somebody else's mail."

They ran through a few of the letters, exchanging comments on some of the interesting ones and then Jessica asked, "Betty, do you know Bonnie Bobby Brooks?"

"Why, yes. He's my uncle! I love him dearly. He's such a wonderful old gentleman. I must tell you more about him when we have the time. What does the old darling have to say?"

"I'm afraid it's bad news! He was murdered about a month ago during a robbery."

"Oh, my God!" Betty put her head in her hands and sobbed convulsively, "What a fool I was! I meant to see him before I went on my trip but I kept putting it off. What a fool I was! What can I do to help? It's too late for tears now but there must be something I can do."

"Betty, there's a special delivery letter addressed to you."

THE DECISION

"Please open it, Jessica! Read it to me."

Jessica opened the letter. It was from Brooks' lawyer. Jessica began to read, "You may well know by now of the brutal murder of Bobby Brooks. It has left us in deep shock. Mr. Brook was more than a client to me, he was a dear friend. He must have known something like this was going to happen, for he made out his will a week before his murder. No matter what the police may call it, I still say it was murder. The will has been duly notarized, registered, and witnessed by the probate court. Mr. Brooks bequested to you the Black Diamond Coal Company and all its assets. He wanted me to alert you to the evil forces who will try to steal it from you. So because of this, he made one major stipulation in the will. In case the burden of operating the Black Diamond Coal Company becomes too great or dangerous to you, and/or the mine is not operating by September 30, 1894, you are instructed to sell it to the highest bidder."

The letter continued, "Mr. Brooks dictated the following to me to pass on to you, "Dear Betty, What I'm writing you is between you and me. By the time you read this, I'll probably be with my Maker. I can almost see the vultures overhead. I doubt if I can hold out much longer against them heathen. I know I'm a marked man, and they have me in their sights. Betty! I'd prefer you kept the mine in our family, but if it gets too dangerous for you, I want you to sell it. Furthermore, if you decide to hold on to it, I'd like you to treat the miners with the dignity and consideration they deserve. Betty, you're a fighter, that is why I've entrusted you with the Black Diamond mine. Love it and its people as I have; the rewards will far exceed your wildest imagination. This is a great responsibility I've given you, but I believe I know you better than you know yourself. You're a born fighter, for as long as I've known you. Don't buckle under their threats and intimidation. Study how to fight them. Deploy the tactics necessary to outlast them. You can trust the miners to back you all the way. When things are the roughest, there is one miner I trust the most of all. He'll be your eyes, and ears! Depend on him, he's a good man! His name is Tony Dinardi. May God bless you and keep you. Goodbye, Betty, I love you...Uncle Bobby."

There were tears in Betty's eyes and she squeezed her hands until they were white. "The greed of such men caused the death of my dear uncle! I will not rest until I avenged him!"

"Betty, what do you intent to do?"

"I'm giving a lot of serious thought," Betty said, pausing a moment to reflect. "You know, Jessica, Bobby Brook was right. It was something he wrote in his letter that moved me. He mentioned dignity and consideration for the miners. He didn't fear so much for his life as he feared what would happen to his men. He must have cared deeply for them to sacrifice his life. I don't intend for that sacrifice to go in vain. I will hold on to the mine any way that I can, using all my resources, if need be.''

"Betty, you're wonderful. Why don't you contact Dennis? I'm sure he would want to help."

"Jessica, I'd rather not for the time being, as he has only a few more weeks before he graduates. I don't want to put him under any additional pressures. Later on we can tell him. By then he'll be in a better position to advise us. Promise, Jessica, that you won't say anything about this to him."

"I promise. Betty, I understand and agree. And as soon as he graduates, we better tell him the whole truth or he'll be terribly upset with the two of us."

"Now, we've got that settled. Here's what we're going to do, Jessica. Get a pen and some paper and I'll dictate a letter to the paymaster at the mines. Here's the gist of it; reword it so it makes sense to them. Authorize the paymaster to send Mr. Tony Dinardi to meet with me as soon as possible at my home in Philadelphia. Make sure, Jessica, you write down my address and the directions or else the poor man will get lost. He will also be given expenses for the trip with full pay, plus an extra fifty dollars for spending money."

"I'm waiting breathlessly until he gets here, Betty. A sudden thought crosses my mind, heaven forbid! The poor man might get lost just trying to find a hotel here."

"Perish the thought! He will be our guest. He'll have no time to lose his way! There are so many things that we have to discuss about the mine. I, too, Jessica, am afraid he'd get lost in the city. Time is of the essence now."

About a week later, Betty and Jessica were in the parlor when they heard a knock at the door. Upon opening it, they saw a medium sized, dark skinned man wearing an old, brownish plaid cap that was perched unsteadily atop a mat of unruly black hair. He wore a too-tight, store-bought brown suit and a pair of brown shoes that had seen a lot of wear. Physically, he was a pitiful sight, with one bruised eye, the other blackened, and a bandage over his forehead. He growled an unintelligible greeting and his eyes blazed with anger. "My name is Tony Dinardi. The paymaster told me you wanted to talk with me about the mine. What do you want to know?"

Betty put him at ease as she answered, "Please come in, Mr. Dinardi, bring your luggage with you," pointing to the old vintage suitcase wrapped securely with two heavy ropes around the middle to keep it from sagging. "My name is Mrs. Patrick O'Shea, but my friends call me Betty, which

THE DECISION

is what I'd like you to call me. This lovely young lady is Miss Jessica Longstreet. We'll call you Tony! As you can see, Tony, we're not very formal around here. You'll be our guest while you're in Philadelphia. Tony, you asked me a direct question. For the present, it would be better if I answered it after you've had the time to rest and clean up."

"So nice to meet you, Tony," Jessica said warmly to the red-faced miner, "How did you like the train ride to Philadelphia?"

Tony grunted, "It was all right! Stop! Go! Stop! Go all the way! They couldn't make up their minds."

Betty laughed, "That is the way we feel about it, too," replied Jessica, "Sometimes I wonder if the engineer had a few fast drinks before he started."

"I never thought of it that way," smiled Betty, "until Tony brought it to my attention."

"Let's go into the parlor Tony, by the way, that's some blackened eye! I'd like to see what the other fellow looks like."

"There were just too many of them, Betty. I mean Mrs. O'Shea."

"You said it right the first time, Betty." I prefer that we keep things on a first-name basis. What do you mean there were too many of them?

The embarrassed man started slowly, intimidated at first by the lavish surroundings and outnumbered by the opposite sex, "Betty and Jessica, we have a very bad problem at the mine."

The warmth and friendliness of the two women gave Tony new confidence. "They have brought in over a hundred professional enforcers to beat us up and toe the mark. They want to shut down the mine. Some of it has been shut down already. What are we going to do about it? Some of us already are getting our heads busted in and some of the miners are in the hospital with very bad injuries from these animal bestas! They insult our women and keep our children from their play. What kind of people are they? Is this the America we have heard so much about? If this isn't the land of the free, then what is it? They've closed and boarded up some of the mines, soon they'll have them all board up! We haven't worked since poor Mr. Brook was murdered by the same group. What do they want from us?"

"How dreadful!" deplored Jessica with anguish as her voice shook with anger. "Betty, if only I were a man."

"I never realized the hopelessness of it for you miners, Tony," Betty said. "The seriousness of the situation you're facing each day at the mine. We are definitely going to do something about it but I'm not free to divulge what steps we're going to take in the future. You can rest assured, Tony, that something will be done to alleviate the situation."

Jessica cut in, "I say, Betty, if it's a fight they want, it's a fight they'll get! Jason will be graduating in June, maybe he will have some ideas on the subject."

Betty went on, "I have an idea who is behind all this, and I suspect the skunks want us to sell them the mine. But I won't. I can't name names right now until I get the necessary proof. If those skunks have the mistaken notice that I'm a defenseless woman, they'd better have another thought coming. You say, Tony, that you haven't worked since my poor uncle was killed. That's over a month ago! How have you managed to live and survive without working? How do the rest of the miners get along?"

"Mrs. O'Shea, I mean, Betty," The words weren't coming out the way Tony wanted. "It's difficult! Some of us are surviving on not much more than bread and water. Our credit with the local food stores is gone. We try to share what little supplies we have with those less fortunate. When the mine was working, there were over two hundred miners on the job; now there are none. We are also over ten thousand dollars in debt owed to different stores and owners. Those no-good bums have even closed the first-aid station that Mr. Brooks had set up for us. Now they've kicked our doctor out of town so we have to go to a nearby town for medical aid. You know what that costs?"

"The beasts!" stormed an angry Betty, "Tony, you and the miners need help right now, and it starts right now. This is what I'm going to do to help the situation. I'll write a bill of credit to cover all your back debts and present bills. I'll also write a personal check. Let me see, yes, I think it will be sufficient for the present time. I'll also set up a fund for the miners for anything that may come up. This will be considered a loan until you're back working again. I'm sure this will be enough to carry you through the crisis. If you have more money problems, let me know. We'll see what can be done about it."

Tony replied in a husky voice, "You know, Betty, we cried when Mr. Brook was killed. I don't believe it was so much because of his death as it was for our fear or what was to become of us. He was like our father and we loved him so dearly. Betty, you are like Mr. Brook and I'm paying you the highest compliment when I say that. I believe he knew he was going to die by bucking all those bad men. He wouldn't sell us out to them. You are of the same stock! I know the miners will be glad to know this!"

"By the way, Tony" Betty asked, "I'm curious, will the miners fight at your side in case of an all-out battle?"

"They all will, I promise you that!" Tony answered with conviction. "And especially my two best friends, Sadar Kominski and Sock Trullas,

THE DECISION

who will be in the middle of it. We call Sadar Kominski the "Mad Cossack" because he came from the Steppes in Poland. You ought to see him do Russian dances! Up and down, up and down, never stopping! I tried it once and I landed on my bottom." The ladies giggled in delight.

"Then," he went on, "there is Sock Trullas, the only Greek in the mines. He's a character. Always saying the funniest things. He's saving his money to bring over his betrothed from Greece. Two things Sock loves to do is fight and make love, Sock says, "I'd rather fight than make love because you don't need as much rest between fights." Excuse me, ladies, I didn't mean what it sounded like."

The women laughed! They were amused with Tony and his anecdotes of the miners. Jessica replied, between spurts of uncontrollable laughter, "We would surely love to meet your two most extraordinary friends."

"Thank you, Tony," Betty smiled at him. "Now I'd like to know all about the troubles at the mine. How did my uncle deal with each situation? These and other questions we will discuss in the next few days. There is so much we have to learn in a short time. In the meantime, I'll show you to your room where you can rest and clean up."

For the next few days, Betty and Jessica invaded the inner depths of Tony's mind with questions about coal mining and the miners. They devoured each bit of information that he passed on like a ravenous animal with its first tasty morsel. They were appalled at man's indifference to man. "Bonnie Bobby" Brooks's death was devastating to Betty, but to the people who loved him, it was catastrophic. If the mines had their way, they would have canonized him for sainthood. He was a man for all people!

Tony, too, was surprised by Betty's and Jessica's knowledge of the coal industry, thanks in part to the research that Betty and Dennis had done. As Tony so naively put it, "Say, Betty, you and Jessica are no dummies. No insult intended! You've taught me things about the coal business that I never knew before. Both of you have been a pleasant surprise to me. Honestly, I mean it! Wait until I tell all the miners when I get back."

On the fourth day, Tony bade them a tearful goodbye as he left for Andura with the encouraging news that Mrs. O'Shea was the female reincarnation of Mr. Brooks's spirit.

A few weeks later, Betty and Jessica were at Dennis' graduation exercises at Cambridge. They sat enthralled in the audience with the rest of the parents, waiting excitedly for their boy's name to be called. Finally, Dennis' name was called and he was presented with his law degree. Betty had a tear in her eye and Jessica's throat knotted up with a lump in it. They savored the moment!

After the ceremonies, they went to their hotel room to discuss Dennis' graduation and the latest developments. Dennis didn't take long to bring up the question, "Mother, what is so important to discuss? Is it about my uncle? How is he?"

"Dennis," Betty started slowly, afraid to tell Dennis what had happened, and more afraid not to tell him. "What I have to tell you is not pleasant. I dread telling it to you! Uncle Bobby was murdered a little over two months ago."

The news shocked and angered him. "What?" he moaned in disbelief. "Why didn't you tell me sooner? Didn't you think that I would care? How could you? Who could have done such a thing like that to a wonderful human being like Uncle Bobby?"

"We haven't the proof," answered Betty, "but we believe it's the work of the Big Seven Coal Company. They're behind it. Guilty as sin, but we have no way to prove it. The last time I talked to Uncle Bobby, he told me the Big Seven had made overtures to buy his mine but he steadfastly refused them. This was punctuated by intimidating threats of what the results would be if he didn't give in. Finally it was this! It's all in the open now."

Dennis demanded, "Why wasn't I told sooner?"

"What good would that have done?" Betty answered, "I felt you had enough pressures graduating from Harvard without putting this extra burden on you."

"Well, maybe you're right, Mother," he acknowledged. "I feel there is more to this story than you're telling me. What is it?"

"Dennis," Betty replied, "Uncle Bobby has made me the sole heir to the Black Diamond mine. There is a hitch to the will, a stipulation that if the mine isn't operating by September 30, 1894, the mine must be sold to the highest bidder. I believe Uncle Bobby had that codicil put in to save me the worry of running the mine if it becomes too perilous for me to continue in its operations. That is just a part of the problem," she continued. "First, we have good reason to believe that the Big Seven is hiring outside goons to beat up and intimidate the miners, and eventually shut down the mines. They have succeeded in doing this by continually brutalizing the miners and their families at every turn, even stopping them from working. I've had to mortgage some of my holdings to keep the mine running, but it's like throwing good money after bad. All I'm doing is getting further in debt. What shall I do?"

"The first thing is quit worrying. Second, let's talk about it." Jessica, I'm glad you insisted that mother confide in me. Mother, what is the latest news from the mines? Do you know of anyone there we can trust?"

"Well, I've had some correspondence with the paymaster and Uncle Bobby's lawyer about the scandalous situation at the mine. It appears our hands are tied but there is a little ray of hope. A couple of weeks ago

THE DECISION

I had a visit from one of the loyal miners. He cued us in on the bizarre happenings at the mines and they aren't good. His name is Tony Dinardi, the spokesman for the miners. I requested that he come there after reading Uncle Bobby's last letter in which he wrote about Tony. "Trust him! He will be your eyes and ears. Depend on him, he's a good man." That is as much as I remember of that letter."

Betty stopped to wipe a tear from her eye, "Dennis!" she said, as she remembered, "He came to our home. What a sight he was! He had a black eye and bruised features. A memento from a confrontation with the paid enforcers of the Big Seven. Yes, Dennis, I know we can trust Tony Dinardi! I know..."

"Mother, as soon as we get home, I must go to the coal mines to find out how desperate the situation is. If it weren't for you, Mother, I would never have had the chance to go to Harvard for my law degree. Now it's my turn to partially repay you. A minor compensation for all you have done for me."

"Flattery will get you everywhere in this world. Now we have to concentrate on the mine. Dennis, this will not be a game that college boys play. You're going against the big boys now and their rules are different. They play for keeps! You're going to bump heads with the most unscrupulous bunch of scoundrels you'll ever run into. They wouldn't hesitate to slit your throat at the least provocation. That was how your Uncle Bobby was murdered! By people such as that! If you're not careful, they'll make you their next victim. Keep a low profile when you go to Andura, at least for the time being, before you decide to open Pandora's box."

"I get the full picture, I think I know what you're getting at. I'll keep my eyes open."

Back in Philadelphia, Dennis said, "Mother, I've made up my mind. I'm going to the mine tomorrow and learn things for myself. I don't know how long I'll be there but I'll keep in touch with you. We've a serious problem there! My first job will be to evaluate the seriousness of the situation. I have to know more about the enemies' operations. I have to know who's for us and who's against us. I'll talk to the miners and get their views. There are so many questions to be answered."

As an afterthought, Dennis said, "Mother, the first man I'll contact will be Tony Dinardi and some of his close friends."

Jessica remembered some of Tony's conversations, "There are two close friends of Tony's you should look up. They are Sadar Kominski and Sock Trullas. I'm sure you'll find them interesting. When you find one, the other will not be too far away."

Mother, I'm going alone." Dennis tried to calm her fears. "But don't worry about me," Then he turned to Jessica, "I'll be careful, Jessica. You're more than a friend to me. I could kiss you!

"Well, Dennis, who's stopping you?"

The next morning, Dennis stole out of the house early in the morning headed for the mine. Within eight hours the slow train chugged into the station at Andura. Dennis immediately checked into a small hotel near the station where he cleaned up, ate dinner, then asked the clerk where Tony Dinardi lived. Dennis set out to find him. After a short spell he located the Dinardi home on the outskirts of town. A pleasant, middle-aged woman answered, "What do you-a-want?"

"My name is Dennis O'Shea. My mother owns the Black Diamond mine. I'm supposed to talk to Tony Dinardi. Do you know him?"

"Do I know-a-him? Are you crazy? I should-a-know him. He's-a-ma-brother. Come-in! I'll call him"

In a few minutes, a squat, compact, swarthy young man in his early thirties appeared and warmly greeted him. "So you're Dennis, Mrs. O'Shea's son? That's good enough for me. We have a lot to talk about before I pin you down with questions. We're still getting our butts kicked by those lousy goons. Your mother's probably told you they've been hired to keep us from working. I hate to say it, but they've done a good job of it. We didn't come to America to fight; we had enough of that in the old country. We came here to work and support our families. We cry with shame when they insult our women and children. What are we going to do about that? Tempers and patience are running short."

"Tony, your point is well taken. Tomorrow morning we'll go to town, and then to the mine. I don't promise you anything, but we'll see what is what. You'll find my mother and I are basically fair people. We believe that you are, too. We've an inkling who is behind all the hardships you've had to endure from those scavengers. Time will take care of that!" Their parting was warm.

Dennis' impression of Tony was good. He found him exactly as his mother and Jessica had described him, a warm, honest and compassionate human being. He liked Tony's simple appraisal of the current situation: direct, forward, and unafraid of the consequences, but still concerned about what could happen. He remembered Tony's final words, "We have many problems here. Lots of bad men to stop us from working. Why do them animal bestas do such things? Why? Why? They call us dirty names. Insult our woman and threaten our children. I ask you, Is this the home of the free? Bah! It was just as bad back home. Nothing has changed! They beat us, tried to have fun with our women and cheat us. Must we always be surrounded by scum like this? What shall we do, Dennis?"

Dennis thought long and hard on this question but he had no ready answer. Maybe with a little thought on it tonight, he might come up with an answer by tomorrow. Being the practical person he was, he held no high hopes for that overnight miracle.

THE DECISION

The following morning he returned to Tony's home, refreshed by a good night's sleep. "Well. Tony, here I am! Good morning, Miss Dinardi."

She nodded her head as she went on with her housework, stopping for a moment to warn her brother. "Tony, you be careful. You stay away from those bad men. Keep away from Dvorak, he devil with horns!"

Tony nodded his head to her warning, listening as he finished his breakfast, put on his topcoat, and bade her goodbye. Walking down to Main Street, Tony greeted a few miners amiably. Dennis asked, "Who are those men?"

Tony replied, "They're miners and good friends of mine. Here we speak many different tongues. Do you realize we are the melting pot of America right here in Andura." There are over a dozen nationalities living here. Some know very little English and there are others who can't speak it at all. We all managed to learn to say "Hi" to each other in English. And for us, that was something special. We knew it was a form of American greeting, and we embraced it, each one sounding different but all meaning the same. Isn't that something? Here you'll find Germans, Finns, Swedes, French, Italian, Irish, English, Russian, and a few more that I don't recall right now. The main thing is we like each other. Why? Because we have the same problems to overcome. We depend on each other. That is the way America should be. We've learned to trust each other "that is where we get our strength! We do have a few weaklings among us who would not hesitate to sell us down the river if the opportunity came up. We haven't found who they are, but when we do....Pow!" Tony slammed a mighty fist in his palm.

They continued down the street, waving at friends, when Tony stopped Dennis with a warning. "Here comes that ugly son-of-a-bitch, Dvorak. He's a mean, cruel bastard. He takes great delight in beating up defenseless miners. Now he's got most of the miners afraid of him. I've had my run-ins with him, and I got the worst of it, but he don't scare me."

Dennis replied with assurance, "To think we should be infested with such vermin is abominable and unthinkable. I don't know why I, or you, or any free man, shouldn't be able to walk down the street unmolested by scum like that. This is American and he doesn't own it! It's still a free country the last time I read the paper."

"Well, well, well," sounded a raucous voice, bringing fear to the onlookers, "if it isn't the monkey tamer and Little Lord Fauntleroy! He-ha-ha, there's a pair for you."

The sneer on Dvorak's ugly face threw a scare into many spectators as he went on with his tirade. "I want both of you off the sidewalk and into the gutter where you belong or I'll put you there."

"If you lay a finger on either of us," Dennis looked him squarely in the eyes as he replied evenly, giving no regard to Dvorak's veiled threat, "I'll guarantee you that I'll sue you and your employer for everything you own and I'll personally see to it that you serve a sentence in the state prison, until you come out with grey hair. If you desire that, start swinging at us."

Dvorak mused that over, thought of the penalties, then let out a sneering laugh, saying as he walked away, "There's no fun hitting weaklings like you. You are not men, you're mama's little boys."

To the laughter of some of the crowd, he strutted off, bellowing, "I told off those sons-a-bitches, didn't I?"

Dennis was disgusted, "Tony, I can see what you have to contend with and it's not a pleasant prospect to look forward to every day. I've got to go back to Philadelphia for a few days to take care of some private business of my own. When I'm through with it, I'll be back to see what can be done with this nasty situation."

"Wait a minute, Dennis," Tony said as he held Dennis back, "here are a couple of good friends I want you to meet."

"We heard of your row with Dvorak and hurried here as fast as we could to help but it appears you didn't need any," said a short, muscular man in his late twenties.

"So glad nothing bad happened with that poostee. It usually does," remarked a dark-faced man who looked like Tony's brother.

"Now, hold it, both of you," yelled Tony, feigning anger, "You always show up when the fun is over. I'd like you to meet Dennis O'Shea, the son of Mrs. O'Shea, the new owner of the Black Diamond mine. Dennis, this one here is Sadar Kominski."

"Hello!" a muscular man said, pumping Dennis' hand.

"And this one is Sock Trullas who claims that his grandfather fought the Turks to gain Greece's freedom. So what else is new?"

The amiable loquacious Greek answered, "Any friend of that spaghetti eater is a friend of mine. I see where nothing has changed here with that big gorilla, Dvorak. Someday he will get his!"

Dennis was having fun, enjoying the moment with his new found friends. He had never come across their like before at Harvard. He had so much to tell his mother and Jessica about his trip to Andura, and especially about those two looney characters, Sadar and Sock.

Dennis arrived back in Philadelphia the next day with mixed emotions concerning what he had seen and heard in Andura. He was vague on how to approach the problem as he mentioned it to Betty and Jessica, "Mother, I really don't know now how the situation in Andura should be handled. I've never encountered anything like this studying for my legal career at

THE DECISION

Harvard. It wasn't part of the curriculum in the course they gave there. It's quite a different ball game and foreign to my beliefs. I don't know how to cope with it unless it comes down to all-out fighting. That wouldn't solve anything, and I abhor fighting at any level."

Jessica was furious. "Your ideals be damned! You've got to fight fire with fire. If it's a fight they want, then it's a fight they'll get. Don't give up an inch to those goons or they'll what more. Battle for your principles all the way! The miners will back you, but you have to be their champion. Remember! That was how America was won a long time ago and how it became the great nation that it is today. The only way you can beat this den of thieves is by being stronger than they are. In the end, you will win, for God is on the side of the right as long as you give it a little push of your own."

"Jessica," Dennis marvelled at her, "I didn't think you had it in you. I admire your grit. Buy the way, I met a couple of Tony's friends, Sadar and Sock, who have the same fire as you. If they are a reasonable representation of the miners, we'll have no worry of the outcome. What a pair of interesting characters they are. Jessica and Mother, you'll have to meet them one of these days."

The next day, while having breakfast, Betty received a registered letter from the St. Louis, Missouri Circuit Court. Dennis asked, "I wonder what this is all about?"

"Dennis," replied his mother, "there is only one way to you can find out. Open it and read it to us."

Jessica giggled, "Betty, it doesn't seem as if they educate them like they used to in the good old days, ha-ha."

Dennis ignored this barb as he opened the letter, and started to read, "Through a Legal Separation Decree of 1875 between Patrick O'Shea and Betty O'Shea, you are instructed as per provisions of that decree to send your son, Dennis, to his father in Broken Bend, Kansas. you are also to expect your other son, Kelly, to arrive in Philadelphia on June 10, 1894 as decreed by this court to said provisions, signed by both parties and witnesses."

The letter left everyone shocked as they looked at each other in stunned silence. Dennis had never questioned his mother before about his father, and Betty had never volunteered anything on the subject.

"Mother," Dennis looked straight at his mother as he asked, "don't you think it's about time you told me about my father and my brother? I believe I have the right to know about them. I want to know everything that's happened in the past. All about my father and my brother, and how it came to all this. Mother, please don't leave anything out."

"Yes, Dennis," she admitted, "you're entitled to that. I'm sorry I didn't tell you sooner. It was such a long time ago. We were so young and gloriously happy. Your father was the hard-working rancher from the west and I was the modern, educated lady from the east with my own ideas on how to rear our sons. My ideas conflicted with your father's views. But I'm getting ahead of my story. We met, fell in love, and got married. About two years later we had twin sons, you and Kelly. That's when our troubles began. We were obsessed by how our sons should be reared. Neither of us was willing to give in. I wanted to take both sons east with me to rear as gentlemen with a far better education than you could have received in the west. All you would have been there was just a sod buster or a horse wrangler or something like that. I wanted greater things for you in this world. I wanted you to become a credit to society and me. Your father, on the other hand, wanted to raise you as a rancher. To be tough, strong, honest, and be able to fight for survival against all adversity that came your way. He wanted both of you to run his ranch and expand his ranching empire."

The emotional outburst was uncharacteristic of the reserved Mrs. O'Shea. She stopped to wipe an errant tear from her eye. "Well, things went from bad to worse until we couldn't take it any longer and any discussion of the situation was hopeless. Finally, it all ended up in court, and you know the rest. It's written plainly in this letter, Dennis, you've read the decree, and you're well versed on its legality. I don't think your father and I ever hated each other. It was a case of differing, uncompromising philosophies. That was the sad commentary of our marriage."

"I understand, Mother. Please tell me more about my father. What was he like? I'd like to know everything about him"

Jessica interrupted. "This is interesting and exciting. Do you mind if I listen in?"

"No, Jessica, we don't mind." answered Betty. "You're like part of the family. There is no mysterious past! Just a wonderful marriage that had its problems. Dennis' father was a wonderful, thoughtful, considerate husband. He was tall and handsome, with a booming voice that bounced off the rafters. He had a spontaneous laughter that brought joy in the house. When he talked, everyone listened. He was kind, yet strong in his way. I'm sure you'll like him when you meet him. I definitely know he will approve of his son. Our separation was something that I've always regretted. It shouldn't have happened but it's too late to cry over spilt milk. When you see him, give him my best and tell him I'm fine. I'll take good care of Kelly when he gets here as I'm sure he will of you."

"Mother, I don't feel too bad now about leaving you. A new world

THE DECISION

has opened up for me and I'm thankful it gives me the chance to make my father a part of it. Who knows maybe my brother can solve the coal miners' problem here.''

"Gee whiz!" chirped Jessica, "What a family you have, Betty! I'm glad I'm part of it, even as a friend.''

"Jessica, " Dennis took her by the arm and led her into the drawing room. His mother smiled approvingly, "I'd like to talk to you alone.''

"You know, Jessica," stuttered Dennis, "I'm having great difficulty saying the things I want to say to you! They're not coming out the way I want them to. We've been real close for a long time. Some may call us good friends and others may say our relationship is more than friendly. We both don't know for sure what it is. Maybe this separation will give us a good idea of what we mean to each other. As it is, we're just dragging along, taking each other for granted. But now, I do feel awful leaving you! What I'm trying to say and doing a horrible job of it is that I care a lot for you.''

"Dennis, you're the biggest, most lovable fool alive! For a man with a college education, you have a lot to learn. Neither of us is sure where our relationship is going, and both of us are afraid to admit it. I don't know whether I love you as a sweetheart or treasure you as a brother. Time will furnish the answer. Maybe, just maybe, when you're in the west, and you're feeling lonely, perhaps you will think of me. Who knows? Until then, how about a kiss to hold us 'til our next meeting? This will have to keep us for the next two years. Times may be tough for you out there.''

At this parting, the wheels of fate began to churn and revolve around the next number on the board. Where it stopped, only time and the spin of the wheel would tell. Betty wasn't quite so sure of her lot in life now as the wheel kept spinning. She reasoned all was lost, especially now that Dennis would soon be gone and there was an uncertain future ahead of her. The arrival of her cowboy son buoyed her spirits somewhat. She pictured him as being tall, bowlegged, and smelling of cattle and manure and bay rum. Perhaps yelling "Ya-hoo!" every time he saw something that was amusing or new to him.

Chapter 9

Patrick, John Logan, Annie, and a few close friends, along with interested ranchers, waited patiently at the depot for the first glimpse of Dennis at the railway station on his arrival from the east. They had one common question, "What would he be like? Would he be anything like Kelly? These questions and more were uppermost in their thoughts.

Logan smiled as he remarked to Patrick, "It's going to be a novel experience for you, seeing your other son for the first time in so many years. How are you going to handle it? It's not going to be easy for you." Before Patrick could answer, Logan added, "It will be a great thrill for all of us. Annie is fit to be tied to the nearest post. I wonder how your son is going to take it? I feel for the tenderfoot! It isn't going to be easy. It will be rough on him, maybe rougher on you! I know just how you must feel at this moment, as if you're going to choke, in a dither with excitement."

"You're right, Pop," Patrick replied solemnly with a husky twinge in his voice. "I grieve Kelly's leaving but, on the other hand, I rejoice seeing my other son. It's just too bad that the timing is off at this moment, especially with the troubles we're having with the railroad. This isn't his fight, I doubt if Dennis cares."

Annie bridles up like an unbroken mustang with a burr in its saddle. "Grass 'a fire! Mr. O'Shea. Give the tenderfoot a sporting chance! Shame on you! I think you're dead wrong about him," she said with a knowing smile on her face. "If he's anything like Kelly, if he's got an ounce of your blood in his veins, he'll care! I'll put my horse on that and back it with all the cash I have."

Someone yelled, "Thar she comes."

From a distance they could see the telltale signs of the smoke and sparks as the engine started to slow down. It finally idled to a screeching halt.

THE DECISION

The moment had come; the conductor sprightly hopped off and placed a stool on the ground for the departing passengers. One by one, the passengers got off. No sign of Dennis. It seemed an eternity for Patrick. Finally, Dennis got off. He was a picture of supreme confidence as he walked down the wooden ramp. Dressed in the finest clothing of the east, he was a magnificent specimen of manhood. In fact, some of the ranchers were so stunned by his resemblance to Kelly, that someone in the rear cried out, "Look, it's Kelly! He's come back to help us!"

Patrick quickly put a stop to that rumor, "No, it's not Kelly; it's my other son, Dennis." He rushed forward to greet him.

Annie replied, "Tarnation! Kelly and Dennis sure look like two peas out of the same pod," as all laughed.

Then Annie made a motion to go over to greet Dennis, but a restraining arm of her father's stopped her. "Not now, Annie. This moment is special and precious for them. It belongs to them only. Your time will come."

Patrick held out his arms as he muttered something with a throb in his voice. "Son, you sure are a sight for sore eyes. It has been a long time in coming but you sure make up for the lonely nights that I've missed you." Patrick's eyes were misty as he hugged Dennis with a feeling that only a parent can have at the sight of a long, lost son.

"Hello, Father," Dennis smiled, "It has been a long time in coming but all good things take a mite longer. In our case, a little too long. You'll never know, in your wildest dreams, how many sleepless nights I spent thinking of you. What you were like? What would you say when we met? All the little things about you! You know what, Father? You're way above all my exaggerated expectations, of how I pictured you in my dreams. Only a son and a father, like we two, will ever feel the joy like we are having at this moment. You're exactly as Mother described you'd be. You are my father and I'm proud of you!" Dennis hugged him again.

"Dennis," Patrick said in a gruff voice that threatened to crack at any moment, "I'm just as proud of you as I am of Kelly. I love you both! You are my son! Bless your mother! She did a good job in raising you, I can see her brand on you."

After their moment together, Patrick brought his son over to meet the others at the station. They greeted him with, "Nice looking son you have there, Patrick!" and "Are you sure you're not Kelly?" and "How're you going to like the west?" Finally, Patrick introduced Dennis to John Logan and then to Annie.

Annie let out a yell. "Grass 'a fire! You know, Dennis? We're going to be great friends! Your brother and I were just like bunk brothers. He used to pull my hair when we were young, but I broke him of that habit! Consarn him!"

Dennis laughed easily at this spunky, tough-talking, bubbling redhead. He was going to like her! She was different from anyone he had ever known in the East. He replied in the midst of the booming laugh, "Annie, you're a delight! I'm going to like you! I can see where you'll be a heavenly bonus for my trip out here. You'll see to it that my days are never going to be dull. May I add further that I'm beginning to like the environment here in the West already. No on ever put me wise to the beauty of it all. The only advice I can give to the brother I haven't seen is don't tarry too long in the East before some fast-talking rogue sneaks up and steals your gal from you."

Dennis gingerly squeezed her hand! It sent chills up and down her spine and prompted her to say, "Whoa! Grass 'a fire! You're a regular stampede on the prairie! Where did you larn all those long words? You're slicker with them than a travelling medicine man. You are one hombre I've got to keep an eye on before the natives hogtie you! Rolling tumbleweeds! You are something!"

The four of them conversed, with Dennis and Annie jousting with words like a pair of unbroken broncs trying to unsaddle their riders. Every once in a while, Patrick would interrupt them with questions about Betty, which Dennis was more than glad to answer. Patrick untied the buckboard and headed back to the ranch with them. The first thing that struck Dennis' eye as they were entering the ranch grounds was a huge sign that read:

BETTY ANN RANCH
OWNED BY
PATRICK O'SHEA AND SON

Dennis exclaimed with delight, "I know Mother would be thrilled if she knew that the ranch was still named after her, Father." He inquired hesitantly, "Why did you keep the name?"

"Two reasons, Dennis!" Patrick explained sheepishly, "Sentiment and economics. Sentimentally, I don't want to forget our happiest times and what your mother meant to me at one time. Secondly, economically, I didn't want to go through the expense of making a new sign!" Everyone laughed.

"Don't let him josh you," put in Pop Logan, "he missed her far more than he admits. I know; I'm his best friend."

"I kind of have the feeling," Dennis countered with a gesture of his hands, "she feels the same way about him! I know, I'm her son!" This brought another roar of laughter.

Patrick excused himself from his guests to show Dennis around the ranchhouse. Then finally to his room. It brought a delighted exclamation from Dennis, "Wow! I've never seen a bedroom as large as this one in my life. What do you do here? Hold a rodeo or rope steers? To say I'm astonished is putting it mildly. Father, this is great! I love it!"

THE DECISION

Patrick replied, "I'm glad you approve. It's going to be yours for a long time. Well, we've neglected our friends too long! What do you say we go down and entertain them? Pop Logan is a wonderful man and my closest friend. Annie, well, she's sort of special to everyone in these parts and to us."

"I know, Father, and I kind of suspect in fact, I know she will be for me, too."

They joined Pop and Annie in the living room where they began exchanging questions about the East and the West. It wasn't long before that effervescent sprite Annie brought up a subject that was uppermost in the minds of the ranchers. "Dennis," Annie said, Let me clue you in on our latest troubles out here! We've got a heap of them with the consarned railroads! You'll find out sooner or later that your dad and all the ranchers in the Broken Bend Territory are up to their eyeballs in trouble with the pesky railroads. I'll start this sad tale from the beginning and that's where it should start. It seems that the ranchers never took the trouble of registering their properties. I reckon they were of the old school, where a shake of the hand made it so. The railroads did business in another way....the sneaky way, and yet it was legal. If you call stealing the coins from a blind man's cup legal! They saw the loophole in the ranchers' claims of ownership of their properties when they hadn't registered them. And so they registered the ranchers' properties in the railroad's name and now they claim them as their own. They're hornswoggling us out of our lands. Right now, it looks so hopeless for us. We have no one to advise or help us. What are we going to do, Dennis? Got any ideas?"

Dennis had listened attentively while Annie was talking about their immediate problem. Patrick exploded in anger, "They're trying to dry gulch us!"

Finally, Dennis asked, "Father, could you get me a copy of the court order of this case so I can review it? The only way you're going to beat the railroads is through the courts. Not through violence. It may look dark and hopeless but it's always darkest before the light. What we're looking for now is the light in the tunnel. Somewhere down the line, Father, I might be of a little help to you. I've just passed my bar examination. I'm now a full-fledged lawyer and I'm looking for my first client or clients. I'd like to be your lawyer, Mr. Logan's lawyer, and the lawyer for all the ranchers who need one at this time. Father, will you retain me as your lawyer?"

Surprise of surprises! Dennis had brought a new lease on life to the ranchers. Hopes lived high again! Patrick, Annie, and Logan exchanged looks of disbelief and wonderment at Dennis' surprise announcement. He was a lawyer? They couldn't believe it! They now had a new ally! The tenderfoot from the East was to be their savior; he'd bring justice to Broken Bend and save the ranchers' properties from the railroads. Patrick hugged him. Annie was jumping up and down as she answered Dennis' question, "Will we retain you as our lawyer? Is George Washington the father of our country? Did Lincoln free the slaves? Praise the Lord! Yes, yes, Dennis, yes! I'm speaking for all here. Do I hear a vote of approval from any of you?"

It didn't take long for Patrick and Logan to agree. "You can count on us as your clients," they agreed in unison as Annie chortled, "Grass 'a fire! Dennis! Now let's beat the tarnation out of them scalawags!"

"One thing" cautioned Dennis, "before we get too hopped up with this. We must first have 100 percent approval of all the ranchers to retain me as their lawyer. We can not afford to have a weak link or disagreement among ourselves before we even start. We must be as one or not at all. It will save us a lot of bickering later on."

"No problem to that, " Pop said calmly, puffing on his pipe, "The only lawyer in the Broken Bend Territory is Squarehead O'Brien and he hasn't drawn a sober breath in ten years. The nearest lawyer outside of him, lives over a hundred miles from here and he is the railroad's lawyer, so we can't use him either. That means, Dennis, we are stuck with you" as everyone laughed.

"In the meantime," Pop went on, "Annie and I will go around to all the ranchers for their permission to retain you as our lawyer. I'm sure that will be no trouble. We should be back in about two days."

Patrick laughed, "You came just in time to get in on the action, Dennis. Once more it will be, O'Shea and O'Shea against the railroads."

Annie piped up, "Correction, Mr. O'Shea, you're dead wrong again. It will be O'Shea, O'Shea, and the Logans against the railroads."

"Touche," retorted Dennis. "Glad to have you on our side or we would be devastated. Now the railroads will have to worry about you!"

"I'll be a burr in their saddle and you'll be a pain in their neck in court Dennis, " prodded Annie.

They all laughed at Annie's spirited reply. Dennis began to look at her in a different light. He liked what he saw as he mused, "Kelly you're sure a lucky guy to have a friend like Annie. It would serve you right if you don't marry her before you left."

The telltale signs of the smoke and sparks
streamed out of the iron horse's chimney

Chapter 10

Back in the East, Betty and Jessica had a long vigil at the railway station waiting for Kelly's to arrive. The train was late and every minute seemed like hours for the pair. Finally they spotted it over the housetops, coming in at full blast. It started slowing down as it neared the station, making a full stop a few feet from the two ladies.

The passengers began getting off the train as Betty and Jessica waited patiently on the ramp to catch sight of Kelly. Betty wondered if Kelly had caught the right train. Their fears mounted as they anxiously peered at each arrival. Finally, he appeared, the last one to get off. He was in western gear.

"My, doesn't he look like Dennis?" observed Betty.

"He sure does!" agreed Jessica.

Needless to say, he didn't have Dennis' ways, but there was an animal magnetism about him that caught the attention of the young ladies on the platform, making him blush in spite of himself. This prompted Jessica to say, "Come on, Betty, let's save him before those female vultures swallow him alive. Let's get him out of here without any further embarrassment to him, the poor guy. C'mon, Betty."

Betty rushed forward, crying, "Kelly, Kelly, Kelly, my darling son," as she smothered him with kisses, Kelly returned her love with a brand of his own.

Kelly smiled, and that smile brought tears of joy to Betty as he spoke, "Dad said to look for the most beautiful lady at the station and that will be your mother. I reckon he was right. You are beautiful, Mother."

While this tender scene of love was unfolding, Jessica remained in the background until the proper moment for her to make her appearance. She then stepped forward and casually remarked, "Before this touching moment goes on indefinitely, I wish someone would introduce me to the tall,

THE DECISION

dark, handsome stranger you're making all the fuss about, eh? Betty? Remember me? I'm the gal who escorted you here."

Betty apologized profusely. "I'm sorry, Jessica. I'd like to introduce you to my son, Kelly. Kelly, this is Jessica Longstreet, a very good friend of mine and Dennis'."

Kelly and Jessica stood there eyeing each other while Betty was making the introductions. What they saw in each other they must have liked, for neither heard Betty. Kelly dreamed on and on, "What a beauty! She looks like a goddess. Shure 'nuff, she's better 'n anything I've ever seen."

Jessica shook his hand warmly and his touch sent a hot flash through her body, "It's my pleasure to meet you, I assure you. Dennis and I were very good friends. I sincerely hope we'll be the same."

She looked at him and envisioned the fabled white knight who came to the rescue of the fair damsel. Inside of her, another voice was saying, "At last, Jessica, the man you have been waiting for. Your immediate problem is to keep him away from the grasp of the perfumed female sirens who love to prey on someone as attractive and manly as Kelly."

The spark was there. All it needed was to be lit by one or the other, and it appeared that both of them were willing to light the match and then fan the fires of a promising budding romance. Finally Kelly replied, "The pleasure is all mine. I definitely assure you, Jessica."

They rode in Betty's carriage through Philadelphia as Kelly whistled in wonder and amazement at the stately colonial buildings, "Wow!" he exclaimed, "I've never seen anything like this before. What is that large building over there?"

Jessica answered, "That is Independence Hall, where the Declaration of Independence was signed. It is one of our most historic and precious buildings."

"I've never seen anything so impressive before."

"That is just one of the wonders of Philadelphia. There are more you will see in the coming days. Right now you must be tired and hungry. You have another surprise due you. Wait until you see your mother's beautiful home. It's one of the most majestic in this fair city."

"Might I add," Kelly cut in, I'm surrounded by Philadelphia's two most beautiful women and I'm in love with both of them. This is more than I bargained for when I left the West. I'd be a coward if I didn't accept you. I reckon I'm a lucky guy."

"Keep it up, Kelly," replied Jessica, "You're not hurting my feelings with all that western sweet talk. Dinner will be at seven tonight. You're escorting two ladies."

Dinner was delicious and the conversation flowered with witty small talk until Betty coyly asked, "How is Patrick taking this exchange of our sons? I mean about your coming here? He is probably in the same state of shock that I was when it came to my attention a few weeks ago. I honestly feel the books are balanced. Your father did an excellent job in raising you."

Kelly answered simply, "Father was quite put out at the time but he rebounded fine, although it did come at an awkward time. You see, the railroad is trying to steal all the ranchers' properties in the Broken Bend Territory. As you know, I was ordered by the court to come here, and I'm sure glad that I did, even though I left troubles behind. I don't know how it will turn out. Poor Dennis, he's inherited a pack of trouble even before he gets there. A prairie of grief."

"I guess trouble is catching," murmured Jessica. "We're having our own brand here. It's like this, Kelly. Betty inherited the Black Diamond Coal Mine from her uncle, Bobby Brooks, who was murdered about three months ago by the same cutthroats who are stopping the miners from working. The culprits in back of this are the Big Seven Coal Company. But we have no proof of it. If they keep the mine closed long enough, and according to a stipulation in the will, Betty will be forced to sell it to the highest bidder. You can guess who that will be? Before Kelly left for the West, he went to the mine to see what was going on. He was in a dilemma on how to contend with their nefarious methods. Dennis had never been put to the test of such a violent situation before. He was brought up by your mother to be a gentleman and go to school and be a lawyer, but not to something like this! If the mine goes under, your mother could be bankrupt. She's mortgaged everything she owns just so she could keep the mine working. One thing is for sure. Betty's up against it but you can bet your bottom dollar that she won't go down without a fight. Now between you and me, how are we going to combat those paid goons who are terrorizing and intimidating the miners?"

Kelly asked angrily, "What varmints are paying those galoots and rustlers to stop honest men from working?"

"As I said, Kelly, we have knowledge of who it is, but we have no way of proving it unless we catch them redhanded," Jessica replied with concern and bristling with anger. "Between you and me and the lamp post, Kelly, they're the same ones who have taken over all the small coal companies in Pennsylvania. Their main objective is to take over the Black Diamond mine because it's the richest in the state. Betty's uncle fought them and ended up murdered. Betty has vowed that her uncle's murder will not go unavenged. These criminals have a past history of harassment, bribery, intimidation, murder, and any crime that you can name that would fill the largest book. They know the value of Betty's mine, and they'll go to any means to acquire it. They've already closed it down. Stopping

THE DECISION

the miners from working and intimidated the townspeople, while the government officials look the other way. Do you want me to go on?"

"No, Jessica, you've covered it pretty thoroughly. It looks as though I've arrived here in the nick of time for an old fashioned hoe down of knocking herds of hardheads together. We used to have these kinds of situations in the West, and Dad always said, "You have to meet trouble head-on before it meets you." We had plenty of desperadoes in the old days in the West, in fact, all kinds of sidewinders. No matter where you go in this world, there are always some around to make it unpleasant for decent folks to get along. Somehow, the good guys seem to manage to round them up at branding time. Jessica, I'm leaving for the mine in the morning. It's almost branding time! Are there any friendly faces I should look up when I get there?

"Kelly, these men are killers! They're worse than your killers of the West," warned a worried Jessica. "Please be careful, stay out of dark streets for that is where they are most dangerous."

"Dennis said," remembered Betty, "when he came back from the mine, "There are three men you can trust with your life: Tony Dinardi; Sadar Kominski; Sock Trullas." You can find them most of the time at the Black Hole Restaurant. They're usually together or at least not too far apart."

Kelly nodded his head, "Good, that is where I'll be! The die is cast! All I need now are some city clothes so people won't take me for a country bumpkin. I think I'm going to enjoy myself at the mine, and most of all, here, when I return."

He winked at Jessica, then warned her, "Don't do anything until I get back."

"I'll keep the home fires burning and, in case you should get lost, I'll keep a light burning in the window," promised Jessica.

Kelly was eyeing her up as she was talking. He was taking inventory of her assets, like a travelling salesman and she was well supplied. The tone of her voice implied there were a lot of good things in store for him when he returned from the mine. Philosophically, he assessed her qualities! "My, isn't she beautiful? I wonder if Dennis has his brand on her, and if he hasn't, I wonder if he'd be upset if I stole her away from him?"

Chapter 11

Patrick received the injunction order filed by the railroad against the ranchers from the territory court and gave it to Dennis. He reviewed it and immediately applied for an appeal on certain technicalities. He based his appeal on the grounds that he needed more time, as newly retained counsel, to prepare his case. Time was one commodity he needed more than anything else, because it was in such short supply. Dennis received an early answer to his appeal. He was allowed sixty days to prepare his case. The trial would be held in the Broken Bend Courthouse on August 29, 1894.

Dennis began immediately rounding up material witnesses who knew of the case, amassing collaborating evidence pertaining to it, and any other necessary documents that the ranchers might find. The logistics of the case were enormous, and the future of it appeared not too bright unless something miraculous happened along the way.

Dennis called a meeting at the Betty Ann Ranch to meet the ranchers and for them to get to know him. At seven o'clock, the room was buzzing like a hornet's nest with angry, belligerent ranchers who faced the prospect of losing their life's work. The heated atmosphere cooled down when Dennis raised his hands. "Friends, we are here for one purpose only, to find the answer to your dilemma. Let's not fight amongst ourselves. Look at your fellow rancher! He's not the enemy! We know who that is! The railroad! That fellow rancher sitting across from you has the same problems as you. Keep your powder dry and watch your temper. We have one common foe, the railroad. Now, that we've established that fact, what are we going to do about it?"

Big, burly Jess Cravath shouted from the rear, "Let's shoot them down like the dogs they are!"

"Yes, yes! Let's string up them ornery polecats to the nearest tree, and tar and feather them," added another.

THE DECISION

With his twirling moustache spinning upright as he railed in anger, Sid Sayd roared, "I'd like to hang them to the tallest mast, cut of their ears, then their noses and then stuff manure into their damn mouths, which would still be too good for them."

Dennis held up his hands. "That's the kind of talk the railroad likes! The way they hope you'll react to their injunction. On the other hand, suppose we did it your way. After you've had your little fun! What have you gained? Satisfaction? Revenge? Both of which will get you nothing! You know who will be the real losers? You, you, and you! You might scream at the top of your lungs, "An eye for an eye," but I say to you, "No!" Don't let them know what you're thinking or planning to do. Get them to worry about your lack of open hostility. My friends, I caution you! Walk softly, beware of traps and, above all, don't take the railroad too lightly. They are capable of doing anything to gain their objective, but we'll not do what they do. Here's the path we will take. If you pursue the cougar, you must be smarter than it. If you desire to continue in the path that some of your have chosen, you might win the battle, but the cost would be too great. All you would have won was a Pyrrhic victory."

Sid Sayd asked, "What the hell is a Pyrrhic victory?"

"Pyrrhus," explained Dennis, "Was a king of ancient Greece who was at war with the Romans. They had many battles, the Greeks were victors in all of them but their losses were so great that King Pyrrhus anguished, "One more victory like that and we're finished." A pyrrhic victory is where you win the battle but lose the war. We will not make that mistake against the railroad. Now let's get our heads together and discuss our strategy on how we're going to win this war."

Dennis scratched his head as he added, "Here's what we are going to do, every last one of you. We have sixty days before the trial, and time is of the essence. What I'm going to ask of you is a lot of hard work. Are you with me?"

A loud roar of approval filled the room and someone yelled out, "Dennis, tell us what you want us to do!"

"Gentlemen," Dennis took time to explain it to them, "I'd like for each and every one of you to go home and go through all your papers at home, schools, churches, the courthouse, or any other possible place that important papers could be found, to help our position. We are looking for any laws enacted in the past fifty years or so in this territory, including all Indian treaties, Homestead, and Territorial Acts, or any laws of that nature that would have a bearing on this case. No paper is unimportant, all have to be looked over. Perhaps one of them is our answer. Our time is short, so let's get with it! May God help us in our search. I thank you. Goodnight!"

The ranchers huddled in little groups for a while, then scattered to their ranches as a hovering rain cloud passed overhead. All left with a zeal to do their parts in locating the right paper to solve their problem.

After the ranchers left, Annie and her father stayed behind for a further study of the messy situation. Patrick asked, "Dennis, does this mean we still have a chance?"

"Right now, Father," answered Dennis, "It's little or none. It doesn't look good. We have to undo the harm that was done years ago when the ranchers didn't register their lands. Had it been done then, the railroad wouldn't have a leg to stand on, or a case today. Now, they have all the aces up their sleeve, leaving us holding the bag trying to prove there is a conspiracy on their part. This will be difficult to do with the evidence we have on hand. Somewhere out there is the answer, but where?"

"Wait a minute, Dennis," Logan suddenly remembered, "there is something out there but I can't lay my finger on it yet...I don't believe any of the Indian treaties or papers of any kind will be of any help. I faintly recall my dad said to me in 1858, just before he died, about the Santee Indians. They had a fine, fearless leader, a Chief Thundercloud, who was suspicious of the palefaces and their promises. According to my father's story, it was in the late forties that the Cross County Railroad Company forced the Federal Government to put pressure on the Santee Indian Nation to make a treaty with the railroad. The Santees were forced to cede three hundred feet of right-a-way through their sacred lands for a future railroad. Chief Thundercloud didn't want to sign the treaty, but with the thread of war hanging in the balance, he complied. However, not before he forced the railroad to include a few of his own provisions in it. The wise old chief never trusted the white man because of his many past dealings with them. The only one he completely trusted was my father who really respected and loved the chief. You see, they were blood brothers for along time! They had etched their respect for each other in blood."

"Then, in 1857," Pop wiped his perspiring forehead, coughed a spell, then went on, "one of the greatest disgraces charged against our American government was the brutal treatment of the peaceful Santee Indians. With orders from the War Department in Washington, wrongs were perpetrated against them by the Cross Country Railroad Company, land developers, and other selfish groups lining their pockets. The Army was sent to forcibly remove the Santees from their homes. The aftermath of this tragedy was that the Santees were sent hundreds of miles away to some desolate reservation. My dad and friendly settlers were incensed with this unfair and unjust treatment of the Santees. They even petitioned Washington to redress the wrongs they had committed, I'll never forget it!" Logan stopped a moment to wipe a tear away as he thought of this

THE DECISION

tragedy. "Over eight hundred Santee Indians sadly marched away on that dark day as my dad tried to console Chief Thundercloud, "My heart cries for you; my people have wronged you! I will fight for your return! Someday, somehow, I will see that your people will return to their homes here in Broken Bend. I promise you that!" Shortly afterwards, my dad died. We all knew it was from a broken heart."

Dennis exploded, "How dreadful! It makes me ashamed to be a member of the white race. Being from the East, we were unaware of all this. We didn't know too much about the Indians, except the way it was reported in the papers. We should hold our heads in shame."

Logan continued, "Dennis, listen to me carefully. Somewhere out there on the prairie or farther West are the remnants of the lost Santee Indian Nation. I believe they can be found! They must be, for they could have the answer we're searching for. Chief Thundercloud is probably dead, but he was a wily chief, and would have left the treaty with responsible persons to carry out its mandate. I wonder, mm-mm, after all these years, whether he and his tribe can be found. If found, how resentful would they be towards a white man? I have made up my mind. Tomorrow, I'm leaving in search of the Santee Indians. I'm taking enough provisions to last me sixty days, plus an extra supply for any starving Indians on the way."

"It means a journey of hundreds of slow miles, with backtracking and countless setbacks. I'll try to be back by the twenty-ninth of August. Patrick, old friend, look over my ranch. Dennis, keep an eye on Annie until I get back."

"You bet, John," agreed Patrick, "You old hornswoggler. I'll have some of my men over to take charge until you get back. Damn it! I wish I could go along with you, John. Good luck and good hunting. God speed you on your way."

"Patrick, "Logan answered, 'two men on the trail is a waste of one. I'll do just fine alone."

"You gave me the best job of all," Dennis said. "I'd like to have that kind of duty all the time."

Annie smiled at Dennis as she softly said, "Dennis, you are a maverick like your brother. Not that I'm against it, mind you, I think it's wonderful! You know, Dennis, before you came here from the East, I thought you'd be a stuffed shirt. Grass 'a fire! You sure fooled me! Jumping caterpillars! Don't let this turn your head, but you turned out rather well."

"You didn't turn out too bad yourself. You're not like the women out East and I thank God for that. If I were an artist, I wouldn't change a hair in your lovely red head. All I can say is that Kelly's lucky to have such a wonderful girl. I wish Dad had chosen me to stay out West instead of the other way around."

Annie replied heatedly, "Well, for your information only, Mr. Smarty Pants, I'm not Kelly's girl or anybody's girl as yet. Kelly and I had a lot of fun growing up but that was as far as it went. He was like a big brother to me. I guess people took it for granted that we were sweethearts, but it wasn't that way at all. That something special between us wasn't there. I'm not anyone's girl....not yet. I'm still waiting for a bid."

Dennis swallowed hard as he spoke, groping around for the right words. "Annie, I didn't have the right to say this before, but now it's different....Oh, golly, I'm acting like a schoolboy with his first love. Annie, I've loved you from the first time I saw your lovely face. You are everything I've ever dreamed about in a woman."

Before he had a chance to say anything more, Annie kissed him. "You silly maverick. I've waited a long time for you to say those pretty words...from the first day we met at the railroad station. Don't be afraid, Dennis, it's all right. This is what we women in the West call love. Dennis. This is what it's all about."

He took her into his arms and smothered her with warm kisses. This was not what he expected to find when he left Philadelphia a few days ago. He was not complaining!

The downtown wonders of Philadelphia in 1894 were many...

Chapter 12

The next morning Logan had two oxen hitched to a covered wagon filled with enough supplies to hold him for his extended journey to the unknown regions of the West. He hoped to meet up the Santee Indians. He came with extra provisions of food, clothing, and arms to cover any emergency that might come up. Wishing Annie, Dennis, and his old friend, Patrick, a final goodbye, he took off for his meeting with the Santee Indians and fate.

Many thoughts crossed his mind. Where would he start first in his search for the lost Santee tribe? Was it just an old man's dream that Chief Thundercloud was still alive? If he did find the Santee tribe, and if by chance the chief was still living, another supposition bothered him. Would the Santee Indians still help the white man? The same breed of white devils that drove them out of their homes a long time ago? Logan was a born optimist, believing what his father had told him about Chief Thundercloud. "He's a wise man, my blood brother, and my friend. If you ever need help, go to him! If it's in his power, he will help you."

He remembered something else his dad had said to him a long time ago. "The last thing that Chief Thundercloud said to me was, "I travel west, don't know where. I cry for my people! Long journey ahead. Many will die! Goodbye, blood brother."

The chief didn't know his destination. The White Father in Washington had told him it would be many moons away. With that in mind, Logan started on a westerly course that would take him to his ultimate rendezvous with Thundercloud or his Santee Indians.

After three days of tiresome riding, he came upon a small Indian tribe whose chief greeted him. "I am Red Fox. What do you want in the land of the Ottawas, paleface?"

Logan answered, "I'm looking for the Santee Indians. Do you know where I can find them?"

THE DECISION

"Don't know! It is said they traveled that way," pointing to the northeast.

With thanks to the Indian, Logan changed his direction toward the northeast, driving the wagon for five days before he ran into a larger Indian tribe, the Omahas, whose chief was Great Hunter. As Logan's wagon neared the Indian encampment, the chief advanced toward him, waving a traditional Indian salute. "How, white man. What do you want in the land of the Omahas?"

Logan descended from the wagon and put his hand in the air, returning his greeting. "Hail, Oh mighty Chief. Could you tell me where to find the Santee Indians? I'd like to make powwow with them."

The Omaha Chief was curt. "We smoke pipe of peace first, then talk. No food to give you. Not many deer. No buffalo! all gone! White man kill them. Left them to rot in the sun. Great Spirit angry. Send no more buffalo."

"I know, wise chief. Your people need food. I bring food and supplies for your people. How do I find the Santee Indians?"

"The Santees are the brother of the Sioux. Find the Sioux. They will know! The Sioux go that way," the chief pointed to the west.

After doling out meat, clothing, and supplies to the Omahas, Logan took off once more, this time on a westerly route, deep into a barren land. After travelling for six days, he ran into a much larger tribe, the Sioux, noted for their farming ability and as warriors.

Their middle-aged chief approached Logan. A swarthy, impressive-looking Indian with copper bracelets around the biceps of his arms, he had a headdress of eagle feathers denoting his bravery, and was clad in breechcloth and leggings. As regal in appearance as he was formidable in stature, he held a spear upright in his arms.

"Greetings, white man. I am Chief Straight Arrow of the Sioux. What do you want in our lands?"

Logan saluted him as he got off the wagon. "How! Chief Straight Arrow. I come in peace. My name is John Logan. My father's name is William Logan, blood brother to Chief Thundercloud of the Santee tribe. You are brothers to the Santee. Do you know where I can find them?

"We smoke peace pipe first, then talk."

They sat down inside the tepee smoking the peace pipe until the chief grunted. "Ugh! No more smoking! We talk now. Talk slow, then I know. Talk fast, only you know. Like rain that falls, get wet on head only."

Logan started questioning the chief in a slow, precise manner that met with the approval of the chief. "Oh, wise Chief, I come to find the Santee Indians. Offer them friendship and peace. My father, who has gone to Happy Hunting Grounds, very good friend of Chief Thundercloud. Do you know where I can find him or the Santee Indians?"

"Our brothers, the Santee, no see them for thirty snows or more. Maybe Chief Thundercloud go to Happy Hunting Ground. He old like the land! A Santee warrior visit us about ten snows ago. He say his people are living on trouble land. Bad times for Santee. He say Santee live where two rivers cross. Go past there for two days travel. You go in that direction, Logan, friend of the Santee."

"Thank you, brave chief," said Logan, as they honored each other with crossed arms.

"We make Sun Dance now. Give you good spirits for your trip to bad lands," the chief announced solemnly. The celebration lasted four hours, time that Logan could ill afford to lose, but he stayed lest he dishonor the Sioux.

After the Sun Dance was over, Logan gave the impoverished Sioux food and clothing with some arms to hunt for food as he bade them goodbye. He set on what he hoped would be the last leg of his journey. He had been on the trail for almost a month, with no sight of the Santee Indians. Were they a myth or did they really exist?

Logan travelled across the barren lands for four days before he came upon two rivers that crossed. Now his problem was in what direction should he go? The Sioux chief had told him it would be almost two days travel from there to the Santee camp, but knowing how Indians travel from year to year, Logan was dismayed. He didn't know what pattern of movement the Santees had taken for the last eighteen years. The chief had suggested he go to where the two rivers were crossing, then keep going west and let the Great Spirit guide him. Logan decided differently, veered his direction to the north, travelling for two days.

After travelling for two days in the dry, barren land without sighting anything, Logan again changed his direction and started to go southwesterly. He continued in this new direction for another two days of hopeless searching. Then he changed his route southerly. Time was running out on Logan. A gnawing fear was growing inside of him that tormented Logan with the belief that the trip was all in vain. He felt so alone and so much in need of help that he knelt down and prayed, "Dear God, why is it when we're in trouble, we always come to you? You are our Father in Heaven! I ask not for myself, but for the other good people who are depending on me to find the Santee Indians. Please show me the way! I need your divine help. Thank you, Father."

Logan rose once more to set out for the Santee Indians on a southerly route. He passed some skeletons on the way that looked like human remains. This dismayed him, but he continued on his way until he heard the sound of a tomtom in the distance, and headed in that direction.

What he saw when he arrived there was deplorable. The camp contained the scrawniest-looking Indians he had ever seen in his life, danc-

THE DECISION

ing an Indian ritual to the sun to give strength for the coming day. When the Indians saw the white man approach, they stopped their dancing and three of the youngest advanced menacingly to the wagon. One of them said to Logan, "Paleface, what are you doing in Santee land? We have no more land for you to steal! You want this land? It is yours with the stones and the snakes! We have nothing else more for you to take. You can die on this land as we will one day."

"Strong Arm," the feeble voice of an old Indian begged, "why do you talk to this white man like this? He may be in want! Ask for powwow with white man first."

Strong Arm said gruffly, "Paleface, I welcome you! Old man right! Must not act like white man."

He followed the three young braves and the old Indian into a shabby wigwam, where all sat down. After a few signs to the Great Spirit by the old Indian to purify the air, they began to smoke the peace pipe. After a while, the old Indian waved his hand to stop, "We talk now!"

"I'm looking for the Santee Indians. They once owned the Broken Bend lands before the white man lied, cheated, and robbed him. Is this the same tribe?"

"Heap strong words by white man," said the old Indian.

"Are you the same Santee Indians who used to live there?" pursued the persistent Logan.

One of the young braves grunted, "Ugh!"

"My name is John Logan. My father was William Logan, who was blood brother to Chief Thundercloud, a long, long time ago. My father grieved when the white man stole his blood brother's land, forcing the Santee to leave their lands. He cried and cried so much for his blood brother that he went to the Happy Hunting Ground the next year to meet many Indian friends. Does anyone around here know of a Chief Thundercloud?"

Logan paused for a while while the young braves conversed with the old Indian. The squalid condition of the wigwam described the hard plight of the Indians. Finally, the old Indian asked, "Did you say your father's name was William Logan? We used to call him "White man with the soul of an Indian." He was good man! Life-long friend to the Santee. You are his son? You, his son? You're friend to Santee? My name is Thundercloud! I have lived for more than ninety snows. Some happy, now all sad. Soon no more my moons are short. They pass before my eyes too fast! What do you want of the Santee?"

"Welcome, Oh wise chief and blood brother of my father. My father talked often of you in highest praise, now it's my pleasure to meet you for the first time. You are a legend! My days are complete! I was too small when the white men drove you out of your lands. Too young to know you, but my father filled me with love for you and the Santee Indians. He told me many wonderful things about you and your people. He loved you like a brother. He fought his white brother in Washington for the wrong they did to you and your people. His efforts went for naught, and because he could do no good, he soon died of a broken heart. His last words were, "Chief Thundercloud, I've failed you." What do I want for the Santee? I say, justice! The same white man who talked with forked tongue to White Father in Washington, who had moved you from your happy wigwams many snows ago. They are again talking with forked tongues to move the white men out of their homes, some of whom are your friends of long ago."

"How can I help?" asked the old Indian. "I'm old, my people are weak and starving. My three grandsons carry on my duties. Tell me more!"

"The Cross Country Railroad Company is forcing us out of our homes by writing on a special paper before we did. White man's law says they own property, though we've lived on it for years. Land that you once sold to my father and other white settlers on your lands. We meet in white man's big, big council. A big powwow that will start within fourteen suns. My father once told me you signed an important white paper with the railroad in 1847 on orders from the great White Father in Washington. He say to you to give three hundred feet of right-of-way through Santee lands to railroad for future use. For a long time, you refused. Both sides threatened to go to war, but in the end, being the wise chief you are, not wanting to spill blood on either side, you gave in to their demands. But not before the railroad granted to you your added provisions in the treaty. My father acted as your counsel, reading and interpreting the English words to you. My father said, "Some day, what Chief Thundercloud has added to that treaty will be the undoing of the railroads." Chief Thundercloud, that day has come. Will you help us?"

"Logan," Thundercloud said, with a smile appearing on his face, "you are your father's son! You make me feel good! You talk straight, like father. I have white paper to help you. Brave Heart, bring box with wampum and paper."

His grandson left and in a few minutes returned with an old wooden box. The chief opened it and brought out a yellowed document that had faded with the fleeting seasons. "Here Logan, read this!"

John read the old treaty, and when he got to the added provisions, yelled out, "Great Indian Chief, my father was right! You are the wisest of all chiefs. Can I have this treaty?"

"Logan," cautioned the old chief, "when you try to pet the rattlesnake, it will bite you. You need more than this paper."

THE DECISION

"What more do I need?"

"You need me! I tell white man the truth of this magic paper. I go back with you! Bring my three grandsons to help me. Maybe Happy Hunting Grounds call me, but they must wait! Not now, me once more chief of the Santee. Make one last raid on white man to help old friend."

"Thank you, Chief. We have two weeks to get back. Time is short for us. Must hurry to make it on time for big powwow in White man's council. I bring clothing, supplies, arms, and food for your people, enough to supply them until you get back from your former home."

The driver passed some skeletons on the way that looked like human remains that had lost their way

Chapter 13

Kelly awoke early in the morning. He heard some mocking birds trilling some happy refrain outside his window sill, a good omen, the start of a good day. He went to the closet, tried on some of Dennis' clothes and was pleasantly surprised that they fit him perfectly. He finished unpacking, went downstairs, and was greeted by his mother and Jessica.

Kelly acknowledged the salutations with one of his own, "Good morning, you beautiful ladies. It looks like a day for a train ride and some unfinished business."

"You mustn't rush until you've had a good breakfast," admonished Betty.

"Here's some coffee," added Jessica. It's good and hot. It will do wonders for your stomach on that cold train."

"You're both spoiling me," protested Kelly. "I won't be too long. I should be back in a few days. Just long enough to survey the situation, see how bad it is, and ask a few questions."

He kissed his mother goodbye, wishing all the while it was Jessica he was holding in his arms. He couldn't do that! She was Dennis' girl! Instead, he shook her hand, giving it an extra squeeze that moved the temperature in him sky high. She didn't object or pull back from his touch. Those kinds of things shouldn't happen with your brother's girl, or should they? Kelly wondered how she felt about him as he pondered it over in his mind. "That can wait until I get back from the coal mine."

Kelly caught a carriage that took him down to the train station, where he boarded for Andura. Within eight hours, the train chugged into the small coal town.

Kelly checked into the only hotel in town, went up to his room to clean up, and then came downstairs. He asked the owner where the Black Hole Restaurant was. Kelly followed the man's direction to the Back Hole eatery.

THE DECISION

He entered, wondering if Tony would be there. How would he know him when he saw him? Perhaps he might even think I'm Dennis and maybe not? That would be a laugh.

Kelly ordered a meal from the comely waitress. In a little while his fears of not being recognized vanished when he was spied by Sock Trullas. "Hi, Dennis, I'm glad to see you back so soon."

Kelly smiled at the great success of his deception. This was going to be interesting. He loved it as he said to Sock, "I've got a terrible memory. I've forgotten everything that happened the last time I was here. I had too many things on my mind at that time. I couldn't think straight! I'd like to be clued in on a few things. First of all, what is your full name?"

Sock threw out his mammoth chest and proudly replied, "Strange that you should ask. You're the first one to ask my name since I left Ellis Island. It's Socrates Demosthenes Aristotle Plato Trullasballinopoulos, but everyone calls me Sock Trullas for short. These poosteethes here don't bother me except when they come at me three or more at a time. That I don't like! There are four things I like doing: drinking, eating, loving, and fighting. It doesn't have to be in that order."

Kelly laughed at the gregarious Greek. "I guess both of us like the same platform."

As an afterthought, Sock asked, Dennis, if you're not doing anything tomorrow night, come over to my place. I'm a good Greek cook. I'll cook my special! This dish will melt in your mouth. Roast lamb with string beans, topped off with Retsina wine. You'll have a try at it, won't you?"

"Okay," Kelly agreed, "It's a deal!"

"Look," Sock pointed out, "Here come Tony and Sadar. Hey you two! I want you to meet Dennis again. Dennis, this is Tony Dinardi, and that crummy looking one is Sadar Kominski."

What gives with you, Sock? You been eating too much of your Greek food? We met Dennis about two weeks ago," inquired Tony, then added with a laugh, "or downing too much of that awful-tasting Greek wine of yours?"

Kelly went along with the good-natured bantering of the trio by saying, "Sock's pretty sociable, he's promised to show me the sights and the first one he's going to show me in his home, with a meal of lamb and string beans tossed in for good measure. Should I take a chance?"

"Baa, baa, baa," mimicked Tony, "the day after you get over your stomachache there, you come over to my place for real meal of spaghetti and meat balls like you've never tasted before, with a touch of red wine to wash it down."

"And the day after that, if you're still living, you're coming to my house for a Polish dinner. Kielbasa with potato pancakes. We Poles wash it down with vodka." Now you're set for the next three days. Tony, tell him the rest of the news. I hope this doesn't bother your appetite."

"Well," Tony began. "That big gorilla, Dvorak, has gone around town telling everyone how he had buffaloed you the last time you were here. He says you won't show your face around here again. Furthermore, he says, he's going to grab you by the pants if you do show up and toss you out of the town violently."

Kelly sounded like a raging bull that missed its mate as he angrily pounded the table with his fist. "That no-good, loudmouthed, yellow-livered polecat and I are due for an outing. I'll have to take care of this nasty business and that varmint pronto, here and now. If you guys want a little action, come with me. We're gong to do some head-knocking."

"Whoopeee!" yelled Sadar and Tony as Sock joined in, "Yahoo, here we come!"

They marched down Broad Street, arm in arm, unafraid, when Sock spotted their quarry. "There he is! That's the guy with that big cigar in his mouth, dressed in plaid shirt and heavy boots. He's heading this way with some of his goons."

Kelly looked him over as he was approaching. Dvorak advanced menacingly toward them with six of his paid goons.

Kelly threw the first barb as he warned his men, "I'd like for you men to stay alert in case some of his goons jump in. I'll handle him alone!"

"We'll back you all the way," they promised.

Kelly jeered at Dvorak, "I understand, you big windbag, you've been looking for me. Well, here I am! What are you going to do about it? I'm not like the defenseless old people and miners you have been abusing. You're nothing but a no-good yellow bastard and I'll prove it to you soon. Come on and take your beating." He continued to bait Dvorak. "Here I am! Name your poison! Fists, alley fighting where the winner picks up the marbles, with no- holds-barred, or do you propose to talk me to death?" Kelly laughed at Dvorak, his feet wide apart, waiting for the bigger man's first onslaught.

It was not long in coming. Kelly's last statement struck a vital nerve, moving Dvorak to a fever pitch. He growled some obscenities, made a desperate lunge at Kelly, who had anticipated such a move. He brought down the power-laden right on the back of Dvorak's neck that sent him sprawling on all fours. That brought a round of laughter from the onlookers. Dvorak got up, livid with rage and embarrassment. He hurled some more obscenities at Kelly as he regrouped for another lunge at Kelly, trying to get him in his grasp. Kelly expected his maneuver as he flicked a couple of sharp, painful jabs at Dvorak's nose and infuriated him more than ever by yelling at him. "You son-of-a-bitch, why don't you stand up and fight like a man?"

THE DECISION

Kelly laughed at him decisively, even sneering at him, "My dad always said, "The bigger they are, the harder they fall," and, by golly, you're due for a big fall."

Dvorak saw red as he made another bull's rush at Kelly, who countered deftly at the big man by bringing up an explosive right hand into the big bully's unprotected stomach. Dvorak doubled up and gasped for air. Then Kelly, in a surprising show of strength, picked Dvorak up in one hand and lifted him against the wall and rained devastating rights on the now defenseless man. All this to the astonishment of the thugs and the enjoyment of the crowd, who were anti-Dvorak. This quick skirmish delighted the miners, who cheered on their new champion. He had given them new hope, and the spark they needed to fight on.

Kelly stood there and dared Dvorak's cohorts with mixed contempt, "Well, which one of you yellow bellies is next? The line forms to the right. Do they call you men? You're nothing but gutless wonders. Your leader is out cold, and you might as well be for all the good you can do. You haven't the brains or the guts you were born with. Let this be a lesson to you," Kelly said to the miners, "One and all. If evil comes your way, destroy it before it destroys you. And you thugs," he pointed to the remnants of the gang, "When Dvorak wakes up, you tell him for us, get out of town with all his men. He is forewarned!"

This surprising turn of events had taken the starch out of Dvorak's goons' sails as they stood there stunned and silent, their manhood berated. Kelly and his friends walked by, unmolested.

Tony queried Kelly, "I no understand. Last time he swear at you, call you awful names and threaten you. You do nothing. All the miners think you're afraid to fight. This time, without a word from this animala besta, you walk up to him and kabong him! Wham! Bang! It's all over in a matter of minutes. I no can understand you, but I love you!" Kelly smiled while the powerful Italian hugged him in his gigantic arms.

"Just like the Cossacks on the steppes, we ride to help the poor and destroy the evil men," philosophized Sadar.

"One for all and all for one, filos," cried Sock in happy delirium as they took turns hugging each other. Kelly laughed at their foreign antics, and yet they reminded him of the wild buckaroos on the Betty Ann Ranch.

The news that Kelly (or Dennis, as others thought) had almost demolished Joe Dvorak, the big bully, swept through the little coal town like a forest fire. No one had ever done anything so spectacular like this before to any of the goons that were terrorizing Andura's miners, much less talk about it. The hired henchmen still commanded a lot of fearful respect due to their numbers and viciousness of their ranks. They were especially craven with their threats of reprisal toward the miners and their families. In spite of all this, some of the miners dared to walk down Main

Street with their loved ones for the first time since the shutdown began. Still it didn't stop them from being on the alert from any vengeful attacks from the goons. The beating of Dvorak had given the miners new found courage; something they desperately needed for a long time.

It seemed like a new era was dawning for the downtrodden miners. The happy beginning to a terrible end. They had a new hero to show them the way! They had misjudged him on his first trip to Andura, thinking he was just a city dude with an extensive education and lacking in a backbone, but they were so mistaken about him! They now saw him in a different light, the man to improve their sagging morale.

That night, the miners held a meeting with Kelly their key speaker. The hall was crowded with enthusiastic miners and their families. Kelly spoke to them in a quiet, yet forceful voice with conviction, "Friends, I know you want to go back to work. We want you to go back to work! You will go back to work! I promise you that!" A loud cheer roared through the tiny hall. Kelly smiled at them, holding up his hands as he went on, "In the days to come, there will be many difficulties to overcome, and overcome them we will. We know who the outside interests are that are threatening our way of life. When the time comes, we'll expose them all. You can bet your bottom dollar on that! We know there are a few yellow-bellied stoolies sitting among you, who will report back to their bosses what went on here this evening. In time we'll learn who they are and we'll deal with them in an old fashioned way that they won't like."

The miners looked at each other, trying to discover the Judases in their midst but to no avail. They had better things to do now, and one of them was to listen to Kelly as he rolled on, "We all know there are paid goons in this town who are trying to keep you from working. This too, will pass. I know it's been over two months since you've worked. This too, will be remedied. I promise you that in due time, the mine will be operating again. This too, will come to pass."

This brought a thunderous roar of applause from the strapped miners, for this was the type of fight talk they wanted to hear. Kelly continued, "This will be a long hard fight! Some of us will get hurt! But in the end, we will win! You have my word on that! I make another promise to you. After this is all over, the new owner will never forget you. This, I promise you!"

This brought a standing ovation from the miners as they yelled over and over again in many tongues, "Dennis, Dennis, Dennis, we love you."

Kelly held out his hands, "There is something else I must tell you. I am not Dennis, as you think, but Kelly, his twin brother from the West. I'm a cowboy by trade, but circumstances have caused a change in plans in our family. In the meantime, I'm fulfilling Dennis' obligations and he's

THE DECISION

taking care of mine in the West. Thank you!''

The admission by Kelly to his true identity brought another round of cheers from the partisan miners, who hadn't lost their spirit because of his revelation, roaring for their new hero. "Kelly, Kelly, Kelly, we love you."

This startling disclosure surprised everyone in the packed hall, some of whom were informants of the Big Seven, ready to scurry back to their superiors as soon as the meeting was over. They wanted to warn them about a formidable new foe, Kelly O'Shea.

You could call this Round One in favor of the miners, but the next one would be more difficult to win. The next day, Round Two began in earnest, producing a couple of startling reverses for the miners and Kelly.

The first reversal appeared in the form of Howard Ainsworth, Betty's family lawyer, friend, and financier. Ainsworth quickly came to the point, "Kelly, your mother is in a financial mess. Did you know that she has mortgaged everything she owns trying to reopen the mine? Well, Kelly, she's down to her last penny. She's actually without any funds right now."

Kelly had never dreamed that Betty had used all her money to open the mine. This was going to be a crushing blow to overcome, but he had a promise to fulfill to the miners! No amount of adversity was going to stop him from doing what he had to do! Something had to be done, but what?

The next day Kelly received additional bad news. He learned from Tony Dinardi that more than three hundred additional goons had been sent to Andura to augment the original hundred thugs. The Big Seven Coal Company was sending in its reserves for the final big push. Nothing was being left to chance. They weren't going to blow this one!

All these developments opened Kelly's eyes to the why's and wherefore's of the critical situation. It was going to be open warfare from now on, and he was concerned about the poor miners. There was a rat in the woodpile, but this was the first time it had stuck its head out in the open. He knew the mine as valuable, but now it appeared it was more than he had ever dreamed of. That was it! They wanted to own the mine at all costs! How was he going to work out of these two new problems?

He had an idea on how to solve the first problem, but the second one really worried him. In the back of his mind, it annoyed him about the predicament he left his dad and the ranchers about the railroad. Betty and Jessica eased his mind and raised his hopes a little by informing him that Dennis was a full-fledged lawyer. If anyone could stump the railroad, Dennis could. At least, that made him feel better.

One other thing worried him the most of all. He was falling in love with his brother's girl. How would he explain that to his brother? How?

Chapter 14

Dennis had his work cut out for him. He never realized how large and vast the many things the case would encompass until he started researching aspects of the territorial laws and Indian treaties. He had a steady stream of ranchers bringing in additional facts and documents. Some he read over and over gain, searching for that small clue or loophole in the railroad's case against the ranchers. Dennis worked well into the morning hours, reviewing paper after paper. In the meantime, he tried to cheer the ranchers. Even the high-spirited Annie lost her composure by complaining about the long hours. "Grass 'a fire! Dennis. I know what you're going through, but I've seen you less and less these past few weeks. Consarn it! It ain't fair! I want to spend more time with you."

"I know, Annie," Dennis agreed. "It's harder on me! How I'd love to hold you in my arms and get away from it all...just the two of us! Forget all about the ranchers and the railroad, but right now," he added, "that's impossible! It wouldn't be right! So, we must bear it and wait until it's all over. We love each other. That's the main thing! Funny, I keep wondering what Kelly will say about us? No use worrying about that for now."

"I'm sorry, Dennis. I let my feelings get away from my better judgement at a time like this. You're right, by golly, you're always right as usual. I guess I'm a little impatient at times. It won't happen again. C'mon pardner, let's get those mavericks in our sights and on the rack. We'll squeeze them where it hurts the most."

"Yes, Annie, right in the pocketbook where it hurts the most."

"Dennis," Annie had that serious look on her face, "Would you teach me how to be a lady like the girls back east? I'd like to speak and act like they do."

THE DECISION

"Annie, Annie, Annie," Dennis replied softly, "I will not try to change what God has created in you. You are very special to me! Do you realize the things that brought us together were your simplicity and honesty? I know, as soon as you spoke, you meant everything you said, and believed it, and made no bones about it. I will not change a hair on your head, nor the words you speak. That would be sacrilegious! Only a Michelangelo could paint a picture like you, and only a Shakespeare could write the words in a sonnet to describe you, and best of all, only God could have given me you. No, Annie, I love you as you are, the ebullient spirit you possess! I will not try to dim it. You are more of a lady than all the ones I knew in the East. How can I better that? Annie, I love you as you are, and I will fifty years from now. I will never change. I'll always love you!"

"Dennis," Annie signed, "Grass 'a fire! As I said before, you say such beautiful things."

With an understanding between them, Annie gave Dennis a playful nudge in the ribs. She artfully dodged his amorous advances, "Not until we win for the ranchers will I give you another kiss."

There was a steady stream of ranchers at the Betty Ann Ranch. They came in with a myriad of paper and ideas. Each deserved Dennis' special appraisal. Perhaps, one of them would provide the missing key to the case.

Days became weeks. Before they knew it, the trial date was nearing and there was no word of Logan. The long hours of preparation were having their effect on Dennis. His calm exterior was fading and his nerves were becoming a jangled mess. He wondered how he could prepare a sound case without a shred of evidence to support the ranchers' position? It was an impossible situation. The rancher's chances were slim at the best. On the other hand, the railroad had retained a professional staff for this trial. Perhaps the most famous lawyer of this delegation was James. J. Hawker, a noted New York City attorney. This case meant a lot in power, money, and prestige to the railroad syndicate. They weren't about to leave a stone unturned. The final decision of this case would determine whether they would control the territory in the years to come.

The fatal day arrived. Like any other day, the sun rose in the east, just as sure as the Pony Express brought in the current news. The soft scent of the sagebrush filled the air. Birds flitted about on the dusty prairie. Strong winds swirled tumbleweeds down the dirt-covered streets of Broken Bend.

Buckboards lined up on both sides of the street. Crowds milled outside of the courthouse, some letting their emotions run away from them. Many wore sidearms. Others carried long rifles, as if anticipating impending trouble.

It seemed as if everyone in the Broken Bend Territory had heard of the trial and was on hand to see it with their own eyes. Some were witnessing a trial for the first time. The federal government had delegated the Honorable P. T. Stone to be the presiding judge. He was a well-known judge from St. Louis, expertly competent in court proceedings, an able judge, fair and stern, who would not stand for no nonsense at the trial.

The Cross Country Railroad was represented by their famous lawyer, James J. Hawker. Some of the most influential officers of the company were in attendance, including the president, J. F. Harlon. As they entered the western courtroom, they were deluged with a loud chorus of boos and catcalls from the spectators. The judge pounded the gavel. He warned the hostile audience against any more outbursts. This momentarily calmed the fired-up crowd.

A few minutes later, Dennis appeared on the scene with an assortment of papers. He laid them on the table. The crowd cheered their favorite son. Their roar of approval could have raised the rafters in the roof. Judge Stone pounded his gavel again because of this second outburst. In reality, he was secretly pleased with it. The judge had studied the transcripts of the case and his sympathies weren't with the railroad. However, he still had to administer the letter of the law within its dictates.

The court opened for the business at hand. The trial of the railroad versus the ranchers. The court clerk read the agenda as the bailiff shouted for order. Hawker rose from his seat, strode to the front of the room, nodded to the judge, then presented his opening statement on the railroad's right to claim the ranchers' lands. He was in complete control for the moment with his flawless oratory. At that moment, Dennis and his clients had grave misgivings about the outcome of the trial.

When Hawker was finished, he nodded his head to the judge, then sat down. It was now Dennis' turn to present the ranchers' side of the case. He carefully described the dangers and hardships these fearless pioneers endured in opening up America's last frontier. He praised their efforts to bring law and order to the untamed West. Looking toward the railroad's side of the courtroom, he spoke about the ranchers' lack of foresight in not recording their property claims. Most of the ranchers, he explained, were naive about legal procedure. Being simple people of the plains, they believed in the inherent squatter's rights, or possession as being nine-tenths of the law. These men, Dennis pointed out, had fought with and protected their ranches from renegade Indians, lawless rustlers, and unscrupulous federal officials. Now, they were forced to battle a new foe...the railroad. Dennis talked about their patriotic devotion to America during the Civil War. They fought on both sides bravely. When the war

THE DECISION

ended, they started carving out a new empire from the ruins of the war. Dennis finished with the words, "To such men as these that I represent, history will one day write, "America's debt to them will never be paid. They ask not except for what is theirs."

Dennis' eloquent representation stirred even the James J. Hawker to open admiration. He mused to himself, "This young man is no amateur. He's good! He's a worthy adversary and bears watching. He's not the country bumpkin I had taken him for."

Judge Stone asked the railroad to represent its case. Hawker spent most of the morning interviewing countless witnesses. After the railroad's lawyer was finished, Judge Stone recessed for dinner.

After the court session, the spectators went outside to discuss the morning events. The hungrier ones gathered in a small restaurant that had never seen so many customers in a month of Sundays. The worried looks on the patrons told the story more than words could possibly reveal. They knew the ranchers' prospects were slim.

At one table sat Patrick, Dennis, and Annie, "Have you had any word of your dad yet?"

"Not since he left almost two months ago, but I feel he'll show up in time."

"The way it's shaping up," Dennis acknowledged, "it looks bad for us. We have limited evidence on hand. We need a miracle to pull it off. We don't have one shred of evidence or one substantial witness to help our case. I'll have to stall during the afternoon's session as long as possible, just to buy us some time. I hope your father gets here in time. I'm going to use a new ploy. I'm going to put the railroad president on the stand and see how he likes the pressure. Don't ask me why? I don't know as yet but I think he knows something he's not telling. I aim to find out."

Patrick advised, "Stall as long as possible. I know John Logan! He'll be back in time. He knows today is the trial date and he's got a clock inside his head. I know John, he'll be here!"

Annie broke down and sobbed as Dennis comforted her. "Don't worry, Annie. I know he'll be back. It's time we got back to the court."

The courtroom was again jumping with noisy spectators. Judge Stone pounded the gavel. "If any of you has any more to say, the guard will escort you outside to say it, but not in my courtroom! Do I make myself clear to you?" he thundered. "Guard, lock the doors; no one is to come in."

The judge talked at length about the railroad's presentation, explaining it from a legal point of view. After he was finished, he motioned Dennis to present the ranchers' case.

Dennis rose. "Our first witness will be the railroad's president, Mr. J. P. Harlon."

This was a blockbuster to the spectators, even more so to the flabbergasted railroad officials, who were not prepared for this turn of events. Harlon's lawyer, Hawker, yelled out, "I object to cross-examining Mr. Harlon on the grounds it has no bearing on the case."

Judge Stone replied, "Objection overruled. I see no reason why Mr. Harlon can't be cross-examined."

Harlon looked flustered as he walked to the witness stand. The bailiff swore him in.

Then Dennis began the questioning, "What is your name?"

"J. P. Harlon."

"What does J. P. stand for?"

"Jesse Paul."

"Thank you, Mr. Harlon. What is your connection with the Cross Country Railroad?"

"I am its president."

"How old are you?"

"On April 24, 1894, I was sixty-five years old."

"To your knowledge, did your company ever had any treaties with the Indians?"

"Yes."

"How many?"

"Three."

"With what tribes?"

"I don't know."

"Do you have those treaties with you?"

"Yes."

"Would you please present them to the court?"

Harlon motioned for his lawyers to get the treaties out of their brief cases. Harlon turned them over to the judge. He looked them over, then passed them to Dennis, who asked Harlon, "Are these the only Indian treaties your company has ever signed?"

"They are, to my knowledge."

"I see they are duly signed by Jack C. Knarles of your company with the Kiowa in 1859, the Sioux in 1863; and by Robert L. Browne in 1869 with the Nez Perce."

"They were presidents of our company at that time."

Dennis walked before the judge and asked, "Your Honor, may I read each treaty to the court to validate its true authenticity?"

Hawker objected. He knew Dennis was stalling for time. Judge Stone

THE DECISION

curtly answered, "I'll be the judge of that. The court's time is never wasted for need of evidence. Objection overruled."

Dennis slowly read each treaty, whereby the railroad was to receive free right-of-way through Indian land without fear of attack from the Indians.

Dennis asked Harlon, "Are these the only treaties your railroad has ever drawn up with the Indians?"

"As I said before, yes, to my knowledge, that is all."

At that moment, there was a terrible pounding on the barred door. The judge rapped the gavel angrily. "What goes on back there? Guard, see who's making that racket."

The court guard brought back a piece of paper for Patrick. He read it and gleefully motioned to Dennis, who came over and read the message. Dennis address the judge. "I respectfully request a thirty-minute recess for an important witness to be heard."

The judge asked, "I'd like to know who is the witness and what are the special circumstances for me to allow a recess?"

"Your Honor," Dennis informed him, "Mr. John Logan wishes to enter the courtroom with four Indians whose testimony is vital to this case."

"Indians," screamed a lady, "We'll all be scalped!"

"Quiet!" thundered the judge, "Not in my courtroom will there be any scalping. Guard, pass the lady some smelling salts. In the meantime, court is in recess until two-thirty this afternoon."

Once more Hawker objected vehemently, but to no avail. The stern voice of the judge overruled his objections. The guard opened the door and John Logan walked into the courtroom, followed by a whitehaired Indian. He was supported by a young Indian on each side and followed by a watchful Indian at his rear. Patrick hugged Logan, "I knew you'd do it."

Dennis and Patrick escorted them to an anteroom, where Dennis asked Logan, "Are these the Indians you were telling us about? By all means, introduce us to your four friends."

Logan began, "This is Patrick O'Shea, my old friend. His son, Dennis O'Shea." He smiled proudly as he turned to the white men. "It is with great pride and honor that I introduce you to my father's greatest friend, Chief Thundercloud and his three grandsons, Strong Arm, White Feather, and Brave Heart. Please take it easy on the chief, Dennis. He's ninety-four years old. That is why his grandsons came along. Chief Thundercloud has brought an important Indian treaty he signed with the Cross Country Railroad Company in 1847. It could be very important for our defense in this case." The chief passed the treaty to Dennis.

"Heap strong paper," murmured the Indian.

The more Dennis read, the more excited he became. In a few minutes he came upon a passage that interested him greatly. He read it again and again, not believing his eyes. He clapped his hands together and yelled out, "This is the evidence we have been waiting for. This old paper will win the case, Chief Thundercloud. We are forever in your debt. You are a special and wise man! Chief Thundercloud, with your permission, I'd like to put you on the stand. Would you be willing to do that?"

The old Indian replied with a trace of a smile, "I come to talk, not visit! Some white men have no honor! Will speak many words, all true! Want to see if white man's justice is powerful as White Father in Washington?"

After the short recess, Dennis entered the courtroom with his four Indian guests. He requested permission from the judge to put the aged Indian on the stand. His three grandsons sat on the floor in front of the old chief. Hawker once more objected.

The judge replied, "Objection overruled. Mr. O'Shea, present your witness."

Two of the grandsons helped the tottering old chief to the stand. The bailiff placed the Bible before him and instructed him to tell the truth before God as his witness.

The chief answered in a low voice, "My days are short. Oh Mighty Spirit. I tell no lies! I want to go to Happy Hunting Grounds with clear heart."

The chief waved a salute to the judge, saying, "How, wise White Father."

The judge replied, "I welcome you! We will listen to your words. Continue with your cross-examination, Mr. O'Shea."

Dennis asked, "What is your name?"

"Thundercloud, Chief of Santee."

"How old are you?"

"As old as the hills where I will soon be."

"Did the Santee live in this area?"

"Yes, many snow ago! From the beginning of time until the white man stole our lands in 1857. No forget! Forced to travel hundreds of miles to a land of darkness."

The judge pondered Jason's ?? request to put the aged Indian on the stand.

"Did you ever have a meeting with the Cross Country Railroad Company?"

"I object," stormed Hawker, "as that blackens the good name of my client."

THE DECISION

"You are the most objectionable man I ever ran into. Clerk, strike my last remark from the record. Objection overruled! Continue with your questioning of the witness."

"I'll repeat the question. Did you ever have a meeting with the Cross Country Railroad Company?"

"Yes, in 1847."

"Will you fill us in on the details. How it came about and the result of it?"

"Make powwow with white man! White man want to bring Iron Horse through Santee lands. White Father in Washington have strong medicine with horse soldiers. We forced to sign treaty. Many young braves heap mad! Want to take scalp but I know it's not good. White man is like pebbles on the mountain. Too many! Me no trust white man! Him talk with forked tongue! After many powwows, we agree to allow Iron Horse to smoke through sacred Indian lands, scaring buffalo. I was chief of our tribe. I sign paper! My white friend, William Logan, read paper to me. I no like paper as is. I make more writing on it before I sign. Logan read back new paper to me. Me satisfied, so I sign! Help to make paper strong! New paper take poison out of forked tongue. Me talk straight!" The chief made a pass across his chest with an open hand.

The chief paused a moment to reflect, then continued. "The white man say Indian don't cry. He wrong! White man stole our lands in 1857. Forced us out of our homes in the middle of the night to go to the bad lands where nothing lives. We cry all the way there! You can't see an Indian crying because he shows no tears on the outside. On the inside, his heart is crying, crying for the land and the home he will never see again."

"I rest a minute. Too much for old man!" The kindly judge nodded his head, then ordered the guard to bring some water for the old chief. The guard hurried back with the water and gently offered it to the chief. The chief took a short sip, then said he wished to continue, "White man hurry, hurry to go nowhere. He destroy the earth. No good! Someday no more! He kill the buffalo. Let him rot in the sun. That no good! Someday no more. White man dirty the water and air. That no good! Someday no more. He chop down trees, scar Mother Earth. That no good! Someday no more. White man kill red man. That no good! Someday no more. Now white man cheat white man. That no good! Someday no more. Soon white man will kill white man. That no good! Someday no more. Great Spirit come to claim all land again. That will be sad for all of us. We all to blame. You, for doing this, and we, the Indian, for not teaching white man to love all that belong to the land."

"I am old now," The chief continued, "My people left this valley over forty snows ago. There were over eight hundred braves and squaws who cried that day. Now we are less than two hundred starving Indian on a land that has no trees, grass, water, animals, birds, just snakes! We are a dying people. Someday we be no more! We die more and more each day until there will be no more Santee living. Does the white man hate his red brother so much to allow that?''

"You have taken our lands!" he breathed heavily as he stopped for a moment to catch his breath, "That is bad! Now there is no more Indian land for the white men to steal. The Indian has no more! He will soon be like the buffalo, all gone! Now it start all over for the white man. The stronger white man steal from the weaker one! Why? To keep in practice? No! He want to own everything. Honor mean little to him. If it isn't that, then what is it? Indian know! It's power! Power of life and death over another man! Indian may steal from the white man, but not from his blood brother! He will be banned from his tribe. Not so with white man. He smart!"

"An Indian," Thundercloud said solemnly, "without honor when he dies, he has no place to go. His spirit is without direction. Is lost in the Great Divide between here and the Happy Hunting Grounds. Bad Indian keep searching for Happy Hunting Grounds in the company of other lost men, mostly white. Some men are lost before they start on trip to Happy Hunting Grounds. Some, I see, over there, "pointing in the direction of the railroad officials, "will never make it."

"I object to his inflammatory statements concerning these honorable men," cried Hawker.

"I'd object too, if my trip to the other world was in doubt," said the unflappable judge. "Objection overruled. Continue Chief, we're interested in what you say."

"I have but a few more words," promised the chief. "Do not want to pound your ears too much. Indian is at peace with the world and himself. He does not want what others have. White man would do well to honor Indian way. I had hoped that white man and red man shake hands across the land, but I'm afraid not to be in my time. Someday, it will happen! Not now! Powwow is over!"

Dennis asked, "May I ask you one last question?"

"Ugh! You may."

"You have brought Indian treaty with you to present to the court. Why did you come back to help the white man after all the wrongs his white brother had caused you to endure at their hands?"

"Some things we do from the heart from want of love. Some we do from hate! Other do it for power. The power of life and death over all. That is wrong! Indian came back to show the White Father that paper is true. I tell story! I remember many snows ago, white man brings news

THE DECISION

by singing wire from White Father in Washington to powwow. We hold powwow! White man want land for Iron Horse to scare the buffalo away. We no want war! Too many deaths on both sides. Too much crying in wigwams for lost braves. Too m any white men, too few Indians. After a lot of angry talk, Indian sign, white man sign paper. Signature right here with William Logan's. Both names say this paper is true. That is good! Written paper heap much better than white man's word. It's like making promises to the wind. White man has no honor! Indian keep word! Here, young white brave," he passed the old treaty to Dennis, "take this magic paper. Pull out poison from white man's fangs."

"Before you step down, Chief," Judge Stone smiled, keeping a sober face, "I thank you for reminding us of the white man's faults. They are many! In all my years on the bench, I've never been so moved by a witness's testimony as I was by yours. Clerk, I want you to put the chief's testimony in the records, word by word, in its entirety! You make me a copy of it. I'll treasure it for life. Again, Chief Thundercloud, I thank you."

With the judge's final statement, two of the chief's grandsons helped him from the stand. He walked unsteadily to a seat in the audience. They rose in a body to give him a standing ovation. The aged Indian understood, moved by the unexpected acclamation. The judge pounded the gavel for quiet.

Dennis handed the treaty to Judge Stone. He asked permission to continue his cross-examination of Harlon. Hawker strongly objected, but was overruled by the judge.

Dennis waited for Harlon to take his seat on the stand before he started his cross-examination. "I remind you, Mr. Harlon, you are still under oath. Before Chief Thundercloud came here for questioning, I had asked you some question that needed clarification. According to you, there were only three treaties signed by your company and the Indians. I asked you that question and you answered, "Yes, to my knowledge, that is all," Am I right so far?"

"Yes, you are."

"According to all your Indian treaties, the railroad was allowed a right-of-way through Indian lands. Is that right?"

"Yes, that is so."

"According to the treaties, the railroad was awarded everything and the Indians received nothing for their part of the agreement. Is that right?"

"Well, I guess that is so."

"Doesn't that appear to be an unfair way to treat your red brother? Someone who is naive and trusting and more honest, but unfortunately less educated than you."

"Sir, I resent that statement. It's an unfair and unjust thing to say about my company."

"Let me rephrase it for you. If the shoe were on the other foot and someone stole part of your railroad because they were smarter than you, would you still say it was good business on their part?"

"That is an ambiguous question. I refuse to answer it."

"The question must be answered, it's a moral one and it has a bearing on this case."

Mr. Hawker jumped up and asked for a thirty-minute recess, which the judge granted.

After Harlon was back on the stand. Dennis asked him once more, "Would you think it's good business on the part of someone who is smarter than you to steal your railroad?"

Harlon wriggled nervously, wiped his brow with his handkerchief, looked at the stern face of the unyielding judge and finally with great deliberation said, "It's hard to answer that in the proper perspective."

Dennis persisted, "You can try."

"There are too many intangibles in that question to be answered fairly," hedged Harlon.

Judge Stone reminded Harlon icily, "That question must be answered."

Harlon murmured, "I suppose it isn't too ethical to do a base deed like that."

Dennis countered, "Then what makes it so ethical for you to do the same dastardly thing to the ranchers?"

"We're not doing anything unethical on our part. It's just good business on our part to record all these properties before someone else did."

"For the time being, we'll get away from that line of questioning. Does the Cross Country Railroad Company honor all Indian treaties that they have signed?"

"We definitely do as we have shown it the three treaties that were presented to the court today."

"Do you believe in honoring all Indian treaties?"

"We do."

Dennis walked over to Judge Stone, "May I have that treaty?" I'll need it for further cross-examination of Mr. Harlon."

The judge replied, "By all means."

Dennis queried Harlon, "Do you remember a treaty signed by your company with the Santee Indian Nation in 1847? On August 26, to be exact?"

"No, I do not."

"It's signed here by the president of the railroad at that time. His name was Jack C. Knarles. Do you know of such a man?"

THE DECISION

"Yes, he was the first president of our company."

"It further states in the treaty, I'll read it verbatim. "We, the Cross Country Railroad Company, are hereby promised the exclusive right-of-way through the Santee Indian Nation's lands. Not to exceed three hundred feet wide and free of Indian attacks and free to build a railroad through at a future date without reprisals from the Santee Indian Nation in the Broken Bend Territory. We, in return, do hereby promise to relinquish all future property rights or to lay claim to any additional land owned by Indian or white man. We all promise to accept squatter's rights of anyone owning property in this territory, and do hereby promise to abide by all future laws for all time in this territory," Mr. Harlon, as an authorized representative of your company, will you honor this treaty?"

Hawker jumped up and asked, "Your Honor, may we have a thirty-minute recess to study this document for verification of authenticity?"

"Recess granted."

The tide of the trial had turned to the rancher's side. If Harlon and his lawyers agreed to the mandate of the treaty, the ranchers would win by default. If the railroad chose to contest it, then Judge Stone would make the final decision.

Thirty minutes later, a crestfallen group of railroad officials and lawyers trudged back in the courtroom with their faces drawn and taut. Harlon stepped to the stand with a prepared statement read by Harlon, "Your Honor, we find the treaty to be authentic. We will abide by your decision. We were remiss in our attempt to take title to the ranchers' properties. What Chief Thundercloud said about us is true, but we were too busy being successful to realize it. We are truly brothers under the skin. It only takes some of us longer to learn it. This too, will be changed, I assure you."

The judge pounded his gavel, "This court is still in session. Mr. Harlon, the court at this time has no penalties for the railroad. I assure you that we will entertain any motion from the ranchers concerning your false accusations. That is something you and the ranchers will have to work out as soon as this court session is over. Now, the most important thing of all. Listen carefully, I'll give the ranchers ten days to record the properties and get them registered, or by God, I'll record them in the name of the federal government. I again thank Chief Thundercloud and salute you for being a real American. Case dismissed."

There was bedlam in the courtroom as everyone hugged each other. Annie rushed to Dennis' side and kissed him. There was even a touch of satisfaction on the swarthy face of Chief Thundercloud.

Patrick grabbed Dennis in a bear hug, exclaiming, "I'm so proud of you, son. Most of all, eternally gratified with the job your mother did in raising you."

"Dad, you know who deserves all the credit for our victory? Not I, for any lawyer worth his salt could have done it with the help I received. John Logan deserves credit for the sixty days of travelling and scouting to find Thundercloud. However, the greatest credit of all belongs to that great old Indian, Chief Thundercloud., He is far wiser and braver than all of us. He forgave all of us despite the wrong the white man did to his people. These two men are the heroes in today's drama. I just happened to be in the area to put it in order. Our greatest debt is to Chief Thundercloud."

"Dennis, we're going to celebrate! We're having a big victory get-together tomorrow night at our ranch. Our guests of honor will be Chief Thundercloud and his three grandsons. Just you wait and see! I'm glad that you and I think alike. Tomorrow morning, we're having an important meeting at Logan's ranch. We intend to spring a big surprise at our celebration. That is all I can say for now. I'm sure you and Annie have something more important to discuss in the moonlight, anyhow."

The judge pondered Dennis' request to put the aged Indian on the stand

Chapter 15

The exciting trial was over. The gloom of the ranchers was a nightmare of the past. A happy celebration was about to begin. The spent emotions of the ordeal had taken its toll. The humidity of the long summer was subsiding and peace was again in the heavens. Chief Thundercloud remarks, "Mighty Spirit heap happy! No more heat to punish white man. Sometime forget, punish red man too! He satisfied white man punished enough. Me happy too! No like hot weather!"

Dennis slept for many hours before he finally awoke. He tossed around in bed for a while before he was totally awake. Finally he dragged himself out of bed and washed up before coming down stairs. Delicious aromas were coming from the kitchen. There he found Annie, with an apron around her waist, cooking up a large batch of flapjacks, ham, bacon, and eggs. Chief Thundercloud and his three grandsons were incredulous at what they were observing, waiting patiently in hungry expectation. Dennis yelled out a greeting, handclasping each of the Indians in friendship. He saved a kiss for Annie that inspired the old chief to say, "Heap good medicine."

After having watched Annie prepare so many good things, the chief exclaimed, "White man know how to live. Paleface squaw heap good cook. Food make me hungry. Grandsons always hungry. White man hunger for red-haired squaw only."

They all laughed at the chief's words.

The food was ready! Annie yelled, "Come and get it. All you braves. Let's eat! But before we begin, I'd like the chief to ask blessings on our food."

"Oh, Great Spirit," began the chief, "you have let me see many snows. Give good medicine to all at this table for many snows to come in their

THE DECISION

lives. No hunger for them, except maybe the hunger for a squaw. May we live in peace, red man with white brother and red-haired squaw."

"Amen," said Dennis and Annie, as the four Indians nodded their heads grunting, "Ugh!"

Dennis smiled at the chief, "Tonight, Chief, we're having a big celebration. All the ranchers and their squaws will be there. You and your grandsons are going to be our guests of honor. Lots of happy talking, good cheer, with friendship and love from all of us to you."

The chief thought for a moment, then answered, "We must get back to our people. They need us! But we can wait one day longer for big feast."

Annie hugged him, "Chief, you're priceless. We love you and your three brave young grandsons. May I be your friend?"

"You have pure heart. Your words ring out of the sky. They make me feel good. I accept."

That night the spacious Betty Ann Ranch was alive with smiling ranchers and their wives, who warmly greeted the four, sober-faced Indians. The Indians watched the festivities with mounting interest. All the guests participated, bringing chairs and tables to seat everyone. There were large quantities of food and refreshments. This prompted the wrinkled chief to comment, "More food here than we see on our lands for three snows."

Everyone was enjoying themselves in a new spirit of love and friendship that had never existed before between the red man and the white man. It brought them closer to each other than either had dreamed possible.

Finally, Patrick let out a loud whistle, "I know we're grateful to Dennis for helping us beat the railroad and save our lands."

This brought a loud cheer from the guests, "Here, here!" It even brought a faint smile to Dennis' lips.

Patrick continued, "We owe a far greater debt of gratitude to our guest of honor, who made it all possible. He taught us a far more important lesson. One we should never forget! I am proud to introduce to you that man, the finest man I have ever met, Chief Thundercloud, and with him are his three fine grandsons; Strong Arm; Brave Heart; and White Feather. Let's all rise and give them a hearty welcome."

With a thunderous applause, they all rose to salute and honor the compassionate old Indian and his three grandsons. A guilty tear fell from the Chief's eye as his emotions betrayed him.

After they sat down, Patrick asked, "Chief, do you remember William Logan?"

The old chief answered, "Him good friend. Him have white skin, but with Indian heart. Him good blood brother!"

Patrick continued, "William Logan made a promise to you that he could not keep because he went to his Happy Hunting Ground. Tonight, in his memory, we're going to keep that promise he made to you and your people. This morning, we held a special meeting. Every rancher was there! We discussed many topics, Chief. The main one was you, and we arrived at a decision. We hope it meets with your approval."

Keeping everyone in suspense, Patrick drew a long breath, then went on. "We, as your white brothers, wish to make amends for the wrongs our white brothers have caused you in the past. The grief, you and your red brothers have endured, for all these crimes and sins committed against you, we all share the blame. From this day on, for all time to come, as long as there's land and sky and water, with the ranchers' blessings, we have made out a deed to you and your people. This will consist of six hundred and forty acres of the finest grazing land. It has many trees, lots of birds, animals, and plenty of water. We are only returning some of the land you gave us long ago for safe keeping. It has been kept in trust until now. It's yours again! My friends and I will love to have you as neighbors again. Let me tell you a little of your nearby neighbors. There is Sid Sayd on the western side of you, Jeff Cravath on your northern border, the O'Sheas on your south side and John Logan, your white blood brother's son to your east. Wait a minute! Here is more! We further agree to give to you and your heirs a boon for your lands. You will receive five hundred head of prime beef and ten bulls to make a lot of papooses." Everyone laughed long and loud.

After the laughter had subsided, Patrick continued, "We also further agree to help you build enough homes to house your entire tribe. We further agree to be a good white brother to you. You taught us the Indian way! We liked what we saw. Chief Thundercloud, would you please stand up and accept this deed?" The chief slowly rose to his feet and Patrick put his arms about him. "Chief, this is more than a deed to the land, it is a deed to our hearts."

Many range-hardened ranchers coughed with emotion. The ladies, overcome at the moment, sobbed at this touching scene.

The chief spoke in a quavering voice. "The Indian, too, has a deed from the heart to all of you. An open invitation to stay at our Happy Hunting Ground when your time comes. Tonight, the white man and the red man have shaken hands. I know your hearts are good. Soon, my trip to Happy Hunting Ground will no be with empty heart, but once more filled with hope and love. Evil spirits all gone! That is good! The good medicine you give to our people will make them happy. We live in peace with white bother. May Great Spirit protect you. I am happy!"

Patrick spoke as the chief sat down. "Thank you, Chief Thundercloud, for your kind remarks. The past events were memorable in many ways. It made us do a lot of soul searching. We learned that not all Indians or

THE DECISION

white men are bad. We also learned a valuable lesson. Your enemy of yesterday could be your friend of tomorrow. We thank you, Chief, for these lessons and for your kind invitation to your Happy Hunting Ground. We gladly accept! No more speeches, let the music play! Grab your partners and let's dance!''

The small band swung into a lively assortment of foot-stomping jigs and reels. Soon Sid Sayd was calling square dances in his inimitable Arabic style. The ranchers kicked up their heels and dosey-dooed to the fiddler's music. It was their moment of exhilaration. Nothing would take its place.

A short while later, Sandy McFee came in and stopped the music. "Patrick, you've got a long-distance call from Kelly. It's from Philadelphia.''

The happy crowd quieted as Patrick answered the telephone, still a novelty in the area. "Hello, Kelly, this is your dad. We beat the railroad. Your brother came in the nick of time to help us beat the railroad. Isn't it terrific?''

"Great, Dad! I'm glad for all of you. That takes a load off my mind. I have something important to say to Dennis. Let me talk to him. He can fill you in later.''

Patrick handed the phone to Dennis. "Kelly wants to talk to you.''

From the other end of the line, Dennis could hear Kelly, "Congratulations, Dennis, on your victory over the railroad for the ranchers. That sure beats all! You know, Dennis, when I was riding the train to Philadelphia, there was another train going west. I had the eeriest feeling, and I thought to myself, ''Wouldn't it be strange if Dennis was on that train going west while I'm on this one going east?''

There was a moment's pause on the line before Kelly went on, "Dennis, you've taken care of your end of business but I'm having a mess of trouble with mine. I reckon it's going to take a lot of doing to straighten out. First of all, we've got money problems! Mother's cash is depleted! She's mortgaged everything to the hilt, trying to help the miners stay afloat and keep the mine open. Mother doesn't know I'm calling you. You know how proud and stubborn she can be. We need at least $150,000 to reopen the mine in three weeks or else we lose it all. That's our deadline! If we don't meet it, the Black Diamond mind will be put up for bid and you know who will pick it up for a song....The Big Seven Coal Company! They're the varmints who are back of all this darn trouble. They're financing the goons who are trying to stop the mine from opening. We have another problem worse than that! The hundred enforcers you left me with have now grown to four hundred, all hired by the you-know-who gang. All I can say, Dennis, is we'll give them one hell of a fight. The miners will fight, but they are too few, probably one hundred, or less. One more thing, Dennis, I don't know how it happened but it did. I've fallen in love with Jessica and I want to marry her. I know she's your girl, but we love each other....What do you say?''

Dennis replied excitedly, ''Wonderful, Kelly! She's a wonderful girl! I too, have a surprise for you. The same thing happened to me! I fell in love with Annie. I'm going to ask her to be my wife. We better keep both women in the family. They're both wonderful!''

Annie blushed as she heard Dennis' declaration of love said over thousands of miles of telephone wire. The guests joined in on the moment with loud roars of laughter and congratulations.

Dennis continued, ''Kelly, I'll get you the money from Dad and bring it personally. I'll fight along side you. Goodbye, Kelly, with love from all of us. We'll see you as soon as we can!''

Dennis put down the receiver. Everyone started to talk and ask questions at the same time. Dennis put up his hand. ''I'll try to answer your questions. First, I think I can do it better if I told you a story about two wonderful people, my father and mother. Once they were deeply in love. They married. Out of this union, they had twin sons. Then their troubles began. How to raise their sons? Each believed their way was the best. My father wanted to raise both of us in the way of the west. My mother, on the other hand, wanted to take us back east and educate us in the finest of schools. Their steadfast beliefs caused them to separate.''

Dennis went on with the story, telling of the divorce trial and the judge's special provisions to the legal separation between his mother and father. Dennis related how Patrick had raised Kelly to be strong and self reliant, to fight for what was right. He described how his mother had him educated to be a lawyer. She also instructed him to use his education for the common good of mankind.

Finally, Dennis summed it up. ''When I left Pennsylvania to come here we were having the same troubles you were experiencing here, except that someone else was trying to steal my mother's coal mine. As you know, I came here, according to the legal decree, and Kelly had to go to Pennsylvania to be burdened with the trouble I left behind. The troubles have now compounded for Kelly and my mother since then, for two reasons. First, Mother had to use up all her money and mortgage her assets to keep open a coal mine she inherited from her uncle, Bobby Brooks, who was murdered by the same people who are trying to cheat my mother. Kelly tells me she is broke and needs $150,000 at once to open the mine or lose it all to the Big Seven Coal Company. The second reason is that if Mother doesn't get the money on time and open the mine, the Big Seven will probably pick it up for a song at auction. The only support that Kelly has now are about a hundred weary, hungry miners who work in the mines,

THE DECISION

who are presently out of work but are willing to follow Kelly to the end of the trail. Their task is most difficult! Imagine them, fighting over four hundred strike breakers the coal syndicate hired. Kelly and the miners are going to try to open the mines in three weeks. I've promised Kelly I'd be there with the money and I would fight at his side. I can't let them steal my mother's mine, no more than I could let the railroad steal your ranches."

Tears streamed down Patrick's cheeks. "Dennis, I've been a stubborn old fool! It took a lot to show it to me. Your mother did a wonderful job in raising you to be a gentleman and a real man. I'm proud of you! I know your mother is. She's a gentle lady. I've got close to $50,000 in the bank. It's all yours to do with as you must. Tomorrow, I'll go into town and talk to the bank about mortgaging my property for the remaining money."

"Wait a minute!" yelled Sid Sayd. "Remember how we were all together against the railroad? As for me, I haven't forgotten how Dennis and Chief Thundercloud helped us. By Allah, I'm in this one, too. You can count on me for the sum of $10,000 right away, and more if you need it."

After the swashbuckling pirate's son spoke, a bedlam of voices erupted as the ranchers generously matched the remaining $100,000 that Kelly needed.

"Hold it right there, Dennis," roared big Jeff Cravath, "if I'm going to send money to the mine in the east, I know what I'm going to do. I'm taking some of my ranch hands with me to protect my investment."

"Me too, me too," yelled the ranchers in unison. Manpower to fight the company-hired enforcers came from an unexpected source, the ranchers and their hands.

In the meantime, Chief Thundercloud and his three grandsons had been listening to what was going on. They went into a little council of their own. Finally, Chief Thundercloud asked to be heard. "What I hear is like the winds of the past. I would like to dance one more war dance and help you, but I'm too old! Too feeble to fight the bad palefaces! My three grandsons want to joint your war party! They heap good warriors, not afraid! Strong spirit behind them! Want to help beat the bad men in the east. Them brave warriors! Will do them great honor to help white squaw of big paleface chief. After this battle, we put down our tomahawks and arrows. No more to use on white brother."

Dennis offered his hand to the chief. "Thank you Chief. I promise that I will fight with pride alongside your grandsons. What more can I say to all of you? You're all great people, every single one of you. I thank you all, including my red brothers, for the pleasure of knowing you. I know when we get to Pennsylvania, my mother will be overwhelmed.

When this is all over, I'm coming back to marry the sweetest girl in the west. Annie Logan, will you marry me?"

Annie piped up, "Grass 'a fire! Dennis, you're not getting out of this proposal. You've said it in front of witnesses. Yes, consarn you, my answer is yes, yes, yes!"

The chief said with a twinkle in his eye, "White man will find fighting the railroad much easier than living with paleface squaw."

Pop Logan and Patrick beamed up at this announcement. They congratulated each other. What a way to cement their friendship!

Logan held up his hand, "We have two tasks before us and two trails to follow, my friends. The first one you will do your way, the other is my obligation. We can accomplish both in our way. I have a promise and a debt to pay to my father's friend, Chief Thundercloud. While you are taking care of the mine situation back east, I'll be taking an expedition of supply wagons with the chief back to his people. These good people are destitute, hungry, old, and weak. I shall leave in the next few days for the long trip. We hope to bring back about two hundred old friends within a month or so. We're going to need about twenty wagons with drivers and supplies."

Sid Says yelled out, "By Allah, we're in this together. Say, John, if you haven't enough men to go with you, I'll donate a couple of wagons with drivers for the trip. I'll have them packed with supplies and sent over to your spread within a few days."

"Thanks, Sid, and may God bless you. I need as many wagons as possible, with drivers to transport Chief Thundercloud's people back to the land we've set up for them. I hope by the time you get back, I'll have accomplished my task and you yours. I expect to be waiting for you with our new neighbors."

"What Sid volunteered goes for me, too. I'll have a couple of wagons loaded with supplies and drivers at your ranch in a few days, John," thundered Cravath from across the room.

Annie was in a fix. "I'm drawn between two loves," she reflected, "Dad, you and the man I love. Grass 'a fire! What am I going to do? Tarnations! Shucks! It's a dilemma, but I guess, Dad, this will be one trip you'll be making without me. I'm going with Dennis to Andura to help his mother fight the coal crooks. My heart will be with you and Chief Thundercloud in spirit."

Logan smiled. He was so proud of his daughter. She was just like her mother, so full of life. "Was there ever a doubt in your mind? You've always been a good daughter to me for nigh onto nineteen years. I've been fortunate so far, for I've shared you with no one until now. You have a new life ahead of you with Dennis. You should go with him to Andura,

THE DECISION

or you wouldn't be the daughter I've raised and loved. Do me proud and go with Dennis. And Dennis, you better take good care of her. She is pretty special to me. After all, in the long run, I'm not losing a daughter, I'm gaining a son!"

"She is also pretty special to me," agreed Dennis. "I'll guard her with my life, although I don't think she needs any protection. She's a very capable young lady."

"Grass 'a fire! Dennis, now's the time for us to be talking about a lot of things."

"You're so right, Annie, my life. How's about a walk in the moonlight? Just you and me under the moon."

"Now it all fits in the plan of the Great Spirit," mused Chief Thundercloud. "The black clouds have passed from my people. We now have hope. Oh, Mighty Spirit, you have not forgotten us. Don't forget the troubled white people who go to the land of the black stones that burn. Give them good counsel and protection. Much good medicine tonight, more when I get back to my people. Indian legend say when man shares his food with others, his crops will grow better. Young red-haired squaw put fire in many unlit camps. Too much talk! I go to bed and dream for the first time in many moons."

Chapter 16

"**Mother,**" **said a** worried Kelly, "Mr. Ainsworth told me your funds are low. I think it's admirable of you to help the miners financially while waiting and hoping for the mine to open again."

"Kelly," interrupted Betty, "I made a promise to myself that I'd avenge my dear uncle's murder, no matter what it cost. What was I to do? How could I forsake those poor, loyal miners? Never in a million years!"

"Mother," Kelly explained, "I'm not faulting you on that, I'm sort of glad that you did. I'd a done the same thing if I were in your boots. The fact still remains, you're pretty near broke. When I learned of it from Mr. Ainsworth, I telephoned Dennis and Dad and informed them of our plight. If all things go according to plan, we're still going to need about $150,000 to open the mine and get it shipshape to operate again. Mother, you haven't that kind of money. I had a long talk with Dennis about our immediate needs. He felt he could get the money from Dad. We have a more immediate problem that's cropped up. The Big Seven have brought in an additional three hundred goons. The Big Seven must consider the Black Diamond mine very valuable to spend so much money, time, and effort."

"What contemptible beasts they are," shouted Jessica, her face red with anger. "We'll never let them do that, even if I have to go to Andura and fight with the miners!"

"Now wait, Jessica, grab hold of the reins! Of course you can't do that," soothed Kelly. "That wouldn't be fair! The goons wouldn't stand a chance with you. But you're right about one thing, Jessica. I reckon they've never battled an O'Shea before. They might not like their first taste of it."

Kelly stopped for a moment to remember one important thing he had to say to Jessica. "By the way, Jessica, when I telephoned the ranch, there was something I had to discuss with Kelly. It was about us! I explained

161

how we fell in love. It's such a beautiful yarn that I'll never get tired talking about it. Guess what Dennis said when I told him about it? He approved of my selection, and guess what else he said? He had some special news for the both of us! He has fallen in love with a wonderful girl named Annie, a dear friend of mine back home. You two, young, beautiful ladies are going to have a bangup time when you meet up. What strange, wonderful tricks life plays on us."

Jessica's answer was simple and to the point, "Of course, it's wonderful! I first saw it in the sparkle of your eyes at the station when you first arrived. I was hooked from the beginning! The moment you spoke, my heart did flip-flops and cartwheels. The touch of your hand set my body on fire. A fire that I couldn't put out, nor had I any desire to do so. Kelly, we're in love! What are you going to do about it? Haven't you wondered why I'm in your mother's company so much? Go on, show me how you western men appreciate your women."

Kelly grabbed her and held her tightly in his arms. He smothered her with kisses that seemed to go on forever. Both forgot they were standing next to Betty, but she didn't mind. She rather enjoyed Kelly's show of affection. The scene took her back about twenty years ago to another age and locale when the man in her arms was Patrick O'Shea. "My!" she thought, "Was that twenty years ago? It seems like only yesterday."

Betty knew there hadn't been any real love between Dennis and Jessica. They were just good friends. This was a hopeful sign for Betty. She liked Jessica and highly approved of her as a future daughter-in-law. Betty had one other concern. She wondered what kind of a girl Annie Logan was. She must be something special to put a bonfire in Dennis and steal his heart so fast. "Come to think of it," she laughed, "didn't Jessica steal Kelly's heart in the space of time? Events have sure moved fast for the O'Shea men."

Kelly was anxious to get back to the coal mine and give moral support to the miners, "Mother, I'm sorry, but I have to get back to the miners. They need me now more than ever! I'll feel better about it. Jessica, don't look at me with those sad eyes. You know I've got to go back and keep up the morale of the miners. It is vital for me to be with them."

Jessica came right to the point, "Drat the miners' morale, how about ours?"

Kelly answered that question by kissing her, "That will take care of your morale for now, but it will have to last until we beat the tar out of the Big Seven."

Kelly packed all his belongings in a grip and caught the train to Andura. He had no sooner left than Betty said to Jessica, "Let's pack and catch the Thursday's train to Andura. I think it's time I forgot my role as a lady and assumed the one that the Good Lord had meant for me, a woman and a mother. If Kelly and those miners are going to fight my battles, then it's high time that I pitch in and help in any way I can. Right now, that means I'm going to Andura to be with my son. Jessica, do you want to come along?"

Jessica was delighted, "Is coal black? Do ducks have flat feet? Want to? A team of horses going down hill couldn't hold me back. I was hoping you were going to do that, Betty. I love you! In this battle, it will be all of us, men and women, against the Big Seven!"

Betty smiled. There was something about Jessica's outgoing personality that made her feel so alive and young. It reminded her of herself when she was her age. She had had the same glow in her eyes with love for Patrick in the early days of their marriage. She wondered why it was so important at that time to be so set about their differences. Time proved to be a great healer, but of the mind and the body, but a sadness remained at the loss of love.

The next day they caught the train to Andura. This was to be their first experience in the realities with, a coal mining town, one that they would never forget. They didn't know what to expect. They soon found out in a hurry! Betty had boned up on coal mines by reading many periodicals and library accounts. The research didn't tell about real life in a coal town like Andura. Soon, Betty and Jessica would learn about it first hand. Betty was appalled at the shabbiness of the miners' homes and the putrid air they had to breathe. It's no wonder so many got the dreaded black lung disease!

There was much more that met the eye. Seeing the misery of the miners was enough to turn her stomach. She vowed that one day she would correct those inhumane conditions.

Betty turned to Jessica, "Don't expect much from the hotel accommodations. Let's be happy we're here to help Kelly. If it's good enough for him, it's good enough for us! We'll survive and be the better for it. I don't want to be a burden to Kelly, as he has enough problems of his own. I'm a lucky mother, Jessica, to have two such wonderful sons. I must admit, Patrick did a superb job in rearing Kelly. He is a fine young man, maybe a little coarse and rugged around the edges, but what a man! Just like his dad."

"I agree with you, Betty. Kelly is all man! Someday I hope to meet your Patrick. I bet he was something!"

They checked in at the hotel and, to their surprise, found it rather pleasant. In fact, Betty found it quite charming. The tiny lobby had two wooden chairs and an old brown sofa, a writing table with a small wastebasket, and a large ceiling fan. They walked up the stairs to the third floor and the clerk showed them their room. It was small, neat, and tidy, with clean linen on a brass-trimmed double bed. In the far corner of the room

THE DECISION

was a small dresser with a bowl and a pitcher of water. Across from the bed were two wicker chairs and a writing table. Atop the table was a green shaded student lamp. It wasn't what Betty had been used to, but she was quite satisfied with the lodgings under the circumstances.

After they had washed up, they went downstairs and asked where they could find Kelly O'Shea. The clerk told them he had gone out about an hour before to a meeting with the coal miners at their hall on Axton Street. Betty asked for and was given directions.

Betty thought for a while, then said to Jessica, "This is my fight, not yours. I own the mine and it's my responsibility to do my part in defending it. You are free to do as you wish. I'm going to find Kelly and tell him I'm backing him to the limit. Jessica, if you want to come along, you're more than welcome, but if you don't, that, too, is all right, I'll understand."

Jessica bristled, "Do you think I'd came all the way to Andura to pass up this night? I'm surprised at you, Betty. I'm going with you, come hell or high water, even if it means we get our noses bent out of shape."

"Good! Let's go. Time's a wasting! That's one commodity we're short of."

They located the old meeting hall on a sidestreet at the south end of the town. They arrived in time to hear Kelly say, "Men! It's time we decided not to take each other for granted! We need to stand together against the Big Seven. Let's look at each of you in the proper perspective. Most of you came here from your countries in Europe to escape tyranny, to be free. Let me tell you something about freedom. It doesn't come free and it's not for everyone. It's for those who want to fight for it and hold on to it. No matter where you go, you will always find tyranny. Varmints trying to take your freedom away from you! You've got to recognize tyranny when you see it, then figure out how you're going to stamp it out. We know who our enemies are. It's the Big Seven who are in back of all this, spending thousands of dollars to hire hundreds of goons to stop us from reopening the mine. If they win and we lose, we'll all be losers and you will be the greatest losers of all. The Big Seven will own the mine and you'll have to go back to work for them, under their rules, for starvation wages. There'll be no safety regulations or health care. You enjoyed these privleges under "Bonnie Bobby" Brooks. You'll be worth less than the coal you dig. Is this the life you want or do you want to fight for a better life? If you want to be free, you'll have to fight for it. No one will give it to you but, if you decide to fight, I'll be there beside you. I promise you that! We have to fight for what we hold dear. I ...!"

Kelly stopped short when he saw his mother and Jessica at the doorway. He motioned for them to come in.

"Men," he proudly explained, "it's with great pride and pleasure that I introduce to you the two most important women in my life. First, my mother, and your employer, Mrs. Patrick O'Shea, and my fiancee, Miss Jessica Longstreet."

The miners showered the ladies with a round of applause. They applauded endlessly and yelled for Betty to speak. Finally, she spoke, beginning slowly, "I think Kelly said it all. I deem it a great pleasure to be associated with wonderful people like you. I have my faults, many of them, but the worst would be closing my eyes to the plight of the miners and their families. Kelly has told me about your background. Why you came to this country and what you want most out of life. It's the same thing we all want, freedom. Freedom from want! Freedom to do the things you want. I'm horrified to think that there are people like those in the Big Seven. I'll not change the policies of my beloved uncle, "Bonnie Bobby" Brooks. He loved you dearly. He gave his life for you! I will avenge his murder! I promised this on the Holy Bible a long time ago, and I mean to keep that promise. In the coming struggle, some of you may be hurt, but not half as much as if you hadn't fought at all. As I look at some of these surroundings, I am dismayed at what I see. Lack of first-aid stations, schools, hospital, and police protection. We must have improvements for the future. First, we have a war to fight and win. I promise you, as God is my witness, that in the coming battle, I will be in the thick of it with you. I will fight in the streets with you!

"Everything I expect of you, I expect of myself. I will work with assist, and comfort your women and children. I speak not only for myself but also for Jessica, my future daughter-in-law. She has come here at this trying time, on her own, to help you and my son. Men, we will win! After it's all over, we'll start rebuilding the houses of your neighborhood to make this a better place in which to live. This, and more, I promise you! Thank you, and may God bless you!"

This speech of dedication by Betty stirred the miners. It brought many a lump in their throats and tears in their eyes. She had touched their hearts. Betty had spoken with sincerity, scoring heavily with the listeners. She gave them hope and encouragement for the days ahead. Kelly and Jessica thrilled to her words. Betty had committed herself and promised a new life for the miners with a brighter future.

As Betty stepped off the platform, she received a standing ovation. The crowd kept yelling, "More, more, more!" It was an ecstatic audience. Betty bowed graciously, thanking them as she sat down with Jessica. Kelly had a few parting words before he closed the meeting, "I think my mother has said it all for us. We're all for one and one for all. Remember our plans! We open the mine Monday morning. Be prepared for the worst.

THE DECISION

I expect each one of you to be ready to defend yourself at all cost. There may be some of us hurt, perhaps badly. Protect your flanks and all fallen miners. Stay in groups of five. Fight back to back so you can see on all sides, like a five-pronged spear. Keep moving to your right all the time. Keep moving. If any of you has family is too old, or doesn't want to fight, you'd best stay home. I promise you one thing. I'll never leave your side. Goodnight, men."

The miners slowly left the meeting, taking time to greet Betty and Jessica in their various languages. They, in turn graciously shook hands and chatted words of encouragement to each one. Then Kelly asked, "Mother, why did you and Jessica come here? I'm sure glad you did, though. The miners needed that pat on the back you gave them, Mother. Much more than you know. You gave them a new hope for the future. That's all they asked for. One thing I definitely ask of you, both of you! Promise me that when the fighting starts you will stay in the background, no matter how bad it looks. Both of you! I like my women rough, tough, and spirited, but not messed up. Don't worry, Mother, we'll open the mine! I only hope that Dennis gets here with the money by Monday. The money is needed for operating costs and food for the miners. You know the story, Mother, you've been through it for the last few months. The miners are broke, have no credit with the merchants. They've used up all the money you have given them for food and doctor bills and, to make our problems worse, we have to defend ourselves against four hundred goons with only poorly armed miners and a few friendly storekeepers. A lot of good men will be hurt. I can only wait until then with hope and prayers. I know the miners. They will fight to the end. Hope is eternal for all of us."

"Kelly," Betty declared, "I promise you before God, if we should beat the Big Seven and reopen the mine, we'll make this a model mine. We'll show these people what the true American dream really is."

"Bless, you, Mother, " said Kelly huskily. "I know you mean every words you say. This will be a new day for the miners. Let's hope the money gets here on time."

Betty replied, "We still have a little money on hand. Maybe we can subsidize the miners' food for a couple of days. Here is some money! Make it last! Pass it along to the miners. Do it now!"

"Okay, Mother, I'll use it the best way I can. The miners will be relieved and thankful for the help."

Saturday and Sunday passed without incident, the calm before the storm. Tony, Sadar, and Sock had learned through the grapevine that the goons were going to use all their weapons to stop the miners. The local police were powerless to stop it.

"Furthermore, Kelly," Tony said in broken English, "We fight! They call us wops and dagos! I cut out their throats! You say "No! so I no do it! They call us other dirty names and insult our women. What makes these men do such shameful things?"

"Well, Tony," explained Kelly with the only logical reason possible, the "main cause is ignorance." Take any one of the goons. Have they ever met you and your family socially? Have they ever gone to any of your festivities or seen you at church? Maybe if they had, they'd have a different impression of you. In a way, Tony, you have to feel sorry for them. They have no roots like you and the other miners. They don't know where they're going and that is the loneliest road of all."

"I think I know what you mean, Kelly. Anyhow, there's one thing you can be sure of, the miners are one hundred percent behind you and your mother. They sure liked that speech she gave. It made them feel good! We're not afraid of their threats. They might get some of us, but we'll make them pay dearly for it. This is the first real chance we've had to fight for our freedom. We intend to stand up and be counted. We're going to protect our rights at all costs. We'll not be cheated out of them."

Tony continued, " talked to Sadar and Sock. They said that most of the storekeepers have given us their blessings. Some of them are going to fight by our sides. They figured it was just as much their fight as it was ours. These are the kind of friends we have, the kind who are there when you need them."

"We won't forget them when it's all over. Give them our thanks and our best to Sock and Sadar."

Betty listened to the conversation. She was thrilled by what she had heard and her spirits were buoyed. These wonderful people would be friends for years to come, long after this terrible conflict was over. Betty learned that friendship can spring up from the least likely of places.

Betty was beginning to understand and appreciate Patrick's ideas. She was no longer opposed to his thinking. Perhaps, a long time ago, she was not ready, but now she was! Wouldn't it be wonderful to have Patrick here right now to help and guide the miners. He was always so patient and strong.

Suddenly, both sides saw each other! The battle began in earnest as they surged forward.

Chapter 17

It was a sunny autumn day, a slight breeze fanned the leaves on the ground. Before the day was over, history would be made in Andura. The townspeople had sealed themselves fearfully behind closed doors. They waited for the inevitable clash between the outnumbered miners and the superior force of the Big Seven syndicate. Otherwise, Monday seemed like any of the countless days of the past. The sun displayed its shining mantle over the horizon, readying itself to warm the earth once more.

The stage was set! The adversaries were prepared for their day of destiny in their anticipated fight. Many a miner and perhaps a henchman or two spent a restless night thinking, thinking what the next day would bring. Anything could and would happen! Their nerves were at a breaking point, but that, too, would have to wait!

To the miners, this was to be the beginning of a new life or the end of the old one. To the goons, this was just another adventure in their misspent life. Both of the contestants had a rendezvous with fate.

At the final meeting, Kelly had told the miners, "This is it! This is the day, men! We've made a change in the plans. We're going to surprise them. Catch them off guard! We're going to reopen the mines at one o'clock instead of earlier in the day. Most of you have had a tough night thinking of what may be. It will give us more time to adjust and prepare our strategy. Don't worry if you're tired. We all are! Even the goons have had their share of nerves. They'd be lying if they said different. Don't forget, this waiting game is just as hard on them as it is on us. Believe me, I know. I've been through this before. It's never been easy! Go home to your wives. I'll see you here before one o'clock."

The miners left. Kelly still had some annoying problems that offered no easy solution. Would Dennis get here in time with the money? Could the miners and the storekeepers hold out against the superior numbers

THE DECISION

of the Big Seven? Was he expecting too much from them? Time would have the answer to all the questions.

It was nearing one o'clock. Kelly was discussing the plans for the coming battle with Jessica and Betty, "Here are a few things I'd like you to do. Under no circumstances should either of you leave the hotel. Listen to me! I don't want you in the streets. I'll have enough problems of my own without worrying about my two best girls. More important, I need you as a lookout on the balcony to keep watch for Dennis and that train. He must get here on time. Please do as I ask."

Betty was beginning to have some thoughts about the battle against the superior forces of the enemy. She was feeling the way any mother feels when her son is sent to the front lines to do battle. As a last resort, Betty said, "I'm willing to give up the mine rather than have you or the miners hurt."

Kelly replied, "Mother, do you realize what you're saying? Do you want the miners to give up? Are you asking them to do that? Are you asking me the same thing? The miners are expecting me to lead them, and lead them I will! The miners and the storekeepers are fighting for their freedom and the right to be Americans. They're not trained to be fighting men; they're just miners and storekeepers. I'll tell you one thing, they'll be damned good fighters. Why? Because they'll be fighting for their jobs, families, homes, friends, and their lives. No one is going to cheat them out of the right to protect what is theirs."

"Kelly, you've made your point," Betty said, "As a mother, I hate to see anybody hurt, especially my own family. I'm all right now! One thing is for sure, you've got the same streak of courage that your father had. That is probably why I love both of you so much. Kelly, you're right! If you want something badly enough, you must make a real commitment to do what you must do. Good luck, son! And may God be with you!"

Kelly walked to the door accompanied by Jessica. She took him into her arms and kissed him. "No matter how this turns out, I'll be waiting for you. If you don't beat them for good, you'll have a bigger fight with me explaining why you didn't."

"I know, my darling," Kelly agreed, "It looks like it will be a long afternoon. Watch the railway depot for any sign of Dennis. If you see him, tell him where I'll be. That's where the action will be."

"Good luck, dearest, may the Good Lord be in back of you to protect you from the rear. God be with you."

Kelly backtracked his way in the opposite direction of the mine to the miners' rendezvous. He took one last look at the hotel and saw Betty and Jessica on the balcony. From their vantage point, they could overlook the entire town and the railway station.

As soon as Kelly was out of sight, Betty walked inside for a glass of water while Jessica remained at her post, eyeing the depot for any sign of Dennis. Sometimes waiting plays strange tricks on the mind. Anticipation is the greatest foe of all. Fear of the unknown allows the mind to imagine strange things.

Suddenly the goons changed their strategy. Instead of blockading the road to the mine, they decided to attack the miners before they had a chance to organize. When Jessica saw this, she was desperate, she had no way to warn Kelly and the miners. She had to stay on the lookout for Dennis!

The well-armed goons poured down Front Street form their position to intercept the miners at their staging area. They outnumbered the miners and the storekeepers by six to one and were armed with clubs, bats, and other fearsome weapons. Unless some unforseen help came along, the miners were in for a rough time.

Jessica could see the drawn faces of the miners and the storekeepers. She silently prayed for them. They were outnumbered in many ways. They were not in the same class as the professional, paid goons. The only thing they had going for them was that they were fighting for their homes and families. Fighting for their freedom! Fighting for what they wanted to do without others dictating policies to them. Fighting to retain their dignity as men! In the other direction, Jessica saw the sneering faces of the paid goons. They had come well armed for this battle.

Suddenly, both sides saw each other. The battle began in earnest with both sides surging forward. Kelly, led his followers, Tony, Sock, and Sadar at his side.

Kelly yelled out, "Close ranks! Don't let them separate you! Fight back to back! Don't let them get between you."

Tony screamed, "C'mon, Greek, let's give them a touch of the Latin flavor."

Sock answered, "I've got my baby picked out as soon as they get here. I'll deck him like a Christmas tree."

Sadar was jumping up and down, "Just watch this Polish Cossack in action. Keep a tight formation! Give them hell!"

Suddenly, both sides saw each other! The battle began in earnest as they surged towards each other.

The miners fought valiantly, but the tremendous superiority of their foes was taking its toll. Jessica and Betty cried tears of anguish as they viewed the battle. It was not going well for the miners. Suddenly, Betty heard a train whistle that caught her ear. Looking toward the railway depot, she saw an unbelievable sight. Jumping out of box cars from all sides were hundreds of men yelling like Indians on a scalping spree. They began running down the street. There were ranchers, cowboys, and my God, even

THE DECISION

Indians! Three of the fiercest Betty had ever seen, with war paint on their faces, were whooping up and down in an ancient tribal war dance. Finally, she saw a familiar figure in cowboy clothes. It was Dennis. He had come in time with the money, but who were the other men? They were yelping like coyotes as they rushed hellbent for the battle ahead of them. They were led by a graying man and Dennis.

"Jessica, come over here quick! Look over there by the depot! Look who's coming! It's Dennis! Who are all the men with him? Isn't it thrilling?"

They looked at the incredible sight below. The yelling group of men! Some, Betty faintly recognized. My! They look so great! Then she saw Patrick! "Oh, my God! It's Dennis and Patrick! My two men! I do, do, do, do, do love both of you! Jessica, those are the ranchers and hands from the nearby ranches. Now, the Indians, that is something I can't explain, but they're sure a welcome sight! Now watch, Jessica! You'll see the damndest fight you've ever seen. C'mon, you men, whip the tar out of them! The O'Sheas are together again. We'll never be separated again."

Kelly was fighting furiously! Out of the corner of his eye he saw his dad. That must be Dennis with him, his brother he had never seen. There were cowhands from the adjoining ranches charging the battle area, just in time to take a hand in the fray. There were even three painted Indians, all fighting together.

"Ya-hoo!" shrieked Kelly. A piercing "Ya-hoo" resounded from the newcomers from the west. Kelly yelled out to the miners, "They're our friends, and they're here to help us!"

When the miners heard this, they took heart, they felt renewed strength at the sight of the reinforcements as Kelly urged them on, "Now it's our turn! Dish it out to them varmints! Let's see if they can take it as well as they can give it."

"Ya-hoo!" yelled Sock at the top of his voice as he leaped high in the air. "C'mon, Tony and Sadar. Look who's coming! It's some of Kelly's crazy cowboy friends. Let's welcome our new friends over here where the action is!"

Joe Dvorak, the devilish leader of the goons, spied Kelly and remembered the embarrassing beating he suffered from him in front of his mob. Now, he figured, was a good time to even the score. He and a couple of his biggest men sneaked up on Kelly from behind to waylay him before he had a chance to retaliate.

"Kelly, look out behind you!" came the familiar voice of Patrick, "Someone's trying to drygulch you. Hold on, we'll be with you soon!"

Kelly turned quickly to fight the onslaught of Dvorak and his henchmen. Dvorak let out a string of oaths as he charged Kelly with clubs aflying. The miners and Kelly edged back to the wall. They fought shoulder to shoulder against the uneven odds.

"You son-of-a-bitch! I'll get even with you for the beating you gave me. When I get through with you, there won't be enough of you left to put in a bag," hissed Dvorak through clenched teeth, glaring with a hateful grimace.

"Well, look what we have here! It looks like Joe, the snake, crawling down the gutters, as usual," shouted Kelly with determination on his rugged face. "Let's continue with the lessons I showed you the last time. This will be the last of the series, so pay close attention!"

With that last remark, he deftly dodged a vicious swing at his head by Dvorak. He promptly got his attention with a rapier-like left to the bridge of Dvorak's nose. It brought another barrage of curses from the bloodied Dvorak.

Suddenly, the uneven battle had taken a new turn for the better with the influx of the unexpected ranchers and cowboys.

The three Indians were like whirling dervishes with their acrobatic style of fighting, somersaulting over the confused goons and scaring them out of their wits with their war screams and flying clubs and tomahawks. Strong Arm shrieked, "This is our last war party against the palefaces, so let's make this one we won't forget!"

White Feather leaped over a charging goon as he cried out, "No scalps on this raid! Use tomahawk only to play the tomtom on their heads."

Brave Heart dodged a charging goon and clubbed him on the head while he was going by. He yelled out, "I see mine! Will send him close to Happy Hunting Ground," as he let out an unearthly screeching yelp that put the fear of God in the surprised goon.

The bravery of the young Indian men would have delighted the old chief's heart. They fought with lightning quickness and uncanny agility.

Kelly yelled to Dennis as he clobbered Dvorak with another quick left to his tender nose. "It's a great way to meet, in the midst of a good fight. I'll be right over with you, brother, as soon as I get rid of this one."

"Knock him over here to me as I have a score to settle with him too."

"Be my guest, Dennis." Kelly spun Dvorak over to Dennis, who twirled him around again with a sweet left hook to the eye.

"Remember me?" he taunted him. "I'm the guy you called Little Lord Fauntleroy. Here's one in payment for the beatings you inflicted on the miners."

With that jibe, he struck him with a hard hook to the eye that opened an inch-wide gash. "You haven't seen anything yet. Here's a dandy for the insults you passed out to the women and children of the miners."

THE DECISION

With that remark, Dennis pumped another vicious left hook to the other eye, opening up another gash. Dvorak was a bloody mess as Dennis kept taunting him. "For the most heinous of all crimes, here's one for the murder of my beloved uncle, Bobby Brooks."

This time, Dennis jabbed him with a series of blows that had him floundering above. Finally, Dennis brought up a thunderous right that seemed to raise Dvorak a foot off the ground. The impact was so great, one could hear the crunch of bones as Dennis caught him flush on the point of the chin. Dvorak went limp, all the fight was out of him.

Dennis yelled out, "Hey, Zeke, bring me that rope of yours. We'll need it over here to bind him up, hands and feet together. He'll have a lot to answer for in court. He'll be one of our star witnesses against the Big Seven Coal Company when we drag them to court. This will be the beginning of the end for them. Tie up as many of these guys as possible. The more the merrier. They'll all sing like canaries before it's all over. We'll gather witnesses by the droves. Now they can have sweet retribution. By the time courts are through with them, the Big Seven will be without funds, property, or power. They will have to make full restitution to all the victims of the past. Furthermore, they'll spend the rest of their days in prison. This will be the end of the Unholy Seven. We'll have built up enough evidence against them by then to put them out of business permanently. Watch now as the rats leave the sinking ship. We'll try to round them up before they do."

"Dennis," cried Kelly as he hugged his brother, "I didn't know you could fight like that. We could have used you out west in the good old days.."

"Kelly, my brother, welcome!" replied Dennis, as he eyed his long-lost brother approvingly. "You don't know how long I've waited for this moment. Ever since Mother told me about you. There is so much to catch up on. About nineteen years, to be exact. My, it's tremendous to wake up and find you have a brother, especially one like you."

The good citizens of Andura had never seen a fight like this before. Their hearts and best wishes were for the miners as they cheered them on against great odds, until the newcomers came on the scene to swing the battle in their favor.

During the battle, Betty had slipped away from the balcony. Jessica saw her going down the street with a club in her hand. She was swinging at anybody that resembled the other side. Jessica rushed down but Betty was out of sight by then. Now Jessica was in the middle of the fray. What a grand free-for-all this was.

Nearby, the spirited Annie was making her presence known to all, cheering on the ranchers and the cowhands. Out of the corner of her eye, she recognized Jessica from the description given her by Dennis. She took a chance and yelled out, "Grass 'a fire! Jessica, is that you?"

"Annie," responded Jessica, "I'd know you anywhere, with that beautiful red hair. Kelly told me all about you." They laughed and hugged each other. They looked at each other again to see if it wasn't a dream, they laughed and hugged again.

"Look, Jessica," pointed out Annie, "there's Dennis fighting that big bully. That is my man!" and both laughed. "Let's go over and see if he needs any help."

They arrived in time for the coupe de grace, applied by Dennis to Dvorak. Kelly and Dennis were hugging each other. "Hold it thar, you two love birds," taunted Annie, "remember us two?" She pointed to Jessica and herself.

"Say, Dennis," Kelly "we're in a heap of trouble again, but it's the kind I love."

"Annie," teased Jessica, "tell me about Kelly, the crazy things he used to do when he was little."

"He was a nut, doing everything on a dare," Annie recalled. "Like the time I was in grade school and he yanked my hair. I was so mad that I kicked him in the shins and punched him in the ribs."

"Jessica," asked Annie, 'between us gals, what kind of a guy was Dennis when he was young?"

"Well, Annie," answered Jessica, "he was no bargain! Dennis was always quiet and so sure of himself that it infuriated me. I'd clobber him also! So you see, Annie, they are twin brothers."

While this was going on, Patrick was felled form behind by a blow to the head. As he lay there stunned, a grinning ruffian was measuring him for a final blow. Out of the blue, came an angry Betty O'Shea, who creamed him with a well-timed blow to the head with a club.

She knelt down beside Patrick. Putting his bloody head on her lap, she tore a piece of fabric from her petticoat and cleaned the blood from his head. She said as his head cleared, "Patrick, you big wonderful man. You darling! What a way for us to meet again! Would you believe that I'd ever get caught in a town riot like this, Patrick? I really clonked that bully over the head and I loved it. Why didn't you tell me before what fun you men have at fights? Darling, we've been a pair of silly fools. I've spent so many wasted nights without you. I've missed you, how I've missed you'! Let's start now! Today will be the last day of the past and the first day of our future. This will be day one for us."

"Betty," Patrick said, "you're still the most beautiful woman I've ever seen. I'd like to court you again, Betty, like I did one time. Betty, I love you."

THE DECISION

"Hush, my love." She kissed his lips lightly. "As your Indian friends would say, "No time to fool around. We no grow younger. Soon, our best days are gone. Time to tie the knot again."

Patrick inquired, "How do you know so much about Indians?"

"Kelly told me all about how he was raised by Shatoma. She did a marvelous job in making him the man he is today. I'm really glad you had someone like that to help out with Kelly at that important time of his life. I'm not jealous of her. A little envious of her, perhaps! I missed all those wonderful years I could have spent with you."

"Betty," Patrick paused for a moment, searching for the right words, "Shatoma was a wonderful woman, thoughtful, caring, and kind. At that time, I was in love with two women. She knew and accepted that! She was the only woman I had an interest in, outside of you."

"I'll accept that," Betty answered tactfully.

"Shatoma came along," Patrick continued, "at the right moment, when I needed someone to care for Kelly. She was the mother he needed at that time and it worked out well for all of us. Betty, ours was a mutual agreement. We were on loan from our first love. Shatoma was on loan to me until she died. I was on loan to her until I, too, would be reunited again with my first love. Betty, there are only two women I've ever loved, you and Shatoma. I was very fortunate to be twice blessed with that special love. Excuse me, darling, for a few minutes while us O'Sheas beat the hell out of those goons!"

A familiar voice rang out in back of them, "Wrong again, Dad, it's the O'Sheas and the Logans to the rescue. Glad to see you, Mrs. O'Shea. Grass 'a fire! I have something important to talk to you about later on."

"A wonderful girl," smiled Patrick, winking at Betty.

Another familiar voice rang out, "Glad to see you both in such an odd position. There is something I've been meaning to bring up with you, Mrs. O'Shea. As soon as this miserable mess is over."

"A wonderful girl," laughed Betty, winking at Patrick.

After hours of fighting, the tide slowly shifted from the goons to the miners and their new friends. Little by little, the demoralized and leaderless goons knew they'd have enough. They fled to the hills while the others were thrown in the overcrowded jail to await their punishment.

Peace reigned supreme. All was quiet again. It was time to clean up, time to reorganize! Time for the contestants to pick up their fallen. Time to congratulate each other and time to rejoice and thank God. Patrick put it simply, "Thanks to all of you, from the ranchers to the cowhands to the Indians to the miners to the storekeepers to the women in back of us at this crucial time who helped us in our time of need. God bless them, our women who stood at our sides during this ordeal. We have one more task to do before our work is through. We must reopen the mine. I would like my mother and father to lead the way. We want you to follow us, as this is your mine. You fought for it! You earned the right, so let's open the mine and treasure the moment."

Arm-in-arm, they marched proudly singing all the way, as they were met by cheering onlookers who joined in the festivities. They marched to the boarded-up mine. As soon as they arrived, Jeff Cravath's powerful arms yanked off the two by fours, one by one, until there were no more obstructions left. "There goes your closing," thundered Cravath with a boisterous laugh that was joined in by the others. "The door's open, Mrs. O'Shea. You have earned the right to enter first."

With a thankful smile on her face, a tear could be seen trickling down her bloodied cheek. A lock of hair feel over her right eye. Her dress was covered with Patrick's blood. Squeezing Patrick's hand, she opened the door and exclaimed loudly, "Men, we've done it!" She thought of the hard battle they had just won, and then exploded, "We've done it, men, damn it, we've done it!"

One of the ranchers yelled out, "You go in first, Betty."

Betty smiled and replied, "I'll go in with my husband. I don't want to lose him again at this late time in life." The crowd laughed and cheered. "We've been apart too long to take any unnecessary chances like that now. Patrick we go into the mine together." He gently took her by the arm and proudly escorted her into the mine.

The celebration that night was one of the biggest parties ever seen in Andura. There was a mixing of tongues and dialects. Each spoke and radiated one theme...LOVE!

The miners' hall was illuminated by a sea of happy faces and flooded with joyful tears. The local band tried hard to play the various types of music beloved by the mixed group in attendance, failing to catch the beat in some selections and scratching the surface in others. No one complained. No one cared as they all enjoyed trying the different dance steps. The ranchers, miners, and cowhands danced to square dances, quadrilles, the Irish jig, and the polka. Even the three Indians got in the swing of it by doing their famous war dance as they swayed to the rhythm of the drums.

There was food and drink galore, and an outpouring of speeches for the occasion by many in different tongues, each praising the other. Who could forget the emotional, unforgettable sight of Patrick hugging Betty, to the great delight of their children.

Strong Arm grunted, "Ugh! Too bad grandfather not able to be here, listen to powwow of palefaces, and see our last war party."

White Feather added, "Grandfather happy. Him bring good medicine to our people."

THE DECISION

Brave Heart mused, "Return trip better. Will hold happy feast with our people. White friends, asked them to come. They will be......what you say.....guests of honor?"

The three Indians cried out, "Oh, Mighty Spirit! You have given us powerful medicine. We thank you."

Betty and Patrick were radiant with happiness as Patrick spoke to the audience. "I never thought in my wildest day that it would end up like this when we came here. It's been a glorious experience and at times, rather painful," Patrick rubbed his head and the crowd laughed, "I'll never forget it, nor the men I met and fought with. They are among the finest and greatest I've ever known! I'm happier now than any man deserves to be. I don't suppose what I'm going to say now will come as too big a surprise to any of you, but I figure that you should know first! I have a public announcement to make, Betty and I are going to be reunited and spend our second honeymoon on the Betty Ann Ranch in Broken Bend. You're all invited to come to the celebration. You're always welcome!"

The crowd cheered wildly and yelled for Betty to make a speech. She stepped forward and said, "Patrick and I learned a lot in the last few hours about people like you that no amount of education could ever teach us. How good people and good friends like you, with their undying loyalty that knows no bounds, can teach us that there is good and bad in all types of people. I also learned one other thing that I'll never forget. I can't live alone without my man, Patrick. It gives me great honor and pleasure to accept his second proposal of marriage. This time it will be forever!"

Kelly jumped to his feet and exclaimed, "I too, want to make an announcement, Jessica and I are going to be married."

Jessica replied softly, "Without a doubt, my love, I accept."

Dennis added, "Without sounding too repetitious, I too, have an announcement. We're going to make it three couples to be married at one time. Annie, will you be my wife?"

Annie cried, "Gras 'a fire! Shucks! You're on, pardner! Once again it's the O'Sheas and the Logans against the world."

"Correction, Annie," offered Jessica in rebuttal, "now it's the O'Sheas, the Logans, and the Longstreets against the world."

THE END